THREE NOVELLAS

TRANSLATED BY PETER JANSEN AND
KENNETH J. NORTHCOTT

THOMAS

WITH A FOREWORD BY
BRIAN EVENSON

THREE NOVELLAS

BERNHARD

THE UNIVERSITY OF CHICAGO PRESS
CHICAGO + LONDON

THOMAS BERNHARD (1931–1989) was an Austrian playwright, novelist, and poet. English translations of his works published by the University of Chicago Press include *The Voice Imitator* (1997), translated by Kenneth J. Northcott; *Woodcutters* (1987) and *Wittgenstein's Nephew* (1988), translated by David McLintock; and *Histrionics* (1990), three plays translated by Peter Jansen and Kenneth J. Northcott.

The University of Chicago Press, Chicago 60637
The University of Chicago Press, Ltd., London

Printed in the United States of America
12 11 10 09 08 07 06 05 04 03   1 2 3 4 5

ISBN: 0-226-04432-7 (cloth)

Library of Congress Cataloging-in-Publication Data

Bernhard, Thomas.
[Novellas. English. Selections]
Three novellas / Thomas Bernhard ; translated by Peter Jansen and Kenneth J. Northcott ; with a foreword by Brian Evenson.
p. cm.
Contents: Amras—Playing Watten—Walking.
ISBN 0-226-04432-7 (alk. paper)
1. Bernhard, Thomas—Translations into English. I. Jansen, Peter K. II. Northcott, Kenneth J. III. Title.

PT2662.E7A25 2003
833'.914—dc21

2002045580

∞ The paper used in this publication meets the minimum requirements of the American National Standard for Information Sciences—Permanence of Paper for Printed Library Materials, ANSI Z39.48-1992.

Contents

Foreword

BRIAN EVENSON

"The feeling grows that Thomas Bernhard is now the most original, concentrated novelist writing in German," wrote George Steiner while the Austrian writer Thomas Bernhard was still alive. Now, more than a decade after his death, it has become increasingly clear that Bernhard was one of the strongest voices of twentieth-century European fiction, on an equal standing with writers such as Franz Kafka, Samuel Beckett, and Robert Musil. Possessed of an eccentric syntax and an incomparably rhythmical prose style, Bernhard's best-known works function as irony-ridden monologues and screeds against his native Austria. They submerge readers deep within a maddened or evasive or sophistic voice and hold them there, not allowing them to come to the textual surface for air. Bernhard's sense of these voices is impeccable and unrelenting. Their habitual patterns of expression are so strong that to read Bernhard is to feel as if you have been possessed, as if the thoughts of others are worming their way into your skull and changing the way you parse and categorize the world. As the sentences stack up and logic begins a relentless and darkly comic spin, you are in danger of being crowded out of your head. This is a dilemma shared by Bernhard's characters as well: "Since my thinking had actually been Roithamer's thinking, during all that time I had simply not been in existence, I'd been nothing, extinguished by Roithamer's thinking."*

The three novellas gathered in this volume, *Amras, Playing Watten,* and *Walking,* offer a vision of a relatively early Bernhard. Of an artist whose major concerns—suicide, life as disease, the collapse of identity, the rottenness of Austria, the looming presence of death and madness—are already established, but whose style is still in the process of developing. These novellas provide many of the satisfactions of Bernhard's later prose while at the same time suggesting other directions that Bernhard might have traveled, other likewise unique stylistic paths he might have pursued.

Amras (1964) was Bernhard's second book of sustained prose, published shortly after his award-winning first novel, *Frost* (1963). Stylistically, *Amras* connects the earlier novels *Frost* and *On the Mountain* (written 1959, published 1989) to the novel that followed *Amras, Gargoyles* (1967). In *Frost,* a medical student is sent by one of his overseers to investigate what has become of Strauch, an ex-painter who has withdrawn to a mountain village. The novel, broken into twenty-seven chapters, which are broken in turn into standard paragraphs, is composed of the student's letters to his overseer giving a daily accounting of his investigation. *On the Mountain* consists of the jottings of a court reporter: notes, fleeting ideas, descriptions of interactions, and so on. It is a single discontinuous sentence, a string of words broken into fragments as if (as Sophie Wilkins suggests) the narrator is "in the grip of a fatal lung disease, struggling for breath."

Amras, on the other hand, is the story of two brothers, one of them epileptic, who have survived a family suicide pact and are now living in a ruined tower, struggling either to come fully back to life or to carry out their suicides. The setting is gothic, with the promise of death hovering constantly. The novella is narrated by one of the brothers, a former scientific researcher, in the days following the suicide attempt. *Amras* offers a synthesis of the severe fragmentation of *On the Mountain* and the epistolary and more conventional structural strategies of *Frost.* Its narrator slips from transcribed letters to elliptical and wandering paragraphs to the recording of his brother's frantic jottings.

*Thomas Bernard, *Correction,* trans. Sophie Wilkins (1979; reprint, Chicago: University of Chicago Press, 1990), 25–26.

Yet *Amras* also possesses qualities that would come to characterize Bernhard's later work. Like *Gargoyles*—the story of a doctor conducting a harrowing set of rounds in the countryside with his son, a set of rounds which culminate in their meeting Prince Sarau, an aristocratic madman—*Amras* employs an extended first-person monologue. Bernhard is already moving toward this narrative style through the medical student's extensive quotation of Strauch in *Frost,* but here the monologue is sustained at length, though interrupted by letters and by the brother's notes. In the use of monologue in *Amras,* Bernhard prepares for an even more extravagant gesture in *Gargoyles,* where Prince Sarau speaks with only minimal interruption for more than 120 pages. *Amras* employs monologue but does not fully pursue it, the voice periodically collapsing into fragmentation. It opts for the modernist solution of using a formal collapse to reflect internal collapse. *Gargoyles,* on the other hand, offers a voice that tears itself apart from within while leaving the edifice of monologue intact. We have the sense that, like Beckett's Unnamable, Prince Sarau is probably only getting started.

Playing Watten, published in 1969, is more humorous, more lucidly written. Its narrator is a doctor who has lost his practice because of morphine abuse. As the book opens, the doctor has signed over his inheritance to the lawyer-mathematician and convict rehabilitator Undt. After accepting the money, Undt writes to ask the narrator to participate in his research by writing *"a report on your perceptions, over a period of several hours, of the day before the day you received this note."* The remainder of the novella consists of the narrator's description of these several hours. He records a visit paid to him by a truck driver trying to convince him to return to his old habit of playing cards every Wednesday, a habit which he interrupted when one of the other card players committed suicide.

The "watten" of the title is the name of a card game played in the Southern Tyrol. Most variations of the game demand four players broken into teams of two with teammates sitting across from one another. After the deal, players are allowed to inform their partners through little signs and gestures, as well as by speech, of the conditions of the cards in their hands. Some of the fun of the game comes in the verbal exchange that occurs, in the attempts to inform one's partner without giving too much away to one's opponent. As the rules of watten vary from locale to locale, the truck driver's invitation to play watten is an invitation to the doctor to come back to local society. When the doctor suggests that watten is not enough to save him, just as it was not enough to save the player who suicided, it is shorthand for the failure of society to save the individual and, considering the Tyrolean origin of the game, the failure of Austrian society in particular: "In this country there is absolutely no work for the brain, it is unemployed." In addition, the doctor's long periodic utterances and the truck driver's laconic responses are a sort of verbal game and can perhaps be read as watten played by means other than cards.

Playing Watten is thematically similar to the book that was published directly before it, *Ungenach* (1968), in which an expatriate Austrian, now a professor in the United States, chooses after the murder of his half-brother to divvy up his family inheritance among lower-class Austrians. Yet *Playing Watten* could not be more stylistically different. While *Ungenach* consists of disparate sections, lists of recipients of the inheritance, and so forth, *Playing Watten* introduces the nonparagraphing that would come to be Bernhard's stylistic trademark (the technique appears as well in the earlier stories "Der Zimmerer" and "Jauregg," but *Playing Watten* is the first time Bernhard uses the technique in a longer work). The novella consists of three sections, each a single, unbroken paragraph. The effect is a compelling one: after beginning to read, readers have no place to pause or breathe; instead, they are swept along by the language. *Playing Watten* paved the way for *The Lime Works* (1970), which is Bernhard's first full-length novel to practice nonparagraphing. There, after ten pages of elliptical paragraphs of the kind found in *Amras,* the narrative offers a single paragraph, which is 230 pages long and is woven out of the many voices and opinions surrounding a murder, submerging the reader in a chaotic tangle of hearsay and madness.

Walking (1971), slightly more abstract, contains all the themes and stylistic gestures of Bernhard's major fiction. In some respects the most overtly philosophical text in Bernhard's highly philosophical oeuvre, it is a seminal work. It feels condensed and at times gnarled, as if Bernhard were trying to cram the thematic concerns of a longer novel into the smaller confines of a novella. In it, the narrator and his friend Oehler walk, discussing anything that comes to mind, but always circling back to their friend Karrer, who has recently gone irrevocably mad. The novella is a meditation on thinking, on the impossibility of truly thinking. The majority of the narrative consists of Oehler talking and the narrator listening, sometimes responding. But Oehler's speech quotes Karrer and others, making the layering of the narrative both maddening and wonderfully complex. Four years later, after Bernhard loosened this structure slightly, covering similar themes but allowing them to develop over four times as many pages and with a more substantial narrative in play, he would produce his finest and most disturbing work, *Correction.*

Like *Playing Watten, Walking* is unparagraphed. The structure of both novellas is tripartite. The middle section in *Playing Watten* focuses on a story about the traveler who found the suicide's body, while the middle section of *Walking* recounts the events leading to Karrer's definitive breakdown. One is tempted to view this tripartite structure in Hegelian terms—as thesis, antithesis, synthesis—but if Bernhard employs such a model, it is fissured and cracked and ironized: the ideas of the sections bleed together and any synthesis is ultimately thwarted. The first and third sections in both novellas are sufficiently similar that they might also be read as a single section split in halves by a trauma rising through it. It is perhaps analogous to Hegel's notion of the night of the world—the bloody head rising out of flux only to be swallowed up again—but twisted free of its philosophical significance and ultimate comforting contextualization: an eruption of a negativity through another negativity. In any case, Bernhard would not remain comfortable with the triad as a structural device (though he would use character triads); his later work moves away from structural triads toward dyads and monads, with longer works such as *Extinction* and *Correction* breaking into two long paragraphs, and shorter novels such as *Concrete* and *Wittgenstein's Nephew* consisting of a single sustained paragraph.

At the heart of all three of these novellas lies madness. As the narrator of *Playing Watten* suggests, "One moment I think I'm mad and the next I think I'm not mad. Madness is a fully instrumented score." In *Playing Watten,* madness becomes a given for the narrator—his only choice is whether he will go mad in a natural or an unnatural fashion, and if that process of going mad will terminate in suicide. In *Amras,* both brothers struggle with madness during their stay in the tower, imagining dead bodies swinging in the kitchen, fearing knives, hearing voices, struggling to maintain themselves as both connected to and distinct from one another. In *Walking,* Karrer's "own daily discipline had been to school himself more and more in the most exciting, most tremendous, and most epoch-making thoughts with an ever greater determination, but only to the furthest possible point before absolute madness." But the difficulty is that "at any moment we can think too far." Thinking, in *Walking,* is like walking, and the characters think their ways along routes, with these routes leading sometimes over smooth ground and sometimes to the edge of an abyss. Suggests Oehler, "It is absolutely right to say let's enter this thought, just as if we were to say, let's enter this haunted house." Indeed, language is viral, infecting through the ear the mind that takes it in: external words rewire internal thoughts. By entering into the thoughts of others we become possessed by their thoughts, potentially annihilating ourselves.

In the move from *Amras* to *Playing Watten,* and from *Playing Watten* to *Walking,* we can see Bernhard's development in miniature. The arc pursued is analogous to the arc taken by Bernhard's novels from *Frost* passing through *Gargoyles* and *The Limeworks* to reach *Correction.* Taken as an aggregate, these three novellas present a cross-section of approaches to Bernhard's major themes, illustrating as well the development of his nonparagraphing and of his recursive and obsessive narrative voice. They provide the best introduction to Bernhard currently available, defining the writer's concerns, preparing readers for the larger satisfactions—and the larger challenges—of Bernhard's novels. In the progression, one can sense Bernhard the artist becoming more and more distinct, his vision more and more precise. Yet never is there a moment when these novellas seem undeveloped or immature; they are successful in their own terms even as they prepare for greater things, enriching and complicating our sense of one of the twentieth century's greatest writers.

AMRAS

TRANSLATED BY PETER JANSEN

The essence of disease is as dark as the essence of life.

NOVALIS

After our parents' suicide, we were shut up for two and a half months in the tower, the landmark of our suburb of Amras, accessible only by traversing the large apple orchard, years ago still a property of our father's, which leads up in a southerly direction to the primary rocks.

The tower, which belongs to our uncle, was a refuge to us during those two and a half months, protecting us from the clutches of people, sheltering and concealing us from the eyes of a world whose actions and perceptions are forever determined by evil.

We owe it only to the influence of our uncle, our mother's brother, that in contravention to the crude Tyrolean health regulation concerning persons apprehended in the act of suicide, condemned to excruciating survival and thereby disfigured, we were spared consignment to the insane asylum and being forced to share with so many others, in the dreadful way well known to me, the fate of those from the Upper Inn Valley and from the Karwendel mountains and from the Brenner villages whose derangement and deformation *was caused by that very institution.*

Our family conspiracy had been discovered and made public two hours too early by a merchant from Imst, a creditor of my father's: we had still, in contrast to our parents, never been dead . . .

. . . at once and, as our uncle did not shrink from telling us, completely naked, wrapped in two horse blankets and a dogskin, we had been taken that very same night, and *still in an unconscious state,* in a speeding car dispatched by our uncle to forestall the health authorities, from our father's house in Innsbruck to Amras and thus to safety, out of reach of accusations and gossip and slander and infamy . . . Like our parents, we had wished our suicide and agreed upon it among ourselves . . . and on the third of the month had not wanted to hear of another last-minute postponement like those we had been forced to accept repeatedly in the course of the winter and each time owing to objections raised by our mother . . .

Left behind by our parents, forsaken by them, the two of us, Walter and I, from the very first moments in the tower during those days following close upon the night of the suicides, days described to us only with embarrassment, in bits and pieces, and therefore shrouded in obscurity, spent all our time lying on the straw mattresses apparently made up freshly for us in great haste on the middle floor of the tower, at first unconscious, later on silent and listening, and then, from the end of the first week on, just walking up and down incessantly, often holding our breath, occupied with nothing but our young natures, totally benighted, betrayed, not yet twenty years old . . . The tower, familiar to us from our childhood like no other building in all of Tyrol, was no dungeon to us . . . on the upper stairs and on the lower, groping and shivering, in our thoughts subjected to utter destruction by abject impulses from every point of the compass, we constantly obeyed our fateful, if sublime, sibling torpor . . . Our watchfulness weighed upon our mood and constricted our understanding . . . We did not look out of the windows, but we heard enough sounds to be afraid . . . Our heads, when we stuck them into the open, were exposed to the vicious gusts of the foehn; the welter of air hardly left us room to breathe . . . It was early March . . . We heard many birds and did not know what *kind* of birds . . . The waters of the Sill plunged into the depths before us and noisily separated us from Innsbruck, the city of our forebears, and thus from the world that had become so insufferable to us . . . Leafing through the books and writings belonging to the two of us, selected most thoughtfully by our uncle and sent up to Amras from Herrengasse while we were still comatose, probably completely out of it and unconscious, at death's door, the scientific ones that were mine and incomprehensible to Walter, the musicological ones that were Walter's and incomprehensible to me, meditating on our own history and that of others, general, *universal* history, which drove us to distraction, on the millions of snowstorms of unfolding events—we had always loved what came hard to us, despised what came easy—withdrawn ever more deeply into our raging heads, we padded our tower with grief.

To a letter from the Meran psychiatrist Hollhof, a friend of our father's, which we had received only three days after our arrival at the tower, we sent the following reply:

Dear Sir,
The time has not yet come for us to inform you of the circumstances leading to the deaths of our parents, as you have requested, in particular to give you a description of the period between our parents' (and our) decision to commit suicide and the execution of *their* suicides, with regard to *ourselves,* our "rehearsal for suicide"; we wish nothing more at the moment than to be left alone.

Thank you for your condolences. K. M. W. M.

We sent a second reply, on the same day, to Kufstein:

Dear Madam, all claims you may have concerning our father's business transactions are to be directed to our uncle, our mother's brother, who is known to you. SINCERELY, K. M. W. M.

Heartened only by the attentiveness of our uncle, who visited us twice a week, every Tuesday and Saturday—his responsibilities would not allow him to come more often, on other days—always in high spirits, as it seemed to us, always bearing newspapers, information, tidings which, however, caused us nothing but dismay, thrown back solely on our dreadful characters, injured from way back, watchful, unpersevering, we suddenly existed in a darkness ever more conspiring against us, impairing our very ability to walk and sit and recline and stand, naturally our ability to think and speak, our general ability to reason, the darkness of the tower whose age, to us, spanned not *centuries,* but *millennia.*

Even there, Walter, as he had throughout his life, continued to receive the regular visits, essential to him and expensive, of the internist, an epilepsy specialist famous and infamous throughout the Tyrol, a brutal, excessively healthy man of forty who, though medically trained without compare through early application and subsequent cunning, had always been hateful to us, also had earlier been our mother's physician . . . When in the tower we were as good as gone from the world and suddenly deprived of our parents and their gentle influence, Walter's illness, from birth nothing but a constant source of chagrin to him, initially undermining only his disposition but later more and more thoroughly his intellect as well, advancing against him, it seemed, with logical cruelty, both furtively and openly, a disease completely unexplored to this day, had intermittently, as was observable in phases and stages, taken very rapid, savage turns for the worse and as a result exacerbated, to the limits of our potential, even our mutual relationship to each other, based as it was on sibling trust as much as on sibling *over*caution . . . But we had to stick together, and thus we tolerated each other . . .

. . . . .

Immediately after the end of our barbiturate-induced coma, detoxified by two Innsbruck general practitioners with, as may be imagined, great solemnity, in the certain knowledge that we were forced to exist again, and against our will, thus all the more detestably, both of us had feared that Walter's seizures, congenital to him, inherited from his mother, fostered by his exostosis, which from time to time molested him with lightning speed, having completely abated in recent months, would now, in the tower, emerge again, under the excessive strain of what had happened to us . . . and indeed, long deferred by dint of his incessant intellectual exertions, emerge again they did after even the first few steps in the tower . . . My brother, one year younger than I, was constituted in a much more delicate mold than mine, subject to a rather fantastical nervous system, his constitution had always been inevitably a more weakened one . . . all his life he had been afraid of his mother's seizures, a fear *he himself* had magnified to himself in the tower . . . having spent days in self-reflection at my side, always mute and, like myself, without food, at a moment when, rising with my help, he wanted to go to the window, he had been gripped once again by his epilepsy, though at first only briefly, in the form of a so-called momentary aphasia without any loss of consciousness at all . . . In the darkness, responding to the vehemence of the attack, I had not noticed how much his face, how much his eyes in particular, had changed *as a result of the attack,* but as I was leading him I had felt in his wrist, by which I was supporting him, his condition when he collapsed . . . We feared a catastrophic worsening of his epilepsy . . . We had been forced to spend all our lives, tied as they were to our parents as though to two poles, in constant fear of that "Tyrolean epilepsy" which had always haunted us, haunted us even in our mother . . . that disease had destroyed all of us, from a time no longer even ascertainable, that epilepsy known only in the Tyrol . . . Our mother had been stricken by it at a curiously late age, in her twenty-first year, shortly before Walter's birth, from one moment to the next, verifiably at the high point of a ball in a Wilten mansion . . . and had changed at once, in a manner immediately wrenching to those around her . . . Walter, probably owing to his childlike *excessive* fear, had very quickly been unsettled and corrupted by it . . . I myself, fatefully without fear as a child, never in the least even brushed by it . . . It seemed that disease, erupting randomly at any time anywhere in the Tyrol, had now, after the death of our mother, thrust itself entirely on Walter . . . Now in the tower, and indeed with a vengeance that grew as the days went by, it reasserted itself in him, just as I had known it in our mother, more vilely than before the death of our parents, fostered by everything, it seemed to me, nurtured by the tower's atmosphere . . . In a way that shocked me I observed how he, Walter, came to resemble our mother ever more closely, even physiognomically, in his taciturnity, his complexion, the inflection of his voice, with regard to emotional reactions, bodily functions . . . The insomnia that all of a sudden, owing to a crude physical law perfectly transparent to us, had befallen the two of us for a period we could now no longer measure, subjected as we were in the tower to pulsations utterly unfamiliar to us, prevented us from finding even momentary peace of mind . . .

It was rare that we mustered the courage to approach the windows and push back the shutters: victims of deceit, or so it seemed to us in the howling of the storm, we looked out on the randomly stunted apple trees, into an alpine terrain numb with all that darkness and enigmatic nature and upheaval of reason, a curiously noisy terrain, as it seemed to us, and as though populated only far below, at the end of the apple orchard, where the circus was, an obstinate terrain, scuffed out of its eccentricity only by its black and brown, and here and there white, reflections, a terrain whose suburban existence forever exhausted itself in punishable offenses, exasperating . . . What we heard were the limpid rivulets of an uninterrupted, moribund chemistry, what we saw, day and night, was nothing but night . . . roaring, deafening darkness . . . We had always and from the start been trained to observe everything that was foundering, but here in the tower, distraught, drawn by all of nature into her confidence, we suddenly felt the wisdom of decay . . . Distracted from ourselves by nothing but ourselves, we beheld ourselves at Amras in our sibling connectedness, seething one moment and petrified the next . . . time and time again asking the question: *why do we still have to live* . . . and were forever without an answer—no illuminating echo ever, always backstrokes like cerebral strokes!—helplessly dependent on each other, even in the paltriest actions and functions, in a double-brained loneliness contracting within us and around us more and more with each hour, and yes, even if it confirmed our humanity . . . even days, weeks later we still did not dare talk to each other about the catastrophe; in animal communion, still below the threshold of any mystification, we stuck only to organic matters . . . everything in us derailed into the potential for extinction, into the deepest natural energies . . . In the moaning of my Walter's half-sleep, I eavesdropped on his frequent painful imaginary homecomings, from the tower down to Herrengasse, into the foehn-swept night of the suicides, into the days preceding our suicide and our attempted suicides, into the Marchlike, sweltering atmosphere that had never once for a single moment been *for us,* always only *against us;* ever more solemn, more inclined towards death: All afternoon of that third of the month, which suddenly seemed so propitious to all of us, we had waited only for darkness to fall as if at our behest, that it be over, that with the daylight we too, parents, sons, quickly, effortlessly, simply go under in our sleep and be extinguished, be gone . . . With inordinate clarity of mind we begged, not without words, for unusual swiftness in falling asleep . . . we begged it from the pills in our water glasses . . . we no longer looked at anything but those glasses, the murky white liquid . . . we no longer wanted to go on, wanted no longer to be, wanted only to be nothing . . . Behind closed windows, drawn curtains, completely isolated and closely joined, we had been quite ready; now and then one more sound coming up from the street, the sound of a carriage, laughter, a distant noise wafting our way from Büchsenhausen, had still mediated between us and the world . . . a door, a window, an easy chair . . . We had no longer taken any food, had no longer drunk anything . . . suddenly, for the last time as we believed, had taken pleasure in our clothes, in our hands, voices, whims . . . in the sweet smell of our food pantry, which was open but had no longer been entered by any one of us . . . my brother had had three, four, five books lying on the table in front of him . . . Stifter, Jean Paul, Lermontov . . . once, my abruptly pulling back the curtains had caused Walter, who was sitting by the window, preoccupied with his books *as if he were studying,* to look up at me in alarm while I was watching some people on their way to the theater, in the street which already lay in nearly total darkness because of the mountains . . . I observed two girl siblings, a pair of brothers, two professors in black overcoats, accustomed to their walking sticks, with gray, black-ribboned hats; at a distance of three or four yards the wives of the professors, likewise in black . . . as other people have their Wednesday or their Saturday night subscriptions, their comedy or tragedy subscriptions, these people have their Tuesday subscription . . . I observed the newspaper man, our neighbor, in an old cape of military cut, a girl from the butcher shop with a basket of sausages, and a stranger . . . What I saw was sad, what I thought was sad, with sadness I drew the curtain shut, the sadness that is guided by reason . . . In the space between the houses across the street I had once more looked out upon the Inn, those flowing waters, constantly changing, yet always alike . . . The Inn, the vein which, for a few fleeting generations, had tolerated a dreadful participation bearing our name, a mysterious babble . . . Turning around, I had then been startled by the ghostly familial abridgment: absorbed in the observation of ourselves, we, our parents and their sons, in our house, which had providently been cleansed, as it seemed to us, of the strangers, domestics, servants, after we had at last let even the yard boy go, released him from the cage . . . had resembled nothing so much as a party of travelers wordlessly awaiting the departure of a train they had boarded a long while ago . . . Our mother had once more left her bed, for the first time in weeks, and sat down by the hearth . . . a taciturn monument to Tyrolean ennui, that was how I saw her . . . In her gray chiffon dress, which had long gone out of fashion, one that like all her dresses, because of her scrawny arms, had sleeves coming all the way down over the backs of her hands, she had been to me the expression of the melancholia in an old family care-worn by illness, the mute concealment of a hell on earth . . . We had offered one another the better seats . . . our father had pretended to be looking through the advertising section of our newspaper . . . my brother from time to time had immersed himself in the writings of Sterne and of Dante and Donne, which he had finally added to his selection . . . in the Diderot volume . . . We were not expecting anyone; if the doorbell rang, so we had agreed, nobody would answer anymore . . . We could not think of anyone who might have come . . . Night fell on the street as we had always been used to it, a huge dead bird of prey . . . we then could still hear the church bells so clearly that we had no trouble distinguishing the origins of the individual sounds coming down, from Wilten, Pradl, Hötting, and Amras . . . Odd that people were going to the theater that evening . . . Each of us being provided with, as it seemed to us, a sufficient number of pills in his glass, we withdrew to our rooms and thus, as we had agreed, *from one another* . . . I could still hear our father's laugh coming from the bedroom, Walter had turned to the wall as early as half past nine, I myself had resisted the soporific for more than an hour, finally without success, had risen and gone out into the hallway and down into the vestibule and back again into the brothers' room . . . for a moment, only a moment, I hoped that someone would come into the house and discover us . . . nobody came . . . when finally I was only drifting through milky images, the waters of the Inn were beating in towering, then intermingling waves against the spot on the bank that had been changed by falling rocks and feared by us children . . . In the city there was suddenly a racket as if people were being shot . . . from the direction of the Customs Office I heard steps, more and more steps, as if the soldiers were now going on parade . . . a bird, growing bigger and still bigger, was suddenly in the room, desperately bumping into all four walls . . . I was afraid I would suffocate . . .

. . . . .

In the tower, which I know had been furnished by our uncle with a taste for darkness, made darker and ever darker by him over the years, apparently for himself, we lived through one never-ending sleepless night, interspersed only with our excruciating physical and emotional pain, with the sounds of water and birds, and the fine art, the noble, so-called sublime science, as whose beneficiaries the two of us, as well and as long as it had been possible, were always privileged to regard ourselves from early childhood on in our parental environment, almost without interference, though in the shadow of our illnesses, now suddenly, after we had at our father's behest without warning been ordered, because of the constantly deteriorating condition of our mother as well as Walter's illness, which during our stay abroad had quite suddenly taken a more menacing turn, to return home from abroad (from England), where we had been sent for purposes of study, no longer served as a means to divert us fundamentally, in a way that would have been salutary, from ourselves, from our horrifying convulsions, from the horrifying bouts with our illnesses, let alone to restore us . . . It seemed to us in those weeks as if my science had died with our parents, as if it had committed suicide with our parents . . . as if Walter's music too had been dead since that day; we suddenly looked at our research, at our astonishing theories and discoveries, at the products of our minds, like two people cheated out of everything looking into a charnel house; with every book that I opened I was opening a coffin . . . our aesthetic achievements, even our earliest fragmentary ones, claims, life privileges, documents of our intellectual development, were lying in a coffin . . . Walter, younger by a year, of a so much more artistic, if diseased, temperament, harmony, no longer heard that occasional music, however distant; music, having been everything to him, who had never been able even to imagine a life without it, which he had made his own through his research, had withdrawn from him, sharing, as it were, his despair . . . My natural science, what it represented, had all of a sudden ceased to be anything to me but a dissociation from what I *had* always been, perturbing me, punishing me for itself . . . The weather all at once obstinately enveloping the tower in those latter days of March consisted, self-importantly, of myriad contradictory moods, mutations, revolutions, explosions . . . so it had, strangely, a dreadful influence on us in the tower, unchangingly morose as we were, being suddenly far behind ourselves without a hint of progress: often, as if by mutual agreement, we crawled off to hide in the farthest corner of the Black Kitchen, which was only a few steps away from our straw mattresses . . . only now and then at dusk, when the deep night had turned into an even deeper one, slandering us, or so we believed, when the mountainsides, the walls cutting into the waters of the Sill, when the monumental canyons, echoless because of the thundering Sill, nefariously darkened, to the point of unrecognizability, the world *around* us and thereby the world *inside* us too, darkened and crippled it, did we venture out of hiding . . . As if mocked by ourselves, by the landscapes, by the sciences, by the human confinements in darkened cells, and by the arts, we would then, with crazy, confused shouts, crumbling sentences, push the tables and easy chairs and benches and cabinets around in the tower, till midnight and later, guided solely by the warmth of our bodies and by their animal jealousy taking root in it . . . once we rammed our bodies under the piles of apples, under the mountains of pears, into the moldering, putrid layers . . . as if we were hoping to suffocate slowly in that kind of stunting of our senses . . . Often, at the times when we believed, when we felt, when we knew that our souls, even our brains, had already become impervious to pain, in an utter frenzy we would inflict injuries on various parts of our bodies, on our chests, on our backs, on our thighs, and on our knee joints, on our palms too and on the backs of our heads, not on each other, but each on himself, sibling fashion, submitting to the impulse of the behavior that sprang from our earliest stirrings of vernal nature . . . in counterpoint, with ever increasing rhythmicity, we would beat our heads against all four walls . . . often in the darkness, guided by smells, which is to say by running sores, clinging to nothing but air, to the diabolical oxygenic, we would wantonly, with invocatory laughter, for fun, tear our clothes, our pants and shirts, into shreds . . . each to himself we were the destructive center of all destruction . . . morbid in our contrasts . . . we soon exhausted ourselves in our raptures . . . More recently we had taken to turning over our straw mattresses, inebriating ourselves in the foul smell of their innards . . . both of us, in the states that were triggered in us by the foehn, on occasions that we generated by mutual agreement, but wordlessly, discovered in ourselves a primeval, catlike nimbleness . . . We were taking revenge! . . . We took sweeping revenge on our own physical and intellectual infirmities . . . It was usually hours before we managed to free ourselves again after such paroxysms, of which hundreds, as I have hinted, remained in darkness . . . In the tower, because of its proximity to the Sill river, it was cold, yet after supper we often stood, as long as we could bear it, completely naked, body to body, leaning against the walls that glistened with moisture, in a tender contact that had long ceased to work miracles for us, in a sort of unquenchable, pubertal invigoration routine that weighed on our minds . . . Walter's skin, unblemished, sickly, awkward, shimmered most beautifully where the radiance of the Sill, at an almost acute angle, shone in, broken by a slim shadow cast by the left shutter . . . timid, even fearful, we were silent at such moments which, from our earliest childhood, could still be made ever more profound and subtly refined by us . . . now they confounded us, ever more painfully, ever more illicitly . . . more and still more we were thrown back, here in the tower, on speculation in our highly developed watchfulness . . . Excesses were what we practiced, no communication came to our aid.

My disquisitions on the chromonema, for example, on endomitosis, on isotopes and mitochondria, on the nucleolus, on pleiotropy, which had never failed to amaze my Walter, to give him pleasure, because to him, in his attitude, so dear to me, to the contemplation of a science that was arcane to him, Correns's and Mendel's formulas and theories had never been anything but poetry, crumbled on my very tongue . . . likewise, Walter's recitations of the verses of Baudelaire and Novalis or even the most ingenuous attempt at an approach to the "Sermon of the Dead Christ Delivered from the Vault of the Universe" only aroused panic in us, for they came to a pitiful end every time as soon as they had begun; our diction, Walter's in particular, which, because I was not forced to hear it from myself, I could judge most exactingly, had in earlier times, in our parents' house at any rate, always been open, our childhood and our years in secondary school until the catastrophe had been filled all along with its beautiful rhythm, it had always been a springboard for many things, for everything, suddenly choked into slavish submission, stomped underfoot, in fragments panic-stricken.

[TO HOLLHOF]

Dear Sir, we detect a curious concurrence in our thought processes, however chaotic they may by now have become in the tower: we condone our parents' conduct, in contrast to the public, in contrast to the Innsbruck newspapers, legal experts, we do not condemn them . . . We know what the newspapers have written, what they are writing, because we read them; know what has been said, what is being said in Innsbruck and what in Wilten and Amras, in Hall and in Kufstein, in Wörgl, in the entire Inn Valley, because our uncle keeps us informed of it . . . How monstrous those tales based solely on communal neighborly speculation, the detestable stuff of gossip spreading through the streets of Innsbruck so prone to detraction, its avenues and public places, what goes from mouth to mouth, from brain to brain, in stores and taverns and in the markets all these days and weeks . . . since the two of us after all are well known throughout the Tyrol, have indeed been well known for centuries . . . How, if we had not been taken to Amras and to the tower by our uncle, we should have had to suffer in Innsbruck and surrounded by people, and how we should still be suffering there . . . and in the insane asylum too, given the conditions still prevailing there . . . As early as our first day in the tower, so Walter surmised, the day we regained consciousness, our Innsbruck household had been broken up: without interruption trucks were driving off, he said, with our beautiful possessions, heavily loaded trucks . . . he could see them, he said, coming now from the left and now from the right . . . without interruption he could see, he said, the "horrible, the inescapable . . ." Our uncle's behavior, he said, also pointed in that direction . . . Our uncle comes to visit on Tuesdays and Saturdays, accompanied by the internist who administers more and more medicaments to Walter . . . to treat his seizures he injects him with a whole new chemistry . . . he keeps coming with larger and larger packages, all of which are so complicated to open . . . Our uncle apprises us of what has been done on the Innsbruck Herrengasse, what is being done there, grievously . . . but it was more than a week before our parents' household, in which you were often our guest for weeks on end, the primal core of our family property that had remained to us over the years, had practically ceased to exist . . . Day after day we heard of objects dear to us that had been carried off, of pieces of furniture, of pictures and books, of mirrors, china, and linens. We learned that, owing to the eagerness of the newly appointed owners, everything our childhood had been tenderly attached to has been scattered to the winds, snatched from us and taken away in every direction of the compass, in large trucks and small, just as Walter imagined . . . All we hear of now is attorneys and undertakers, cemetery administrators, tombstone masons, death certificates . . . clerical and secular infamy, dismissed servants, Tyrolean pigheadedness . . . the business practices of hundreds of creditors, Innsbruck newspaper leeches . . . We are told that in June we are even to expect court proceedings against us, that various unexplained circumstances have given pause to the Tyrolean justice system: our parents were found not *in,* but *beside* their beds, that is to say on the floor . . . Walter and I, nestling against each other, in Walter's bed . . . Our discoverer is Lugger, a merchant in Imst . . . Our uncle has made the best possible arrangements for us in every way: petitions, apologies, a myriad of declarations . . . appearances before the provincial legislature and before the bishop . . . appearances before the mayor . . . court appearances . . . our correspondence, suddenly immense . . . consultations with physicians . . . As our appointed guardian he had taken care to protect us at Amras from any harm by the outside world . . . We are happy about what he saved for us, even though it consists of little that belongs to us . . . the liquidation came too soon, the haste with which the creditors proceeded really did offend us . . . We have had to part, by order of the court, even with our bicycles, birthday presents from our uncle, because nobody in the entire Inn Valley was so deeply in debt as our father . . .

. . . . .

To think coherently about our fate, in a manner that would have helped us to move on, was beyond our courage, let alone to explain its causes . . . We avoided the words, the concepts, that aggrieved us . . . but we did not succeed in making ourselves pain-free, even intermittently, stricken as we were time and again by the most unbearable pain of all: the memory of our parents . . . Walter would often go to the window and look out and say, "It's nothing!" even though to him there had obviously been *something* out there under the tower window, a sound, a voice . . . because a voice had *drawn* him to the window . . . the voice of our mother, the steps of our parents in the garden, at any time of the day, often at night, again and again . . . but each time that same "It's nothing . . . ," it happened daily, repeating itself at shorter and shorter intervals, that he jumped up from his straw mattress and rushed to the window . . . then his silence, as though signifying a dreadful resignation . . . Our childhood, which was associated most intimately with our parents, precisely because we had never been shocked by them, but were always left to our own devices, not without their guidance, a very liberal and therefore exacting guidance . . . was present to us in those weeks as it had never been before . . . crazy in itself, it was a consolation to our craziness . . . Often, averting our faces, we would be sitting facing each other in our catastrophic physical and mental condition, after long periods of cerebral turmoil, when suddenly my Walter would jump to the window, startled by a call . . . which, after a certain point in time, *I too* heard . . . but in the garden there was never even a hint of a person calling to us . . . yet for many weeks we always heard the call at the same time . . . quite clearly the voices of our parents calling.

Floors and Walls

Through the floors and walls, not only the air, we were connected most intimately to all of nature, that is to say to all of nature in a doubly rational way . . . we would listen for hours at the most distant shores . . . we heard the mingling of all imaginable languages, the mingling and droning of all sounds filled our cranial cavities, which at times were completely emptied of flesh, of blood . . . at a certain ratio between our temporal bones and the center of the earth, which we were able to determine for ourselves and for everything, we were privy to the processes of creation, to the willpower of all of matter . . . Thus we were conscious of ourselves as of two double mirror images of the universe . . . celestial phenomena, reflections of hell . . . In oceans and deserts simultaneously the tremors of the atmospheres . . . often we truly rose to such heights in the contemplation of the constellations that the cold made us shiver, *ourselves* water, rock . . . in the privilege of mortality, when we listened and thus understood . . . we felt and we understood . . . no longer thrown back on speculation, we beheld the calculations of the lucid human mind . . . how fine, not mentally exhausting was the hush in which we could communicate, renew ourselves at such moments . . . We took care not to mention what we had seen . . . The fantastical unveiled everything to us for seconds, only to plunge it back into darkness *for itself* . . . the most exalted moments, naturally, were always the shortest, indeed infinitesimal moments . . . Pressing our temples to floors and walls, we observed the revolution of millions of light years, far away . . . gyrating cones, spherical celestial bodies, the precise elasticity of mathematics . . .

. . . . .

We were amazed that we were still alive . . . still existed, dared exist again, had not been taken away with our parents, removed from the world . . . still not on the point of transformation . . . We had been ready to die . . . we had completely trusted the judgment of our parents, obeyed our father . . . We had already been sure of ourselves in our deaths . . . we had not *been allowed* to die . . . Parties to the suicide conspiracy, we had in truth already been liberated during those last few weeks at home in the knowledge that we should die, be allowed to die, the prospect of soon being dead had pacified both of us . . . To be sure, the sultry weather had precipitated our resolution, permitting us no further delay, but the decision had already been taken before Christmas Eve . . . The lives of all of us had become unbearable because of the fatal illnesses of our mother and my brother, if a person knows the things constantly *caused* by such illnesses . . . which are beyond cure . . . And Walters's fatal illness, the twofold fatal illness, the fatal illness of our mother and his fatal illness combined . . . and our father's business going to ruin as a result . . . all that commotion mortifying all of us . . . all that legal blather mortifying all of us . . . the large, beautiful estate at Lans, the timber at Aldrans, the vineyards, the sawmill and the maize fields at Fulpmes: suddenly, while we were still children, it had all gone to ruin, been leased out, lost . . . in the end only the two apple orchards at Wilten still belonged to us, but they too were soon in the hands of total strangers . . . for the last ten years our father had gambled and boozed his money away in the beautiful Italian cities of Mantua and Turin, where he had friends, in Rome, Venice, and Genoa, in Trento and Bolzano . . . the first loss, the most painful of all: the Mutterer pasture, the Passeier quarry . . . The mortgages, the debts in Vorarlberg had darkened our lives early on . . . our parents, to be sure, protected us from the darkness, yet even as children we stumbled time and again into the shadows cast by our parents . . . The permanently bedridden state of our mother in particular, who had required constant help and ended up, however gently, making her sufferings the center of our lives, was a source of constant depression to us . . . because of the monotonous wretchedness of all those years we had soon been beyond retrieval for a healthy life . . . what destroyed us too was the going and coming, so constant that we had become inured to it, of all manner of megalomaniacal physicians, Innsbruck psychics, creditors in our parents' house . . . Naturally we had soon been left with no other recourse but suicide, eradicating, liquidating all four of us . . . What a blessing that our parents no longer had to live *through* us . . . Only now, enlightened by our uncle, who always brought many documents when he came up from the city to the tower, the two of us realized how riddled with holes the existence of all of us had been from the start.

. . . . .

In the tower, which had suffered no damage from the countless shocks of perennial earthquakes, and which we had always bolted with a solid oak beam to protect it from the criminal rabble, there were provisions piled up for several years, in the cellars as well as the attic, in anticipation of disasters dreaded by our uncle . . . but we never touched them, contenting ourselves instead in the morning with the milk and the accompanying fresh bread that one of the orchard hands would place outside the tower door as he had been instructed; at midday we ate apples and pears, with which the upper as well as the lower floors were filled; in the evening we would use the open fire in the Black Kitchen to heat up a jug of wine (Lebenberger, Küchelberger, Greifener . . .), which we would finish off in silence on our straw mattresses; with it we ate some of the smoked meat hanging in the Black Kitchen . . . to us, living as we did at that moment in constant mortal fear, by nature inclined towards a compulsive contemplation of everything fantastical, the Gothic fantastical, to the two heads that we were, brains, shut up in the tower, to us, who were compelled all our lives, in the delirium induced by the high mountains, to feel and think everything *to pieces,* the smoked meat hanging from the ceiling of the Black Kitchen was a fantastical image of killed military bodies, of dead asses and heels and heads and arms and legs hanging down out of the darkness of the kitchen ceiling . . . a fiction, generated by our predisposition towards magnifying everything horrible, of dead bodies, of dead male bodies swinging against one another in an incessant rhythm . . . Our uncle had given us permission to partake of the smoked meat, had encouraged us to do so on the very first day, when both of us were shocked by the sight . . . I would cut it every evening into paper-thin slices as skillfully as I could and dip it in our wine . . .

The Augsburg Knife
or The Knife of Philippine Welser

I would slice the smoked meat as well as the bread with the knife that Philippine Welser had brought from Augsburg to the Tyrol for Archduke Ferdinand in 1557 and that hung on the wall of the Black Kitchen, two yards away from our straw mattresses. Walter did not dare handle it, he was afraid *even to pick it up,* but he was delighted when I, much more skilled in the use of my hands, used it to cut into the smoked meat . . . the uncommonly fine "philosophical chasing" (Walter) on both sides of the sharp blade, representing the spires of the city of Augsburg on the Lech, interested us, appealed to us . . . at night Walter's fantasies would often revolve around the knife . . . he feared that in his own hand it would only be used to "inflict pain that would not otherwise occur," that was the idea that haunted him as far as the knife was concerned, he feared that the "artwork from Augsburg that belonged to our uncle" would become a stabbing weapon as soon as it was in his hands . . . and therefore he did not touch it during the whole time he spent in the tower, until his death . . . there was a morbid expression around his mouth when I took the Augsburg knife from the wall with a swift motion . . . with a concentration so great that it gave me pause, Walter followed every step of mine: the way in which he mustered his courage to say to me, "The knife is freshly sharpened," was revealing, made me think; how he kept walking around it, how he was afraid to look at it longer than was "healthy" for him, as he called it; he did not look at it in the way a person looks at a knife . . . whatever he said with regard to the Augsburg knife made me think, but then everything said by Walter in the tower made me think . . . it stirred up the most sinister sibling thoughts in me . . . Already as a child I had seen the Augsburg knife in its accustomed place in the Black Kitchen; it had always been there to cut smoked meat and bread; curiously, Walter, as I remember, even as a child refused to touch it when we had come to the tower, at Easter, Whitsuntide, Epiphany . . . on late summer days, chased by millions of honey-seeking bees, seeking refuge in the tower from the gnats . . . buried in the same straw mattresses that were now our resting places . . . seeking shelter and finding shelter from the obscene advances of an angry nature . . . The Augsburg knife or the knife of Philippine Welser: my uncle did not understand my brother's continuous fear of that knife, which was the sharpest of all; once he tried to force it on him, pressing it into his hand with the swiftness of an adult, but my Walter had recoiled from it . . . the knife shooting to the floor, I remember it clearly: I had been gripped by its glitter and sparkle the moment it came to rest on the floor . . . I immediately remembered that event at the renewed sight of the knife . . . right away, on our very first day in the tower, I myself suggested to Walter that he be *spared* its presence, that it be taken off the wall . . . I was going to give it to our uncle so he could take it away with him . . . but my brother did not want that . . . With the shutters closed, it gave us the illusion of a "Turkish" crescent . . . In Walter the sight of the Augsburg knife, Philippine Welser's knife, in contrast to myself, in whom it produced nothing but the pleasurable impression of unusual sharpness and high art, fantasies evoked by the beauty of its elements, must have triggered only perplexity, something frightening to him, incredibly frightening, a dreadful horror . . .

. . . . .

What we were preoccupied with above all in the tower was our childhood, which we had lost with the catastrophe . . . it lay, to us, behind a dark forest of disappointments, through which there was no way back . . . in our dreams we breathed its air, heard its burbling brooks . . . there they were, the naively soaring thoughts, arabesques on the terrifying outer façade of life . . . left to our own devices, our childhood had been guided for us by our parents *with inconspicuous consistency,* in accordance with their knowledge and feeling . . . then, later, by sophisticated medical regimens, paternal as well as maternal desperations . . . a sad degeneration of everything in which we were allowed timidly to thrive cast its shadow over the last ten years our family spent together . . . around us and in us and with us everything was crumbling, we could see it in the people, in the houses as in our thoughts . . . read it in the buildings, which were already averting their faces from their owners . . . Soon the grass was no longer so fresh, the grain no longer so tall, the books had suddenly ceased to be quite so insurmountable . . . less and less often we had gone to the country, less and less often to Italy, to Munich, hardly ever any more to relatives . . . no longer to the lake . . . everything had to go to seed . . . For many months in succession we were condemned on Herrengasse to a grayer and grayer emotional life that embittered our studies . . . epilepsy cast its black shadow over us.

[TO HOLLHOF]

Dear Sir, our university studies, lasting all of five and a half months, had been a traversal of Leopold Franz University and its institutes adjacent to the Botanical Gardens, stifling our natures arbitrarily no less than radically, the daily passage through a full millennium of our rotten world of learning . . . the very awakening in our parents' house had been sheer torment to us, for in truth it was already an awakening in the high-ceilinged and gray and answerless courtrooms of dull curricula, world views, of dusty theories and philosophies, an awakening in the stinking laboratories and auditoriums of our gloomy provincial capital . . . In those months we had soon exhausted ourselves in the memorization of the depressing conventions of pseudointellectualism, in the nauseating subdeliria of academia . . . We could find the wellsprings of our music and our natural science not in the soil of the state system but only in ourselves . . . After all, so-called *education* as well as so-called *higher education* had always been hateful to us, had been hateful also to our father . . . With the day-to-day ingestion, imposed on us by the state, of the viscous poison of erudition that contaminates the whole world, destroying all subtler traits in our young brains so utterly unsuited to coarseness, we had soon overtaxed our natural talents . . . Our time at the university was probably our worst time, hardly a time of life . . . just think of the weeks spent plowing and harrowing through immense writings and books by our own professors, tomes whose noisome smell simply took our breath away . . . underlining, as we were ordered to do, sentences that destroyed the entire philosophical scheme of genetic mutation, that was how I spent those student days . . . yet the two of us persisted in clinging to the girders of those research bridges that we ourselves had invented . . . With Walter it had been no different, as far as education, higher education, was concerned . . . I had had to spend one whole long winter only on the "primary process," on the "accessory substance which, in the transporting form of the chromosome, appears first and foremost as the so-called intercellular substance (matrix)" . . . and had to exist like that . . . exist like that with unheard-of exactitude . . . Walter with his twelve-tone technique . . . but as soon as we allowed ourselves, in obedience to a glorious intuition, blithely unconcerned about higher education and higher educational coercion, relying solely on our innate intelligence, to be abruptly transformed into primeval rock and into family, with our penchant for illuminating, together with nature, every cranny in the gloomy edifice of our thought, in the respective fields of study that seduced us, yes, soaring up and away into higher regions, indeed the highest, we were out of the woods . . . The weekdays of our university period were a sad example of those institutional martyrdoms that are subject to the enforced paralysis of the educational realm and that we never managed to elude . . . Our time at the university had been as monotonous as its methods, which were bound to destroy, annihilate us, accustomed as we were to loving and preserving the creative element in everything and everyone . . . But the Sundays of our university period too are something I do not like to remember, they too were dominated by its weekdays, futile our efforts to repress them . . . like a fatal disease it ruled our lives . . . In our inability to shut out our weekday martyrdom on Sundays, we were in no way different from the others . . . instead of shunning the lying, the thick, lying tomes, we *immersed* ourselves in them on Sundays . . . Only before going to sleep, a feat in which we succeeded less and less often automatically the older we grew, indeed had no longer succeeded automatically even in our early childhood, did the two of us sometimes have the strength for a stroll in the garden, along the Inn, through the city . . . We never knew the athletic intake of air enjoyed by most students, budding academics, young people . . . we loved the stinging air on the banks of the Inn, the long nocturnal cemetery visits . . . to the cemetery adjacent to the Anatomical Institute, to the cemetery at Mühlau . . . with the passage of time, because Walter's illness brought us yet more closely together every passing day, we were permanently shackled body to body in an often truly unbearable fashion . . . Walter's epilepsy ruled our lives . . . Not a step without Walter . . . no longer a thought without Walter . . . I was his brother, was his brother with utter consistency, if a person knows what that means, into the darkest crannies of his head, which was killing him . . . For years I was never alone any more . . . the university period a dreadful ordeal . . . It was late February, one day before the seizures of our mother *and* Walter, both of which lasted for several hours, that we entered the building on Angerergasse for the very last time . . .

. . . . .

Between Walter and myself only a semiconscious state continued to prevail, in that semiconscious state we existed side by side as though in and as though against the misapplied reason of our acquiescence: *henceforth we only obeyed* . . . Our mutual relationship was not without enmity . . . indeed our natural innate mutual aversion was in truth the source of our affection, of our sibling commitment, our petrifaction . . . We lived at the highest degree of difficulty at which two human beings who are painfully joined can bear to exist . . . on many days we were as soothing to each other as humanly possible . . . which drained us as time went on . . . the high art of coming to each other's aid was something we had mastered early on in peerless fashion, and we had been able to develop it further still after the catastrophe . . . In the tower we had suddenly become fully conscious of the deepest darkness, at moments . . . of the inanity of possibilities . . . *in the tower* we had become conscious of ourselves, it was then that we looked at ourselves, for the first time, from the outside *and* from the inside . . . Rhythmically, for a celebration however agonizing, we joined, after the deaths of our parents, in constant fear of ourselves, of our own divinations . . . the time we spent together was a time without closed season . . . we kept on living through it without joy and, as if we ourselves had been our own power of observation, apathetically . . . Subject only to physics, not harmony ourselves, we were our own misfortune . . . In Walter this process reached even deeper . . . We stood in manifold contrast to each other, for instance: while *I* was occupied with my science, Walter was *ruled, undercooled, overheated* by his music . . . for Walter everything sprang *out of himself,* but for me *not the least little bit sprang out of me* . . . That alone would be sufficient reason for the disquisition "About Us" . . . But even after that disquisition, what we were, are, will be will remain in darkness, everything remains forever in darkness . . . everything is always, *is not* . . . our simultaneity, temperaments, geometry . . . from the bottom up, in order to be higher *at the bottom* . . . We lived consistently, often insistently, if truth be told, in mutual physical aversion . . . the physical element in Walter, his eccentric physical side, had been the eccentric physical side of our mother, *alien to me* . . . *My* physical side that of our father . . . all our lives we *mediated* between the two of us . . . As a result of Walter's illness our aversion (for each other) had become affection (against each other) . . .

. . . . .

In the last three weeks we did venture out . . . but did not dare distance ourselves more than a mere few steps from the tower . . . We conversed with the gardener and with the orchard hands, who, because the season was propitious for the task, were pruning the apple trees . . . they were turning over a section of the lower meadow, repairing the two embankments . . . all of them were doing their jobs with diligence . . . the older ones we knew, new arrivals had been introduced to us . . . as early as four o'clock, when I was awake, I could already see the lights in their quarters on the side where the circus was . . . Their conversations revolved around their jobs, which, as I could see, they enjoyed (they had all been well chosen by our uncle, well overseen), their relations, love interests, wage scales, unrealizable dreams . . . Since our uncle understood agriculture better than the lot of them together, they entrusted themselves to him of their own volition, without inner reservations, obeyed him . . . our uncle was someone everybody got along with . . . those people of course knew of the catastrophe, which inhibited our interaction with them . . . Nature, which was still holding back, already putting on color, was the subject of our conversations with them . . . they were pleased when we called them by their first names, when we showed that we were familiar with their families and problems . . . Our uncle's estate was one of the finest in the entire Inn Valley, and still is to this day, in the last two decades he has been able not only to preserve but even to enlarge it: we learned that the workmen were building a hunting lodge for him at Aldrans, the place of our earliest childhood, the birthplace of our mother . . . the forests around Aldrans belong to him . . . for the summer he was planning his own paved road to Rans . . . He has many friends and is a shrewd Tyrolean provincial politician . . . during the period in which he was able to double his property, our father lost everything . . . Wherever our thoughts turned, it made us sad . . . On two occasions we shared lunch with the orchard hands in the shed down below, treated them to a whole ham, on the bone, two bottles of wine . . . After that, Walter demanded every day that I take him down to the shed, but the orchard hands were in the orchard only for four or five days, then they were ordered to move on to Aldrans . . . The old man who placed the milk and the bread outside the tower door for us in the early morning was "the only human being" besides our uncle . . . he was past sixty, looked like eighty . . . But we did not dare admit to our uncle how lonesome the two of us were in the tower, how great in the end, after five, six weeks, our need for human contact had become . . . Our uncle had after all forbidden us to leave the tower, as well as conversing with the workers, which of course we did behind his back, at a time at which we were certain that we would not be caught in the act by him . . . Then suddenly we were apprised by him that we could no longer afford the sums charged by the internist for coming out to see us at Amras, and we had to go to the internist's office in the city of Innsbruck for our appointments . . . We declined the use of the car put at our disposal by our uncle for the visits to the internist and always walked to the city, agonizing though that was for us . . . Nobody can imagine how those visits to the internist affected us . . .

[TO HOLLHOF]

Dear Sir, three days before Walter's death, which has cast its pall over everything, destroyed everything for me, we paid our last visit to the internist . . . having finished dressing quite early, in our boots because it had rained without interruption the four preceding days, we had left the house a little after three o'clock and, afraid of being stared at by everybody in the overheated, overpopulated afternoon, for it had been a market day, had not walked along the bank of the Sill straight to the road . . . from our orchard we had gone into the orchard adjacent to it, and so, agonizingly, from one orchard to the next, again and again through orchards, through all those apple orchards, which really were off limits to us, through the endless apple orchards of total strangers, not without using force, shoving and cursing . . . then directly downtown, without detours . . . through Dreiheiligengasse, where, continuously inflicting reproaches and lies on each other, the whole gamut of irritations and depressions . . . we bickered all along the way to Marktgraben, the internist's building . . .

In the darkness prevailing there, between the walls and on the stairs, thresholds, pedestals, window sills, on the projecting banisters and their ornaments, we tried to calm ourselves, thereby to strengthen ourselves; but *here,* of all places, especially horrible scenes were still played out between us . . . it was the most dreadful day we ever spent together . . . at the top of the stairs, and totally exhausted, you may be sure, I had to wipe Walter's spittle off my clothes, for in his morbid attitude towards me and against me he had spat at me . . . had tried to hit me in the face . . . in the epileptic's chair once described to you on an earlier occasion, in the internist's waiting room, Walter, owing to his enfeebled brain mass, owing to the sultry afternoon weather, was completely unable, to a degree downright excruciating to me, to recover from the exertion of climbing those stairs . . .

Every one of our visits to the internist involved that terrible climbing of stairs . . . sitting in the raised epileptic's chair with its many belts and chains, as though constructed especially to accommodate him and his by then shocking infirmity, that chair, which was even bolted to the floor, welded together, as I have learned, by a Hötting metalworker to the internist's specifications, for the benefit of all Innsbruck epileptics, clearly showing, particularly on its sides, the traces of many desperate people, he was startled when quite suddenly the door to the consulting room was opened from the inside and the summons to enter the consulting room was issued to one of the people waiting on the chairs, not always the one who had waited longer than anyone else . . . Walter always waited patiently for the young woman to call his name . . . The only thought that occupied me was the question whether, by now a wreck with sleeplessness, I found myself at this time with my poor Walter on the fifth floor of the internist's building, as I believed, or only on the fourth; that question had occupied me here every time that I was engaged, in the first few moments, in the initial scrutiny of the waiting room patients, one that I had turned into a veritable science, protecting my ever more helpless brother, protecting *and erecting* him, beside him, or rather *below him,* flushed with the illicitly philosophical element of our sibling existence . . . and with the rigor of that kind of thought process I calculated to myself the number of stairs existing in the internist's building, depending, from where I was, whether they led either up or down, those iron constructions artfully defying their architectural period, calculated again and again, without for a single moment taking my eyes off the company of sick people assembled in the waiting room, forever obsessed with that "Tyrolean epilepsy," though at first still wordlessly, that crowd of people constantly setting traps for us . . . in a manner finally confounding me, heating my body from the inside out, I listed in my brain the stairs in the internist's building in a vertical column, like numbers, in order to add them up . . . I multiplied and divided, meanwhile connected to Walter by a remark ("Then we'll go home *quietly* past the Sill farms . . .") that calmed him, pacified him . . . I calculated to myself the number of stairs from the ground floor to the top, then from the top (what top, how high a top?) back down to the ground floor, without reaching a conclusion . . . finally, in the nerve-wrenching recklessness of my brain, I thought that the office of the internist, and psychic, as I was to find out after the fact, who had made a name for himself even abroad, had to be on the fifth, if not on the sixth, on the seventh floor of the internist's building . . . calling my thoughts to order, which were struggling forever with only the strangest, craziest things, I duly resolved to cast an upward glance as we were leaving the internist's building in order to ascertain on what floor the internist was really located, or, better yet, I told myself, I shall count the stairs as we go down, count them *carefully,* even more carefully, I thought, than the last time, when I had lost count as I always did, as I did after every visit to the internist . . .

[TO HOLLHOF]

Dear Sir, as soon as my brother sat in the epileptic's chair, myself beside him as though being punished, often in a *canine position,* he would calm down . . . I would touch his knees and his thighs . . . now and then I would gaze, without his noticing, into his childlike face, forsaken with unconscionable cruelty by the whole world and *even by me,* as I was aware, that face whose changes no longer reflected anything but resentment . . . every time, without exception, I started thinking about the stairs in the internist's building, about the crazy location of the internist's office . . . it was always the same for me, and then the epileptic's chair: Walter, when he sat in it, would sigh, "There, yes, my seat . . . !" That "There, yes, my seat!" repeated every time we visited the internist, gave him relief . . . When, after the hour-long torment of the walk from Amras down to Innsbruck, through the parentless city by then already alien to us, we were suddenly in the waiting room, which, dark and windowless, without ventilation, calmed nobody's fear, lessened nobody's pain, Walter's seat, the epileptic's chair, was always vacant, without fail . . . I had to *watch* over Walter . . . Many people, over time, have fallen out of the epileptic's chair . . .

Walter had from the start resisted the tying, chaining, shackling of his body in the epileptic's chair . . . once, when I attempted to tie him to the epileptic's chair because I feared a sudden seizure, he rammed his knee into my face . . . Any assistance I rendered to Walter weakened me . . . I think the reason nobody in fact dared sit down in the epileptic's chair, the only one to be found in the waiting room, was our power of suggestion, mine and Walter's, which, on the laborious walk leading from Amras to the internist, straight through the brutal Innsbruck rabble, invariably asserted itself with energetic violence as soon as we came within a few hundred yards of the internist's building: *my Walter,* and on Walter's side, *I, I must, sit in my epileptic's chair just as I always do* . . . as soon as I and my brother, I thought, as soon as the two of us on our way down through the orchards get to the low ground, wherever, even still in the tower, *before* the Sill, and have the wish that the epileptic's chair be vacant, vacant for us, vacant for Walter . . . and as soon as we invest all our strength, not only physical strength, also my mental strength, all the strengths at my disposal combined, Walter's strengths too, as soon as both of us invest our collected strengths in this wish and intensify, indeed *over*intensify that wish to the extent to which we draw closer to each other, often inflicting on each other *unthinkable agonies,* so I told myself, Walter's epileptic's chair will be vacant, it will *be there for him* . . . When we entered, the patients in the waiting room were always silently startled . . . later more and more excitedly talkative, absorbed, it seemed to me, in the ignorance of their fatal illnesses . . . It was unclear to me on that afternoon why the building, one of those buildings in the inner city of Innsbruck harking back to the Secessionist school to which they owe their desolate appearance, did not have an elevator like all the others of its height and vintage, like those many other buildings crammed together, reducing the mountain city to the basest imaginable level of despair, rendered preposterous, indeed intolerable, by their projecting oriels, and inducing and seducing anybody forthwith to crime and wantonness . . . unclear as well how a physician could hit upon the idea of keeping an office on a fourth, fifth, sixth, even seventh floor without an elevator leading up to it, an *epilepsy specialist* at that . . . the waiting room, overcrowded at any time of the day, made everything even more inexplicable . . . the four walls displayed (display) the so-called, by us, "epileptics' pictures," hung in vertical pairs, representing men, women, children, foxes, cats, dogs in the throes of horrible epileptic seizures . . . all imaginable forms of epilepsy . . . a whole series of the famous-infamous "Inn Valley Animal and Infantile Epilepsy," painted by Schlorhaufer . . . What's important, I told myself, as indeed I always told myself, is that the internist be a good internist . . .

[TO HOLLHOF]

Dear Sir, when my Walter had calmed down in the waiting room, I thought of the walk I had taken that day, around noon, two hours before our visit to the internist, down to the circus, the Sill farms, Tantegert, etc. . . . I had left with several letters I had written that morning, the first letters in a long time . . . in them I expressed thanks for the countless letters of condolence we had received . . . Shielding myself from the intrusivenes of those of the internist's patients who were known to me, whose curiosity we attracted almost constantly, I watched the flies, which were slurping the sweet exudations of the patients from the walls . . . Imprinting on my memory a person who had entered before us, a girl not even out of school yet, but already, and this made the sight of her so sad, succumbing to the gloom of womanhood, mutely brooding to herself, preoccupied with a section of the hardwood floor measuring two or three square inches, but probably far away in a forsaken state, helplessly preoccupied with her forsakenness, I, who in recent times (which in every imaginable respect have only been bent on destruction and death—our timid, fearful world was no longer capable of outwitting time and its machinery . . . wherever we looked, it was coming to grief, everywhere and in everything and everybody, in the cities as well as in the country, in these times which people would have preferred to sleep through, if that were possible, over such long stretches of desolation), I, who in the weeks after our catastrophe, *before* Walter's death, had found nothing more irksome and nothing more difficult than breathing, who for weeks, when I lay sleepless, was forever forced to register every breath of my lungs and to whom my breathing appeared noisier, was more illicit, than the breathing of others, than all unconscious breathing, all unconscious breathing of youth and of health . . . set about reconstructing, in a way solely my own, proceeding with a downright miraculous sense of wonder, the *afternoon that was no longer anything but a fading memory* to me . . . seeing through the patients, at a distance of fifteen, of twenty yards, cleverly separated by myself from everyone else, husbanding my steps and my thoughts, just as I have always loved to do, alone with myself, I was walking on the road leading from the orchards of Amras to Wilten, where I had not walked for half a year . . . guided by sounds and colors . . . a person suddenly no longer attuned to anything but parting and death, not yet twenty, hesitating ahead, marveling back, with a penchant for solicitude, unsuccessfully resisting jolts and disappointments, in the certain knowledge that I should have to perish along with Walter . . . I am walking, I told myself, *to the post office* . . . I am walking while Walter, enfeebled by the imminent visit to the physician, watches me from the tower window, watches me until the moment when the only way he can watch me is through the *power of his imagination* . . . I am walking under the bell jar of our sensations . . . pointless attempt at a swift escape from hopelessness . . . with my head schooled in darkness, welded to darkness, from one extreme to the other . . . conflicts . . . forever into *the depth through depth,* guided by the *power* of imagination . . . In that thought I pursued myself for a while . . . To avoid suffocation, I suddenly turned back in that thought . . . as if for dear life I had run back *into myself in that* thought . . .

[TO HOLLHOF]

Dear Sir, today I am sending you the selection you have requested of the writings composed by Walter in the tower, which he kept secret from me and which I found under our straw mattresses.

Circus

Woman on the Tightrope

In her center I could suspend my world, if I were not corrupted by academic learning. I could have used, misused her for my theories, taken her all the way, even before she became *a possibility*. For which both she and I lack the intelligence . . .

Ringmaster

The moment says that the human being is an artful human being. Every lash of the ringmaster's whip against the animal (the leopard) puts the concept of two brain *halves* to shame. The victorious one—since nature is a law—refuses to do truth's bidding. We assume *the* standpoint, the leopard's standpoint.

A Book about All the Observations that I Made in the Tower
A book about all the observations that I made in the tower would of course have to be a book about *everything*, about the *totality of possibilities*. For that reason, it is impossible to compose a book about all the observations I made in the tower.

. . . . .

The tragedy, the tragedy of tragedy, which has always been but an attempt at tragedy.

The Idea of the Burning Circus Tent in the Human Mind
The idea of the burning circus tent in the human mind causes, in most people, the roaring of the lions and the tearing of the tigers' claws to appear *exhilarating*, the ability simply to exchange in the human brain the high points of a circus program, trading balancing acts for magician's tricks, the animal act for the clown act . . .

(The death of the animal trainer is embarrassing because the trainer is not immortal.)

The Clown and His Partner
The moment in which the clown enters with his partner is fatal, to the moment, not to the clown and his partner; but all moments are fatal to the clown and his partner, which is why *at this moment* I can *hear* everything. Between the clown in his silver costume and his partner in the red one, everything aims at *dazzling* the audience (in exchange for their money and *for their minds*); an artful trick only for the human eye, for the naive human soul; nothing but millenary *fatal tradition.*

. . . . .

Everything that amazes has its method, until we notice that the amazing is not amazing, has no method. The best seats are those in which the imagination plays itself out. (There are only lead actors in the minor roles.)

The Man on the Tightrope
The man on the tightrope is famous because on the tightrope he can perform a leap that is famous; we are already watching his leap for the fourth time,

for a single leap would be too little for all the people, for the curiosity of *all* human beings—at the ringmaster's behest the man on the tightrope *always* performs *four leaps,* stopping short of the fifth, for it would *already* be *flawed;* the time between two performances is *only just* sufficient for the man on the tightrope, acclaimed by all, to collect the exact measure of strength that is necessary to perform four leaps "of such stunning precision."

[TO HOLLHOF]

Dear Sir, . . . on the chair beside the epileptic's chair, on the chair *beside* the door, *behind* it when it was open, the faces had changed, I noticed: where there had been an old fat one the whole time, apparently incapable of moving, I now perceived, now registered, like Walter (who was constituted of much finer centers of perception), a young thin one in that spot where there was an imperceptible but continuous draft through the crack in the door . . . What aroused my interest at the moment was this: simultaneously, that is to say, while I was watching the young thin face, completely new to me, a country face, a country face created by generations of *judges of faces,* a maidservant face created by millions of female employers, *I saw myself* . . . saw myself over and over (now pressing Walter's hand) on the road to Wilten, myself under the apple trees on the edge of the cemetery, myself at the wall of the cemetery, myself under the door of the cemetery keeper who was eating, drinking, arguing with his wife . . . I saw myself examining the exit ramp of the lumber mill that once belonged to us, the din of the saws, the smell of moldering wood . . . While I was seeing the country face, I saw myself on the hill from which one can take in all of Innsbruck with a single glance, the stultifying city . . . I saw myself in the woods, I saw myself in the potato field . . . For me the young thin face (while I was seeing myself) was all young fat faces and consequently all young fat faces and all old thin ones and old fat ones combined, all faces in the world, which was constantly expanding and constantly contracting: all human faces forever simultaneously existing, forever simultaneously changing . . . on my stroll . . . with its brief downpours refreshing everything except me . . . saw myself, occupied with ideas and with the ideas of ideas, the organs of rotten and concentrated thoughts, theories, procedures, confronting myself with them . . . on that steaming afternoon, that sultry, steaming, forever pouring afternoon . . . an incredible desertion on my part, as far as my brother was concerned; I was constantly deserting from everything and everyone . . . I saw myself in the brutalized Innsbruck streets, forever *turning away* from the houses of butchers, from the houses of writers, from the houses of actors, from the houses of court-appointed individuals . . . I was forever turning away . . . I saw myself fleeing from the sluggishness of the city, the sluggishness of the world, the sluggishness of my brain . . . and time and time again, behind the country face, the maidservant face, the thin young face . . . the *back*ground of where I was strolling . . . the *fore*ground . . . I was strolling and *pretended* to myself that I was strolling . . . I no longer had the strength for a stroll, I had pretended to myself that I was strolling to Wilten, pretended all afternoon, my abject misery, *our abject misery nothing but pretense* . . . within myself I had treated myself *as if I were myself,* as in a bad novel . . . because a pretended stroll is not a stroll, even though it is indeed a stroll . . . only appears *as* a stroll, as the *stroll of a stroll* . . . so, at Walter's side in the internist's waiting room, I reenacted for myself that stroll I had taken, that is to say, the pretended stroll of a stroll that *was* not a stroll . . . sitting beside Walter, who had to wait a full hour before the young woman finally called his name, grudgingly called his name . . . And observing, from a distance that was best for me, every detail about myself, critiquing myself with relentless acuity, making a spectacle of myself . . . I was making a spectacle of myself, I was here making a spectacle of everything, everything (even Walter's morning fatigue, Walter's midday nap, Walter's groping-through-the-tower) . . . so while at Walter's side in the waiting room I was sauntering on the tree-lined road all the way to Wilten, sometimes striding, not sauntering, crawling and striding, sauntering and crawling, striding and sauntering, I was only making a spectacle of everything . . . but most of all I was making a spectacle *of myself,* a spectacle of myself through myself . . . crazy, vulgar, artificial . . . in a jinxed attempt to bring nature into alignment for myself with the spectacle of myself . . . with my modus operandi, which in this instance was once again completely philosophical, on the road lined with apple trees, in the waiting room, in my brain, in the brain of the brain . . . because of my wretchedness, because of the wretchedness of all of us, I was coached for such brain possibilities in nature . . . the spectacle out of which I was observing myself there, from the ambush of my brain, sauntering and jumping, hopping and standing still in a flash, quite often in a puddle that instantaneously covered me with mud from top to bottom, in my crazy emotional state . . . hardly protected by either the background or the foreground, was after all the spectacle too of observing my representation and, no less, of observing the observation of my representation (during which I continuously corresponded to the background, to the overground as well as underground of my representation . . .) . . . I was a huge number of existences, a huge number of devastating *possibilities* of existence signifying everything . . . the walking one and the one appearing to walk, hop, jump, stand still in a flash, be half crazy . . . I have been all existing existences combined, *I have* been . . . but on this last afternoon I spent with Walter I had controlled myself as a continuous affect, in the end effect, continuously interrupting me, interrupting my sufferings . . . all those existences you may imagine: the highest symmetrical tension of which I was capable . . . then the crumbling of my conceptual world when, having posted the letters, left the post office, concluded the ruminations about my countless letters (badgering letters, begging letters, mean-spirited letters, intelligent letters) I was returning to Amras, the shortest way, the shortest possible, through the blackness of Lemmen Woods. I was still seeing myself (in the internist's waiting room) chucking out of my path shreds of paper, rubber, newspaper pages (a section of the *Times*!), chunks of wood . . . I grew morose in the confused current of air, in the currents from infinity into the Inn Valley. This is what I felt: nothing but spring breezes of an unimaginable world intellect . . . the logarithms of fleeting celestial bodies, the macrology of age concepts . . . along with the young thin patient's face, I saw all patients' faces combined: all patients' faces, assistants' faces, internists' faces . . . all inventions and sensations, exaltations, deflations . . . as if in a transformer station of all desperations, I saw everything . . . All my life I tried to free myself from myself and from Walter, from our family, from the many generations of our family, tried to free myself from them by dint of physical tricks, mental tricks, without success . . . always from one form of chaos into another . . . I have always had to wither away with the fatal illnesses of the Tyrol, with the fatal illnesses of our family . . . so Walter too withered away of the many fatal illnesses of the Tyrol, of the fatal illnesses of our families . . . for Walter everything had always been a double torment, double energy, double tradition, dissipation, cause of death . . . all our lives, the two of us were at a monstrous disadvantage . . . always had to obey the nature within us . . . On that afternoon the walls of the waiting room had contracted to such a degree that I grew afraid . . . contracted around *me,* contracted *around the two of us, around the two of us within us* . . . In Walter's face there had never been anything but sorrows, the ALWAYS called forth by his *excessive* intelligence, which of course only needed to liquify everything . . . Both of us had mastered the art of insinuation like no other . . . we hated, despised everything explicit, everything that had been talked out to the end . . . We were, as you know all too well, *sworn enemies of prose,* we were sickened by that loquacious literature, by that stupid narrative vein, especially by the historical novel, by the regurgitation of dates, historical coincidences, even by *Salammbô,* for example . . . We had never had a taste for stories . . . in Walter's face, as though in a house in which deaths have occurred, a charnel house, and more visible than ever on that afternoon, the mortifications had succeeded one another, those mortifications reflected in human faces . . . a necromancy no longer even perceptible to the sciences had been in his face, his face of a child, on that afternoon that already from the very first moment had been *his last afternoon* . . . that whole time, for hours, I myself, surrounded by the many patients, had thought only of my stroll: Wilten, Sill, circus . . . dogs, cats, pigeons, ducks, pheasants, of the bustling, deferential makers of suburban history . . . then, behind that, the conversation of the patients, simultaneously *in front of me:* the religious imbalance on the sixth floor (or the seventh?) . . . I saw the flying buttresses of our forebears . . . *This* is where I wait and *that* is where I stroll . . . adjusting to the laws of life, obedient to them, for better or worse at the mercy of nature's power of attraction, through the afternoon that I love . . .

"Propositions" of Walter's

AMRAS, MARCH

With me, entirely new surfaces, entirely new circles, entirely new rectangles, with me an entirely new architecture has *come into being.*

. . . . .

The soundlessness of the brain . . .

. . . . .

The air penetrates and corrodes . . .

. . . . .

That of which death *would be* made . . .

. . . . .

Everything rhythm: thought-endowed mountains, thought-endowed rivers . . .

. . . . .

All through life: I do not want to be I, *I* want to be, not to be *I* . . .

. . . . .

What mars the mode of representation in antiquity is *the human element.*

. . . . .

. . . that I call attention . . .

. . . . .

The reality in the interstices of truth.

. . . . .

Pathogens: philosophical sophistries of death.

. . . . .

To treat the dead as one treats life. Life as one treats death.

. . . . .

I am the border, continuous, *death.*

. . . . .

Death, when all is said and done, is something only for higher mathematicians.

. . . . .

. . . death is *that simple.*

. . . . .

I stand in an ideal relation to my death.

. . . . .

The ideal king. The ideal one *is* king.

. . . . .

The generation that no longer marvels at anything.

. . . . .

The head that understands everything . . . *and then* dies.

. . . . .

A great plan born of fear . . .

. . . . .

The transitions are a mystery . . .

. . . . .

Daily question: why am *I out of myself?*

. . . . .

In logic it is (precisely) the connections that lead to nothing(ness).

. . . . .

Births: introductions of superstition.

. . . . .

The demonstrably *extrahuman* illnesses at the center of the human being . . .

. . . . .

The insensitivity of nature . . . (Fahrenheit, Celsius, etc. . . .)

An Actor

An actor appears in a fairy-tale play in which he plays the part of the evil sorcerer . . . he is encased in a sheepskin and in a pair of shoes that are much too short and pinch his feet . . . *nobody sees that* . . . he *so much* enjoys playing in front of children, because they are *the most appreciative audience* . . . The children, three hundred of them, are *naturally* frightened by his entrance, because they are completely taken with the young couple, whom the sorcerer, casting a spell, changes into two animals (*crawling mammals*) . . . What they would like best is to see only the young couple, nothing else, but then the play would not be a good play, and what we have here is a good play, a good fairy-tale play . . . a proper, good, fairy-tale play (play) requires an evil (evil-*minded*), inscrutable figure who has (strives) to destroy the good, the scrutable, or at least to make it look ridiculous. Now as the curtain rises for the second time (and the play takes its course), the children go completely wild, they rush from their seats onto the stage, and it is as if there were not merely three hundred of them but three thousand, as if there were a million . . . and although the actor as sorcerer weeps behind his sorcerer's mask and pleads with them to stop hitting and kicking, they are not to be moved and rain such blows on him (with hard, pointed objects, scissors and knives) and stamp on him for such a long time that in the end he stops moving, he *is dead* . . . when the other actors, who have been standing backstage waiting for their cues without having noticed any part of the tragedy in this fairy tale-play, suddenly rush in and realize that their fellow actor, the best of them, is the sorcerer, the actor as sorcerer, the children who have killed him burst into monstrous laughter, so great that *in it everybody* loses his mind . . .

. . . . .

In nature, nature represents *death in the future.*

. . . . .

The natural element, the mechanical element in nature.

. . . . .

Art: life as infamy.

. . . . .

Religion *through* infinity, but . . . as soon as the epochs have become extinct, the religions are extinct . . .

. . . . .

The distance is the shortest.

. . . . .

Desolation in the human being, desolation in the world around the human being, desolation . . .

. . . . .

Where so much of the world has been destroyed in us.

. . . . .

The poetic days, the unnatural ones.

Journal

13th. The rain casts a pall over everything . . . Above three thousand feet, snow has fallen, it is cold, no heat, but it is better to be in the tower . . . the dog has been howling, his chain kept rattling, I couldn't get used to his persistent warning; as if someone had climbed over the wall and were already down there and into the apples. 14th. The orchard hands are digging a pit, two yards deep, two yards long, two and a half feet wide . . . 15th. The dog has bitten the child . . . 17th. Our uncle has managed to overcome the obstacles to our parents' burial. Reading, *non*reading of our books . . . The dog will not obey commands. 18th. Both of them, our uncle as well as the internist, I don't understand either one of them . . . 19th. *I, Walter?* A brother constantly watches his brother . . . 21st. With the window closed, reading to each other is impossible. A few steps to the window: *nothing* . . . but the parents did call . . . The ecclesiastical trait in our parents . . . 23rd. My failed spring . . . went to see the circus people, conversed with them, talked about their illegitimate children, roasting corncobs on an open fire . . . the *leopard that died* . . . Our apples for the children, the pork suet for the animal trainer's wound . . . ten of them in a caravan, sunk in a deep sleep . . . CIRCUS WINTER QUARTERS, title for a novella. 24th. Somebody asks for me, whether I am registered at the university, probably the man from the chancellor's office, and my brother says, "Of course . . ." 26th. The fear of Philippine Welser's knife . . . 27th. A pig taught him to cry . . . (Our uncle). 28th. There really is an individual who dreams of a *lifetime job* in the brickyard, as I have just learned . . . In the afternoon suddenly the picture before me of my brother and myself being driven to church in a sleigh, calling to the coachman to drive *twice as fast as the last time*. 29th. I: A cut-off dick as a symbol of faithfulness? He: Whose dick isn't . . . Nothing interests me any more, for I know what interest is, I *no longer have an interest* . . . Is something possible at nineteen that's only at eighty? If every day, though different, is still the same, same length . . . 30th. Our life concluded at 6 Herrengasse, our two existences concluded, broken off, at 6 Herrengasse. 4th. Why parents? Children . . . Yesterday not one seizure but two, one right after the other. To the parents the children probably say nothing, the children nothing to the parents. 5th. That primitive immortality, what other kind of immortality . . . ? Or: through the world in a chunk of ice . . . 6th. They have poisoned the dog. A railway conductor with the brain of Montaigne? 7th. *Your* acumen, which triumphs *there*. 12th. The dog is *our uncle's dog* in what respect? Dark night, that from the eye his function takes* . . . 13th. A brother is a continuous spoilsport. 17th. Death quite simply takes a bite out of *my soul* and casts *me* aside. On the way home from the internist, down in the woods, I always expect to be accosted, I know that it is something evil that will accost me. Don't ask.

[TO HOLLHOF]

Dear Sir, I cannot evade your inquiry: *I saw* the disorder in our tower, which was placed at our disposal by our uncle, I looked into the Black Kitchen, even while I was looking at the half-opened door to the internist's consulting room . . . into the tower, in which the chaotic conditions of a pair of brothers chained to each other *unto death,* spoiled by learning and by dreams,

*Bernhard gives this quotation in English (from Shakespeare's *Midsummer Night's Dream,* act 3, scene 2, line 177). *Trans.*

forsaken by their parents, prevailed among mountains of books and hopelessness . . . I had the feeling on *that* afternoon, the last one we spent together, that my Walter distrusted me . . . The day before he had fallen head first out of his chair by the tower window and remained unconscious for two hours . . . At that juncture we had made up our minds, in the course of the night, not to wait until the appointed Tuesday to go to the internist but to go as early as Friday, that is to say the very next day . . . At times I noticed a truly *deathly calm about Walter* . . . I was shocked by that deathly calm (about Walter) . . . until in the end the internist behind the door to the consulting room probably dropped his stethoscope . . . The examination, like the twenty-seven preceding it (during our time in the tower), had shown "no cause for alarm" (according to the internist) . . . On *that* afternoon our uncle took us back to the tower in his car . . . when he had left, Walter lay down, I myself, because I simply could not stay in the tower any longer, went into the orchard, at once to the circus people . . . An hour later I came back (to prepare our supper) and, having searched in vain for Walter for quite a while, found him *lying below me,* his head shattered, directly *below the open tower window;* not until two o'clock in the morning did I run over to the tavern to report what had happened so suddenly . . .

[TO HOLLHOF]

Dear Sir, for the second week now, my brother has been the object of speculation at the Institute of Forensic Medicine. The body, which had already been released, is to be examined, inspected once again, by two of the three Innsbruck pathologists (not by H.) . . .

An accident, but also an *in*cident of a seizure, must be ruled out . . . If you were to let me have the watch that my father gave you as a present, in Mantua I believe . . . A visit on my part to Merano is not possible.

[TO HOLLHOF]

Dear Sir, it was suicide, that is now the official ruling as well; there exists a short note to that effect in a journal of Walter's that I found yesterday; I am thinking of letting you have that journal too, for your purposes, as well as the notebooks that my brother filled with his writing since he was thirteen, among them a final one while he was already in the tower. I shall not be in the tower much longer.

[TO HOLLHOF]

Dear Sir, my brother's burial was performed after all, against the wishes of the Innsbruck church authorities; it took place on the twenty-ninth, at four o'clock in the morning; besides my uncle, a lady unknown to me but, according to her assertions, formerly on intimate terms with our father, and the cemetery staff, there were no mourners present . . . not the lowliest cleric. My uncle immediately took me to Aldrans, where he owns a large tract of forest and a hunting lodge built just last summer and where I believe I can be of use to him. It will be sufficient if you address your letters to "Hunting Lodge at Aldrans," nothing further.

At Aldrans

In the evening the woodcutter comes down; at first I thought, an animal . . . , but then very clearly, an animal that is human, that human who is the woodcutter and who hides from me as if he *were* an animal . . . I myself hid, watching him, listening: he takes three or four steps to the left, then to the right, but I cannot see anything but his shadow, which is *down* one moment and *up* the next; when he jumps, I jump too, when he peeks out from behind the tree, I have already pulled back my head . . .

. . . . .

What kind of people are those (the young lady) who are staying at the manor house? That's the question asked by those who are not staying at the manor house, and those who are staying at the manor house and walk through the woods wearing spats(!) ask themselves: what kind of *people* are those who are *not* staying at the manor house? Those of the one group keep running into those of the other behind the cemetery, they do not know what greetings to exchange, *whether* to exchange greetings, because any greeting seems ridiculous to them . . . as if those staying at the manor house and those not staying at the manor house belonged to different planets . . . the one wearing spats and the one not wearing spats, each claims the privilege of being in a world entirely alien to the other, being of another spirit . . . being further along than merely existing . . . those afternoons, to the people traipsing through them every day, are one of the great errors of humanity.

. . . . .

At bottom, only that exists which has tormented us and which is tormenting us, which is forever tormenting us (for us); what has seduced us, who has seduced us . . . everything else, everyone else, has never existed, for us . . . not a single person who did not at least once torment me *and* seduce me . . . The greater the torment inflicted on me (by him), the greater, etc. . . . Our mother caused us our greatest torment, *her* greatest torments, nothing but incessant torments down to the small and smallest details . . . torments precisely calculated in advance (calculated in advance by her) . . .

. . . . .

On the Schladming range up to the larches, all the way to the timberline; a herd of roe deer suffocated under the avalanche; right away I remembered the terrible rumble after midnight.

. . . . .

Walter's shadow, which explains to me the speed his figure is putting behind him, his face, *already receding* . . . his body, present no longer in anything but his torturous, laborious *attempts at locomotion* (Walter) . . . He comes into the tower and rushes directly to the window . . . his figure, which then leaves behind numerous figures, he who no longer coincides with any one of those figures . . . But there is no first and no last figure of the brother . . . no brother . . . Walter *is.* Where have you heard that before? Thought it? That a hundred thousand figures, millions, billions . . . death after all does not interrupt . . . My relationship to Walter *now:* he simply takes off his jacket a hundredfold, goes into the Black Kitchen a hundredfold, lies on the straw mattress . . . is afraid of the Augsburg knife, a hundredfold . . . but not like *you eternal* a hundredfold . . . At Aldrans everything is connected to Walter.

. . . . .

The word crows and the cawing of the crows and the downward swoop of the crows and the black of the crows, that is all you feel . . . The word crows is the past seasons and the future ones, the present ones . . . The word crows, like the downward swoop of the crows, etc., makes everything possible, impossible, etc. . . . For days on end the word crows (even in sleep, which is a half-sleep) ruins everything, devastates everything, extinguishes everything *around you.*

. . . . .

A coffin is carried past: the priest walks behind the coffin, the sister of the deceased walks behind the coffin (behind the deceased), the intended of the deceased, the children of the deceased, the *more distant* relatives of the deceased, whom they *assume* to be in the coffin, finally the band.

. . . . .

Our year in Folkestone with its monthly visits to London was our best, as it now turns out; the study of a *higher uncertainty* . . .

ALDRANS, 7 NOVEMBER

Dear Uncle, it took me four days, after you brought me to Aldrans and left again so soon, to become accustomed to myself, to the person I am, to myself, who is now without Walter, has always been without Walter; I always only thought I was alone, I was never alone . . . not until now have I really been alone . . .

The house, surprisingly, since after all it is only a few months old, is easy to heat from top to bottom; I provide for myself in every way; manual labor brings me back to myself *simply,* suddenly my thoughts understand me . . . My food, my clothes, I take care of everything . . . Your people are solicitous, but they do keep their distance from me, to them no doubt there is something about me now that frightens them. Perhaps they are now blaming me . . . they are all good people, I observe them as they work, eat, converse, what I observe in particular is their relationship to you, to their master, who, they say, has lately come out to them but rarely; I believe it is a good relationship.

Be advised that the oldest of your woodcutters and the youngest are sleeping together, not only at night . . . it is *not un*natural (yes, unnatural like nature), no, but since there are after all others in the dormitory, you would do well, in my opinion, to transfer the old man up the mountain to the larches . . .

Playing cards is a diversion to me, the many different possibilities of the game, the finest human game, it affords me peace, even if it is a peace that is dangerous in the long run.

My computations concerning the timber logging are all correct . . . I am enjoying my new occupation . . . the fatigue that these days causes me to fall into bed at eight, half past nine, along with the others, is not the fatigue of my recent years . . . Hollhof continues to take an interest in us, but what I write to him is hardly helpful, and even that I do only out of a sense of obligation because he was a friend of our father's . . .

It is often frighteningly quiet in the hunting lodge. As I am still a long way from studying what is, to me, *new nature,* I am once again beginning to make discoveries of my childhood that were long forgotten (e.g., the geometry of crystals) . . . As for reading material, I need the book "On Primary Rocks" by Bergonzi; I look forward to devoting some time to Seume, feel like reading "Moby Dick," the Descartes . . . When you come up here, bring two cases of beer, a liter of kerosene, and a padlock for the shed.

. . . . .

The consciousness that you are nothing but fragments, that short periods and longer ones and the longest ones are nothing but fragments . . . that the duration of cities and countries is nothing but fragments . . . and the earth a fragment . . . that *all of evolution* is a fragment . . . there is no completion . . . that the fragments have evolved and are evolving . . . no trajectory, only arrivals . . . that the end is without consciousness . . . that then there is nothing without you and that therefore nothing is . . .

. . . . .

The people who die without having known their illness, their fatal illnesses . . . Walter's illness, the illness of our mother . . . the mystery surrounding our "Tyrolean epilepsy" . . . nobody notices the onset of his fatal illness . . . life would then be unbearable, no longer an oenothera lamarckiana.

. . . everything a question of the shortest of periods, not of temperament . . . in the notion: I can remember, that is where I went wrong, then as now.

. . . . .

Grandissimi fiumi corron sotto terra

. . . . .

On Herrengasse the room where the theater costumes hung: Pantalone, Columbina . . . Our tragedies, *fun* plays, *show* plays . . . Bavarian-Italian plays . . . how much I should like to be in that attic with the costumes, but I am enjoined from entering "our" house . . . It is "for good reasons" that our uncle did not buy it at the auction . . .

. . . . .

As if only the woodcutters had a rightful claim to the landscape . . . as if I had no claim to it . . . If I told them, which I am completely incapable of doing . . . *no rightful claim at all,* huh?

. . . . .

. . . if I renounce them *of my own accord* . . .

. . . . .

Our father, an unhappy person like our mother, but because of our mother; then, because of our mother, the family . . . when Merano was still the capital, that's what I could say . . . commerce, academic degrees, a certain secular prince-of-the-churchliness . . . in dealing with people *lavishly grand-inquisitorial* . . . carriages, saddle horses, hunts with the Primas Germaniae . . . in summer, the many artists in the house, objects of perpetual scorn in front of us . . . *The artists, those wretches* (father) . . . Excesses, breaking with the church, war . . . in connection with our grandfathers the names Cattaro, Solferino, Pontebba, Venice, Riva, Monte Cimone . . . Our father often used the word London; Paris he hated . . . "The misfortune into which we *have been* plunged" (father).

. . . . .

Everything shriveled to a few headstone inscriptions in the Wilten cemetery.

. . . . .

La vita bene spesa lunga è

ALDRANS, 18 NOVEMBER

Dear Uncle, today I received a bill from the internist in the amount of forty-five thousand shillings, which I ask you kindly to review and then to remit the sum out of the Flirsch account . . . I should also like to ask you to give me the real name of the lady who was at Walter's funeral and whose acquaintance you made, as you say, back in your days in Padua . . .

. . . . .

On completely ordinary days our father would order the horses . . . in the landau, which had been converted for the winter, across a frozen Lake Achen . . . the horses could get hardly any traction on the icy surface . . . sometimes I wake up because for hours the pounding of their hooves, helpless at first, then suddenly racing, strong, has been ringing in my ears . . .

. . . . .

"If on top of everything else someone can still afford a cook and a caretaker and a gardener and a wife who has been ill for twenty-two years . . ." (Lugger).

. . . . .

Secretly, so I thought even in my earliest days, I shall leave the world . . . all alone I have survived them all.

. . . . .

On the other hand, I might have developed quite differently without Walter . . . Something is wrong when I am *there,* something is wrong also when I am *here* . . . With the crossing of the (invisible) boundary, everything is always lost . . . Because I *then do* take sides . . .

TO MR. L. T. AT RUM

Dear Sir, in your possession, stemming from our estate at 6 Herrengasse in Innsbruck, there are, among other things, several piano scores that belonged to my late brother Walter, among them, as I am certain, some bearing the signature of Michael Haydn, especially one, most valuable to me, of Mozart's "Titus"; also a copy of "Zaide." I am especially interested in the return of our Hofhaymer edition, and I should be obliged to you for giving me some indication of the basis on which a negotiation between us concerning the above-mentioned items as well as the others from my brother's collection, which was awarded to you by the District Court, might be effected . . .

. . . . .

On the way back to the hunting lodge it occurs to me how good it is no longer to have any rights . . . so in that thought I walk around in circles for quite a while.

. . . . .

Like the poacher last week, that is how everyone looks at me; when we were children, probably the most horrendous thing to us was a person who was said to be a poacher, an illicit taker of game.

. . . . .

At last, you think, at long last—the next moment (after two hours of *total* loneliness): it's unseemly to accost someone who is kneeling . . . and you walk on . . .

ALDRANS, 27 NOVEMBER

Dear Uncle, O. left at four o'clock to go up to the larches, not even reluctantly, he has no idea why you have transferred him . . . the kid does not understand . . . his injury, the ulcerated wound, opens every day now because we are working so hard at the logging . . . Yesterday a major repair on the scale, which we did ourselves . . . the ice on the creek has closed, and I can go to the feeding station without taking the detour past the power plant: two hinds, always the same . . . our trial in the Innsbruck Juvenile Court is now to proceed with me alone in the dock, not until spring . . .

. . . . .

In Hall a woman is said to have testified in court that she was related to us and to have made several untrue statements about us, which are now on record.

. . . . .

As a child, dragged together three dozen frozen deer in a hollow, covering them with brushwood . . . lay down crying and freezing with the dead animal bodies without freezing to death . . .

. . . . .

The wound that the old woodcutter inflicted on the young one always causes the young one the "most horrible" pain at those times when the old one enters the young one's space *in reality,* enters his brain, the atrium of his brain, which is open in every direction.

. . . . .

The ice on the creek has closed, the spring has closed, the summer has closed, people, animals, sensations, everything . . . the spoken word, which simply shuts the world down.

. . . . .

You open a door, a second, third, fourth, fifth one, you close every one of them again behind you und keep running (forever recurring notion of Walter's) . . . you open more and more doors, finally they *slam* shut behind you and squash you every time . . .

. . . . .

Batteranno il grano

. . . . .

On the milk platform before the fork in the road leading to the city, the woodcutter squats, in a drunken stupor . . . so he did venture down from the larches . . . I lead him back up again halfway to the larches . . . Dragging logs has made a cripple out of him, or so he says.

. . . . .

Long-lasting sight of the dead crow in front of my window.

. . . . .

A branch snapping back startles you . . . for days, pain in *that* part of your body which is the fatal one for you.

. . . . .

The "Tyrolean News" writes: ". . . who committed suicide last winter . . . were held in high *esteem* . . . were convicted . . . creditors . . . excesses . . . lavish lifestyle . . . *smart* sons . . . who perished as a result of his mother's epilepsy . . . ," etc. ". . . who was enrolled in a science curriculum at the university . . ." (still is).

. . . . .

The mountains are against human beings; the cruelty with which the high mountain ranges crush human beings . . . *the methodical terror* of the rock, when it has intruded into the brains of human beings.

. . . . .

No alibi, if you muffle up like them, don their jackets, their pants, put on their hats . . . mittens, hard hats . . . adopt their gait . . . they constantly trip you up in contradictions . . .

. . . . .

Every year a person who has drowned in the creek, his tubular boots *jutting* out of the water.

. . . . .

Burned out, frozen to death, with the head welded to the sky, condemned to walk . . .

. . . . .

"You know," says the young lady, "why don't we take a quick walk through the cemetery, didn't we go to the cemetery last Tuesday too? . . . to the uncles' family plots" . . . We walk through the gate and then take a left in the direction of the plots, she says: "I've always enjoyed going to the cemetery." With her grandmother she always visited every cemetery "within reach" . . .

Her grandmother was an actress, wife of a big-game hunter, African explorer . . . Neither of us says anything during the two hours we spend in the cemetery reading names off the headstones . . . then, when we are already on our way to the manor house: "If I died here, just imagine, if I died *here* . . ." Meaning, if she *died* five hundred miles from home . . .

TO MR. L. T. AT RUM

Your letter has destroyed my fondest hope; so, because you are one of those odious, cruel lovers of old musical manuscripts, the "items that are in every respect priceless" are lost to me.

. . . . .

No longer any other walk than the walk to the cemetery; with or without a book in my hand . . . I am thinking: *the profound meaning of cemeteries* and of the *world outside of cemeteries;* the countlessness of dead people . . . the many diseases of young girls laid out in their coffins . . . dead boys, men, victims of leukemia . . . I think of the touch of the blue boy's black lips in our gardener's bedroom . . . the great stir caused by the body of the late gravedigger falling out of the glass hearse . . . the sudden draining and drying up of superficial figures of speech . . . the cemetery, Walter's favorite retreat too in our childhood . . . the buzzing of the bees in the cemetery, flies colliding in the air of the mortuary chapel . . . the fountain forever running and the wreaths forever wilting . . .

Part of the way up to the larches with the stranger; as if he were luring me into an unfamiliar, *mysterious* trap: the side-by-side uphill walking of his face and *me* . . . with the sudden voice that did not fit into that body . . . and the notion that the man was not wearing anything under his sheepskin . . .

. . . . .

. . . most people wish for a sudden, surprising death, surprising *them,* painless . . . end of all excesses . . .

. . . . .

What will you do when you, who have been humiliated, die . . .

. . . . .

What remains of the dead is often nothing but the acrid smell of their urine, a smell closely related to us . . . the urinous smell of the men in the hunting lodge reminds me of certain dead people of my childhood . . . of the landscape evoked by them . . . the steep slopes, at night disfigured by the foehn's predator claws.

. . . . .

The road builder is found dead in the street, . . . they carry him into the vestibule and then deposit him on his bed; I help to undress him, to wash him, to put his clothes back on . . . a large puppet wearing a leather suit . . . tubular leather boots in the candlelight . . . the glassy face of the road builder . . . next to his deathbed the two woodcutters and I finish *his* booze; I drink two glasses, then I notice the blood coming from his left ear . . . A corpse that stays warm for a long time; we eat pork rind to go with the booze; outside the door the priest asks whether the road builder has been *washed* yet; I tell him, "Yes, the road builder is washed and ready, *we* washed him . . ."—"Good," says the priest and walks into the house; the two shivering servers fold the road builder's hands.

. . . . .

Forever seduced into memory, into the memory of memory.

. . . . .

Smell, gait; gradually *he* is becoming the outsider . . . the young woodcutter who soon *will be* the old woodcutter . . . woodcutters, heirlooms of generations that knew how to maximize profit . . . he had "suddenly felt his foot grow warm . . ." The injury refuses to heal; Aldrans is far removed from medical science; a case of blood poisoning without the least medical ministration . . . but anyone may, if he dare, cut into the leg and drain the blood . . . a person walking through Aldrans does not see woodcutters, only woodcutter *suits,* woodcutter *hard hats,* woodcutter *mittens,* woodcutter *footprints* . . .

. . . . .

In a half-sleep saw the orchard hands who are carrying Walter ("The handsome dead man" [L.]) over to the tavern, how, under the apple trees, they lift the body onto their *shoulders* . . . the circus people had knelt down by the orchard fence . . .

. . . . .

I am walking in front, trying to clear the way through the undergrowth in the woods for the young lady . . . she has scratches everywhere . . . pulls me by my coat sleeve out of the *new* growth and pushes me in among the spruce trunks . . . I want to follow her, but she zigzags . . . *I* hide, *she* hides . . . *I* shout, *she* does not answer, *she* shouts, *I* do not answer . . . In the manor house she shows me her room . . . the whole large house well heated . . . I wonder about the way she was raised . . . manor house past, manor house smells, horse smells, apple smell as in the tower . . . mockingly she addresses me in the *formal* way; to her father, in the vestibule, she says, "*He* (I) hurt his knee, in the new growth"; she is always afraid of uttering the word "Türkenschanzpark" . . . as she tells it, she "grew up in Türkenschanzpark" . . . She keeps saying, "pity about the morning . . . pity about the afternoon . . . pity about the half-used evening . . ." Once, in the vestibule, "The masses are becoming *incredibly* stupid . . ."—"But how *was* your brother?" twice, "Your mother, *poor woman,*" three times; *nature bores her.*

. . . . .

Gradually my clothes too are beginning to exude the characteristic smell of Aldrans, my shoes, etc. . . .

The most striking foreign body in Aldrans besides me is *myself;* nobody can tell from my appearance *who* I am, *what* I am, *how* I am . . . I cannot tell from anyone's appearance *how he is* . . . only *what he is made of* . . . Amazing, the possibilities suddenly opened by a word like the word *Constantinople,* which I impart to a few people who have never before heard that word, like the word *Afghanistan,* the word *monomania,* the word *aphasia,* the word *plastidome* . . . To top it all, I say to our woodcutters, *Bosphorus,* and they are scared.

Procker farm, Prandl farm, Gaßl farm, Starken farm, Taxer farm . . . Sistrans, Ampaß, Ampaß, Sistrans . . . and always back to Aldrans for supper, for the preparation of supper.

[TO HOLLHOF]

Dear Sir, your publication has whetted my appetite to read more such publications by you; what gave you the idea of *The Reflexivity of the Brain*? Not the slightest hint of perplexity in your thoughts, which fact, as you may well imagine, at first sufficiently shocked me *to make me capitulate* . . .

. . . . .

A meeting with Hollhof would be unbearable to me . . . Especially having to listen to what he *knows* about our father . . . and having to suffer the pain of the injuries that would cause, without being able to run away from them in front of Hollhof . . . those revelations *that I can imagine* . . .

. . . . .

Walter's birthday without even the shadow of a thought of Walter . . . when Walter was alive: week-long *pre*parations, *after*effects of his birthday.

. . . . .

In re anatomy: yesterday, in a dream, *all to myself,* I slaughtered an object, by turns porcine/human . . . as a pig, it (my object) bolted from me through the orchard . . . I caught up with it and dragged it back through the orchard by both ears, hauling it to the slaughtering block . . . the whole orchard (at Amras) full of spattered blood . . . After the last squeal let out by the object (as a pig), it (as a person) was suddenly still; all through the night the clanging of the buckets filled with blood . . . Cause: the slaughtering that took place on the 22nd.

. . . . .

With Walter in the horse-drawn cart (in winter in the horse-drawn *sleigh*) at five in the morning, taking the fresh milk down from the farm at Aldrans to the milk platform at Rans; back again with the pig feed, then: *the lavishly set breakfast table out in the open air* . . . the first morning view of the Hafelekar . . .

. . . . .

Absurd idea of a Christmas Eve without parents and brother, without Walter's reading of the biblical nativity story, without *us* . . . A letter from

Schwaz in the Tyrol, in which I am enjoined to pay eighteen thousand shillings owed by my father to a horse trader (and cement producer) who lives there.

. . . . .

Death, appearing in so many shapes that it makes one shiver, and making all sorts of propositions to everybody . . . death coming up from the railway station, coming over from Wilten, climbing down from the larches, coming out of the air, dwelling in the hunting lodge . . .

. . . . .

Death, constantly set in relation to a particular number referring to me . . . with the *weight of the moment.*

. . . . .

Because nothing happens . . . continuous touching, palpating of bodies from which all warmth has long gone, brains from which all warmth has long gone, congealed nerve centers, ossified body cacophonies.

. . . . .

Mountains, resistances, generators of destructive decades . . . your candidacy for suicide perpetually ignoring you.

. . . . .

Studying and carrying *further* a large part of Walter's thoughts, which are your thoughts; the criminal aspect of our depressions . . .

. . . . .

Through Aldrans in the evening . . . not a soul . . . I call, nobody hears me . . . out of fear I converse with the echo that I am producing . . . that way, with the voice that is mine and remains unheard, nothing inspires confidence.

STAMS, 21 DECEMBER

Our existence, no doubt about it, was created by this Tyrolean landscape and atmosphere, corroding the finer nervous systems, brain systems, the phlogistic ones . . . Forever *feeling* ourselves, frightened at ourselves, we had been products of the life-threatening inhalation of the Tyrolean hydrogen . . . slowly killed by the confluence of bodies adverse to creation . . . We were instantly constantly led astray without a knowledge of the organs of cold nature's bodies . . . What guided us was only meteorological influences, meteorological reversals, rising temperatures, falling temperatures . . . victims of constant incisions, incitations, irritabilities, of thousands of years' unhealthy calorics, of the most unreliable mercury column in Europe.

Children of mountain crags and gorges, of the pornography of nature, we always lived only in the divinatory chemistry of the Tyrolean Alps, which is giddy with clairvoyance, each of us a diviner of misfortune, a hygrometer, a health indicator between Hafelekar and Patscherkofel . . .

. . . even as children we existed in constant fear of apoplexy, in abject dread of earthquakes, fear of collapsing buildings, rabies, in constant dread of being beaten to death, of being run over . . . Only under the shield of nature's forgetfulness, which was very great during our childhood, did we dare venture under trees, under oriels and projecting roofs . . . Never did we go with the others, *like them,* up into the mountains, the sheer drops, glaciers and summits . . . out of fear that we would hurtle down, freeze to death without mercy.

Any departure from home, from our parents' house, had been possible to us only in pain . . . because of the fear of injuries . . . The truth is that all our lives we were constantly afraid, a monstrous fear is what our parents had instilled in us . . . that fear, in the course of time, with the fatal illness of our mother, with Walter's fatal illness, had reached deeper and deeper into us, then extended within us to ever new and different regions of our natures, our physical natures, especially with regard to Walter, with regard to me, my existence which, after all, had been caused by him, our spiritual, our intellectual natures, so different from each other . . . soon, with the passage of time, we were afraid to open our books, our writings and letters, afraid to enter those gloomy, unventilated churches of the various philosophies, the monstrous dynalogies of cathedrals . . . fear of the trap doors in philosophical tunnels, the mills and lumberyards of the arts and sciences . . . even when we were still children, opening doors and windows had caused in us an impaired sense of balance, headaches, and fainting spells . . . later those things had happened to us frequently when turning a page in a book . . . with how much greater torment in Walter . . . Beginning with our very first thoughts, we had always lived in a kind of spiritual alpine incest implanted in us by our parents; on the altars they had erected everywhere we sacrificed our finest talents . . . but it is true that our parents themselves had been the products of those dreadful Tyrolean oxidations, timid viscera of the Upper Inn Valley that took millions of years to come into being as though precisely *for them* (as for us), the *unconscious ones, driven by a death wish* . . . They too had been forced to spend their lives in the perusal of our penal code Tyrol . . . which deprived them of the opportunity to study in detail, with the rigor of a scientist *not born to the disease unto death,* that Tyrolean terrestrial surface, continuously freezing them and scorching them, with which they were born . . . the beauty of the Tyrol had not been possible for them either . . . we had lived in it only to suffocate in it, rid ourselves of our lives in it . . . if we had offspring, they too, because out of us, would suffocate in it . . . Rejected by everything early on, seeking refuge, we had all our lives been locked within the hylozoism of all of us; that fact, with natural logic, overshadowed and darkened our relationship to our external environment, most devastatingly while we were at the university; it has darkened mine to this day . . . Walter and I had always been deceived; in a desolate composition of the air, in a patriarchal, fatal, antihuman galvanism caused by the perfidious heights and depths of its *architectural nature* . . . How many of our talents might we have been able to develop to amazing greatness in ourselves if we had not been born and raised in the Tyrol.

. . . . .

Spent a long time in my room, in which I can no longer feel myself, reflecting, against the backdrop of the woodcutters, first drunk and then asleep, talking in their sleep, calling women's names, names of tools, names of trees, names of children, terms for articles of clothing and leather, *dreaming off-color dreams,* on the labyrinthine aspect of my science, on its scientific aspect . . . How in it and out of it and in me the many, the thousands, but thousands of designations, *anesthetizations* are forever changing *in themselves,* how the ones (often rather seedy ones) have turned into the others, yet others . . . those uninterrupted tradescantia, bellevalia, oenothera and drosophila . . . crepis capillaris, epilobium . . . colchicine, datura stramonium, citrus maximus . . . the translocation of semichromatides demonstrated by myself . . . back mutation and lethal mutation . . . and now nothing left but araucaria, podocarpus, ginkgo, oxalis, myrtillus and calluna, the querceto-fagetea, the betoleto-pinetea, the alnetea glutinosae . . . primary and secondary types . . . tertiary types . . . the treeless tundra age, high glacial age, late glacial age, subborealicum . . .

TO NICOLUSSI

PROFESSOR OF NATURAL SCIENCES AT INNSBRUCK

Dear Professor Nicolussi, our misfortune has brought about, in a terrible manner I must say, a probably permanent separation of my person from Innsbruck and thus also a final separation from you and your science, which was already a lost cause to me. My thoughts are impotent, are no longer thoughts, likewise my feelings . . . The dark period which, in obedience to the rules, I was forced for months to spend in our auditoriums, was suddenly followed by one that was the darkest of all . . . I no longer pursue any studies, with a totally impaired sense of balance I walk through a forest of stifled experiences, fatal clues to the intellect, everything is dead, all books are dead, even the air I breathe is dead . . . How many times, countless times, have I been killed already, now that I suddenly observe myself *in myself* with the greatest human control of which I am capable . . . I thank you for your often rude silencing of my thought processes . . . for the instruction you offered me, often even late at night, in your house high above the terrible dark city, in your "metaphysical" house, as you used to say.

TO RATTEIS, BOTANIST IN PARTSCHINS

Dear Sir, the time during which, in complete secrecy and most assiduously, you taught me botany and other things besides, the time of my great affection for your art and for your personality, to which, as I know today, the whole province of Tyrol, and not just the natural sciences, owes such a great debt of gratitude . . . was the most beautiful, most successful, most valuable time of my life.

To me nothing exists any more now but the numb, sad toiling of my fellow human beings; I am no longer receptive to the magic of the *theoreti-*

cal . . . The questions I used to ask you have often come back to me with a terrible vengeance recently, and particularly at night . . . Back then already, on the Brandjoch at our first encounter, you explained many things to me that were then, later, to destroy me.

. . . . .

Aldrans: seeing that there is no longer anything left of you . . . not having to say anything any more because of the double sufferings . . .

. . . . .

On the way to the hunting lodge you discover that your despair was only an idea of despair. You were always afraid that they would exclude you from their card game . . . yesterday they did exclude you.

[TO HOLLHOF]

Dear Sir, I cannot accept your invitation to come to your estate at Kaltern. The watch, for which I extend my heartfelt thanks to you, was a present of my mother's paternal grandmother to my father and was originally among the possessions of the Fugger family . . . I thank you and bid you farewell.

. . . . .

The crow whose attentive gaze distracts me, stuck as it is on the ice, and which I thrust into the air in a flash with the point of my walking stick.

Readings of Walter, sensations of Walter, desperations of Walter.

SCHERMBERG, 11 FEBRUARY

Dear Uncle, I left Aldrans and, indeed, the Tyrol eight weeks ago; *if* a human being can, *you* will understand me . . . that I suddenly, without the possibility of even the slightest Tyrolean existence, hurt you so deeply . . .

. . . forgive me and forgive me for Walter as well . . . even the company of the workers was in the end nothing but one long torment to me; *the mere sight of those people* . . .

. . . if I was of use to you at the hunting lodge, even in the most laughable way.

. . . now I can claim a certain measure of experience in timber processing as well.

. . . supposedly safe, to make an attempt to explain my inappropriate conduct.

My plan is not to abandon my studies, just to pursue them solely *within myself* in future . . . the conditions prevailing in our insane asylums an *embarrassment* to all of us.

PLAYING WATTEN

TRANSLATED BY KENNETH J. NORTHCOTT

At the end of September I realized quite a large sum of money from the sale of the Oelling property, which, after the death of my guardian, was split equally between my cousin and me. I had no wish to use it for myself, but I wanted to devote it to some good purpose, and in fact, inspired by reading several of the lawyer-mathematician Undt's writings, all of which deal with the hopeless situation facing prisoners who have just been released from jail, I decided to write a short letter and simply, as a matter of course, offer the sum of money that had unexpectedly fallen to me to this man, who, not only in his writings but even more immediately by his personal intervention, placed himself, at any time and with great devotion, at the disposal of those outcasts among men. On 11 September, I communicated to Undt, who, devoted as he was to his task, had for years been established in Gars am Kamp, which, though a small and modest place, was extraordinarily helpful for his purposes, my decision to place one and a half million schillings at his disposal, and on the thirteenth I received the following reply: Dear Sir, If you intend to place at my disposal, with no other condition than that it be used exclusively for the purposes for which I have been working for almost three decades and, as I believe, not totally without success, I would ask you to remit the sum by return mail. Very sincerely yours, F. Undt. On the very same day, I arranged for the money to be sent to Undt. Two days later the recipient confirmed receipt of the one and half million. He wrote: Dear Sir, I shall use the sum that I received today to adapt Castle Thunau, with which you are familiar and in which I intend, before the beginning of winter, to house eighty men who have been released from Suben. Very sincerely yours, F. Undt. Two months later on 17 November, Undt replied to a letter that I had mailed on the thirteenth in which I asked him for the titles of writings that had appeared under his name. Undt had published them but, because of the circumstances surrounding the seclusion in which I live, they had until then remained unknown to me. He wrote: Dear Sir, my most important works, and I shall only mention those, are *Books:* Decrepitude I, Decrepitude II, Decrepitude III; *Articles:* Compensation for Unlawful Arrest, The Judged and the Condemned; *Essay:* Body and Chaos. Sincerely, Undt. The following day (yesterday) I received the following note from Undt: Dear Sir, since, as I assume, you are familiar with my intellectual work, it will not come as a surprise to you if I ask you *to write a report on your perceptions, over a period of several hours, of the day before the day that you received this note.* As you know, I only ask for a self-description of this sort from persons who, I feel, are without any shadow of doubt extraordinary and absolutely ideal for my scientific purposes. Sincerely, Undt. Since my work on chronic subchronic nephritis (*morbus Brightii*) is not yet complete, I hesitated at first, but then immediately set about doing what Undt had asked. I swung round in my chair and, using the windowsill, not the desk, as a suitable writing surface, I wrote: Dear Sir, when I wake up I usually think: why am I alive? and why do I live in this hut? and people ask, why do you live in that hut? and I reply: because I live in the hut, sir. As I am getting up, I think to myself that I have, for the longest time, been unable to walk as far as the gravel pit, in fact, even with the utmost exertion, I cannot get as far as the rotten spruce tree. In the last twenty years I have walked that way with terrifying regularity: hut, rotten spruce, gravel pit, rotten spruce, hut. Now and again I would make a detour over the pond, dear sir. In the midst of the gravel pit, with no thought in my head but catching my breath, I would catch my breath. I would breathe deeply in and out. This habit I think saved my life. I walk, and while I am walking I count the number of steps I take. Four thousand to the rotten spruce, eight thousand to the gravel pit. When it is very hot. When it is very cold, dear sir. Signs of exhaustion, of course. Daily as far as the gravel pit; on Wednesday I go and play watten.* I now no longer walk to the gravel pit. No longer to the rotten spruce. Do not leave the hut at all any more. *Yesterday:* got up, washed, dressed, and then the truck driver comes by and asks me why I no longer go and play watten, and I try to explain why,

*For a description of the game, see p. ix. *Trans.*

but I cannot explain why. I say: no, no more watten playing. You knock, I say, I open the door for you, you come in, I say, you come in and sit down without ceremony, stretch your legs out, and you always ask the same question: why don't you go and play watten any more, doctor? I say: would you like something to drink? You say: no! no! and you repeat: why don't you play watten any more, doctor? I say: no, no more watten playing. Today he's wearing his winter cape, I think to myself, that means it's winter. I do not go to play watten any more I think to myself, I say: Look, I don't even go to the rotten spruce any more, let alone the gravel pit, let alone to the inn. Of course, I say, I've tried to go to the inn but I didn't even get as far as the rotten spruce. There's no sense in trying to persuade me. I say to the truck driver: I don't go and play watten any more, it's impossible. But he acts as though I hadn't said anything. It's about time to go and play watten again, he says. It's always the same, dear sir, he just sits there and keeps saying, at short intervals, that I should go and play watten again, and I keep answering: no, no more watten playing. When he's gone, I swear that I will never let him in again. But I do open the door to him again, he comes in, and the scene is repeated: why don't you go and play watten, doctor? and I say: no more watten playing. Yesterday: the winter cape was his father's, I think to myself. I start putting my papers in order, even though I know it is pointless, but all the same, out of the pile of papers on the desk I select those that belong together—notes, letters, bills, old prescriptions, notices, drafts. Even though I know that the mess gets worse and worse. If I've told you a hundred times, I say, I don't go and play watten any more, I don't go and play watten any more, there's no point in your coming to see me to try to persuade me to go and play watten, but the truck driver hasn't been listening. You come here every week and waste your time and ruin mine while you're trying to persuade me. He doesn't listen. But even if I did suddenly feel the need to go and play watten again, I wouldn't go. Leave me in peace, I say. Find yourself someone else. Everybody round here plays watten. *I* don't play watten any more. A lot of people are just waiting to be asked to play watten. Why don't you leave me in peace and give up on me? I say. All they think of around here is playing watten, I say, you would find someone to play watten with you in a second and you'd see that I'm superfluous. They all play watten better than I've ever played. Just think of Urban, the hardware merchant, I say. You keep pressing me to go and play watten. I don't understand why you've got it into your head that I should go and play watten again. If I don't play watten any longer it doesn't mean that the whole group doesn't play watten any longer. One man for Siller, the suicide, and one man for me, it's easy enough to find two people who play watten. Go to Urban the hardware merchant, I say. I know that Urban plays watten better than anybody. And you get along like a house on fire with the hardware merchant, I say, and the schoolmaster gets along well with Urban, and the landlord, all of them. I don't play watten any more, I say, but the truck driver reacts quite differently from the way I had expected, he says: come and play watten on Wednesday, doctor! I am quite determined not to go and play watten any more. I'm pretending to arrange my papers, but in reality I am creating even more mess among them. The presence of the truck driver makes me behave in a totally stupid manner. This whole pile of prescriptions, notes, notices, thoughts, I say. But it's true, I think to myself, that I always had my best ideas, my best thoughts, on my way to play watten. I've got to sort out this pile of papers, I say to the truck driver, but all the while running through my head is the thought: every time the truck driver comes, the mess on the desk is worse. Actually, dear sir, on my way to play watten I always had a clear idea of matter, the outer and the inner world both withdrew from me; they did not continue when I was on my way to play watten. A head full of learning! Do you know what that is called, I say to the truck driver. The truck driver says: the landlord has bought some new chairs. The watten table has new chairs, he says. Already on Monday I would have calmed down at the thought that I would be going to play watten on Wednesday, dear sir. Tuesday was entirely given over to preparing for Wednesday. I say to the truck driver: playing watten was always crucial for me. And crucial above all, I think to myself, the moment my practice was closed down. Suspected of, you know, I say to the truck driver. The law, I say. Morphine, I say. There's some truth in it, I say, but the fact that I was no longer allowed to practice is a rotten trick. Not to be allowed to practice, to deaden the nerve. To forbid someone to practice is to kill him, dear sir, it destroys him. Instead of going to my consulting room, dear sir, when I was forbidden to practice, I went to play watten. I had a refuge, dear sir. Rotten spruce, gravel pit, playing watten. I didn't want to trouble the high court.

Nothing but unpleasantness from the highest authority on down. Without a doubt, a good doctor, I could have said that straight out if I myself had not been the doctor. Other people said I was a good doctor. Closing down my practice only helps my competitor, I said. The truck driver sat motionless the whole time, as though he were surprised by the fact that today, for the first time, he was wearing his winter cape and as though he were incapable of the slightest movement, at least of his head. His father was a well-known butcher, but disgust at, and loathing of, animals that had been slaughtered made the son develop the father's business, one of the largest butchers in the province, into a trucking firm that was just as reputable. I say to the truck driver: playing watten every day at that time. But the truck driver does not understand me. He looks at me, notices that instead of tidying up my desk I am making an even greater mess. First of all playing watten *three* times a week, I think to myself, then playing watten *twice* a week, then playing watten *once* a week. Human beings are probably constructed for a world quite different from their own, I say. The truck driver says: it's time you went to play watten again, doctor. He said that the last time I played watten I left my hat in the inn, going to fetch it would give me an opportunity to play watten again. Come and play watten tomorrow, says the truck driver and picks up a piece of paper for me that has fallen off the desk. A letter I never mailed, I say, a reminder about a fee, a very large one admittedly, but quite justified, addressed to the major German industrialist, I say. Rich people take their time about paying, they don't pay anything for months, years even, and then they suddenly pay a ridiculous sum, which has nothing to do with the sum you originally demanded. But to go to court, I can't do that, I say. You would have to go to court every day and go to court about everything and everybody and finally waste all the strength you have on legal matters, a person could easily exhaust himself by spending his whole life doing nothing but litigate, litigation that he would always have reason to pursue. Basically, everyone ought to be litigating against everyone else all the time, I say. Hundreds of decent fees, I say, but none of these wealthy people give a thought to paying. When they heard that my practice had been closed, all these people thought that they now had a reason for not paying me. People are mean, because the world they live in is mean. Everything about people is mean. Meanness and nature, as the nature of meanness, complement one another,

I say. Now and again people speak out, but there's no point in speaking out. The only thing in their heads is the lust for profit and the malice of deception, I say. If you take nature apart, it is easy to recognize that its construction is a deception in all its parts. And the megalomaniacal person is the same in his natural meanness. The line that stretches in a philosophical idiocy towards the horizon always turns out in the end to be a perversion, I say. Every day at the same time, I say to the truck driver, in the evening before I went to bed, I thought I would go and play watten. *Lying* in bed and *sitting* in bed, I imagined I was going to play watten, while in reality I was completely engaged in making *one* philosophy out of *all* diseases. This is something the truck driver does not understand. But I say to the truck driver: I shall go *then* and I shall go *there,* I enter the wood from all sides, if I go *into* the wood to go and play watten. Actually, if I come into the middle of the wood I approach myself from all sides to go and play watten. Actually, all the selves that are coming into the wood are going to play watten. And the only thing they are thinking about is going to play watten. But that is the strange thing, I say: they are all thinking they're going to play watten, but they don't go and play watten. They want to go and play watten, but they go to play watten and they don't go to play watten, I say. Always the idea, especially when I am busy with diseases, that I would go to play watten, I do go to play watten, hundreds and thousands approach me to go to play watten at the same time as I go and play watten. The fact is, I say to the truck driver, the schoolmaster has the same idea. While he is at home correcting exercise books, he has the idea that he is going to play watten *as several selves.* But while, in my imagination, Siller the suicide is absent, I say, in the schoolmaster's imagination Siller the suicide also goes to play watten. In the schoolmaster's imagination, Siller is also sitting at the table, while in my imagination he is not sitting at the table. In the schoolmaster's imagination I too am sitting at the watten table. If he can't get to sleep, I say to the truck driver, the schoolmaster imagines that we are all going to play watten, even Siller the suicide, which is really very interesting, because Siller the suicide is no longer present in my imaginary view of playing watten. In my imagination thousands of people who are all *me,* I say, are going to play watten. Not Siller the suicide. In my imaginary view, the schoolmaster says, hundreds of people who are all *me* are going to play watten, Siller the suicide as well. It is quite simple, I say to the truck driver, to replace one of us. The hardware store owner will play for me and, in place of the suicide, you could have the man with the wooden leg (also a mill hand) who is already pensioned off, which is an advantage, I say. If one of us doesn't want to play watten or cannot play watten, someone else will play for him. Siller the papermaker hanged himself, so someone else plays watten for Siller, I don't go and play watten any longer, not because Siller the papermaker hanged himself but because I no longer go and play watten, and so someone else plays for me. But the truck driver says nothing, dear sir, and remains motionless. For two or three hours I breathe regularly, dear sir, I think to myself and totally forget that I am breathing and then suddenly everything within me is in chaos, and I hear that I am breathing, and I watch how I walk and I breathe in too shallowly or I breathe out too shallowly and I take steps that are much too short. I either breathe in too heavily or I breathe out too heavily, or I walk too quickly or I walk too slowly. My head doesn't move though it should move. I keep thinking: stand still, sit down, lie down . . . in the hut, I immediately lie down and stretch out, *I try* to stretch out, but without success. *I scrunch up* but I do not stretch out, I think to myself. The truck driver watches me while I am thinking: I draw my legs in, I draw my head in as part of the bodily tension which is the source of my mental tension. Breathe regularly, I think to myself on the bed, and I try to breathe regularly on the bed. Then I remember the writings that I have totally neglected. Breathe regularly, I think to myself, but I cannot breathe regularly, because you cannot walk regularly either, as you know, if you think: walk regularly. If you watch how you walk, it is a hopping movement, not just walking along the street. The fact that I have not learned the necessary regularity in breathing is depressing. I tried to compensate for this incapacity by visiting the spa in Hall, I think to myself. But my stay in Bad Hall did me no good, I think to myself. My condition got worse. All I have to look forward to, and I have thought this ever since childhood, is deterioration. But at least I had the strength to go to Bad Hall, I think to myself. Look, even taking the waters is completely pointless, I say to the truck driver. Indeed after a short stay in a spa like that people get strokes and spas are well known for having the largest cemeteries. They're full of people who have come to the spa from far and wide in order to improve their health. Names from the whole of Europe in the cemeteries of the smallest spas, I say. Dear sir, at my age, just imagine, I actually fell for the spa quackery. I say to the truck driver: spas are a swindle. You let yourself be persuaded to take a cure and that means a short and fatal process that costs a fortune. Taking a cure is like falling into a trap, and the greatest stupidity of all is visiting spas, and every year millions of people go to spas and persuade themselves that it is a good idea. Actually I think my condition is *now* much worse than it was *before* the cure, I say to the truck driver: You yourself took me to the station, when was it exactly that I went to Bad Hall? The truck driver says: six months ago. Yes, I say, six months ago. Shortly after that the papermaker committed suicide. *Before* Bad Hall, I say to the truck driver, I could breathe regularly for a whole morning and for a whole afternoon and that means walk regularly, but that seemed to me too little and I went to Bad Hall; *before* Bad Hall, I could actually walk to the gravel pit with ease, actually in extreme heat and in extreme cold actually. *Before* Bad Hall it was the easiest thing in the world, my greatest pleasure, to walk as far as the rotten spruce, whereas *after* Bad Hall I couldn't even get as far as the rotten spruce, let alone go into the gravel pit to play watten, I say. I actually thought *before* Bad Hall that *after* Bad Hall I would get to the rotten spruce more quickly than I did *before* Bad Hall, more quickly to the gravel pit and be playing watten more quickly. The truth is I don't go the rotten spruce any more. I can't go and play watten any more. It's not the suicide's fault. I can no longer go and play watten. And yet the distance from the hut to the rotten spruce is laughable. But of course, I say, if I increase my extreme effort, increase the most extreme of all efforts, if I make myself into nothing but a single ruthlessness towards myself, etc., I say, even if I could walk to the rotten spruce again, I still would not go and play watten. No, no more watten playing, I say. Dear sir, it often seems to me that I have suddenly gone to play watten again. The truck driver comes at shorter and shorter intervals and asks why I don't go and play watten any more. He came today, I wasn't even dressed, I think. I hadn't had breakfast and the truck driver was already there. *Commotio cerebri* I suddenly say, *contusio cerebri, compressio cerebri*. Of course all of that is a mitigating circumstance, I say. People can bring up anything as a mitigating circumstance, I say. Would the truck driver like something to drink? I ask. No, nothing, he says. The poor devils can testify in court that they were poor, and the rich that they were rich. All of them with the same justification. And the stupid that they have been stupid all their lives. Some declare that they have been *disadvantaged* all their lives, others that they have been *privileged* all their lives. *Everything* is a mitigating circumstance. Some say that they have seen the whole world, others that they have seen nothing. Some that they have received advanced schooling, others that they have received no schooling at all, the philosopher says he was a philosopher, the butcher that he was a butcher. All these people always have an alibi. Every existence is a mitigating circumstance, dear sir. Before every court, before every self-judgment. At this point I stood up, and the truck driver rose, in his winter cape he seemed to me to be even smaller, his head jerked as if he were frightened, his whole body gave the impression that my suddenly standing up had taken him completely by surprise, had given him a start, and I went over to the picture of my maternal grandparents and put it straight, because the whole time I had been sitting opposite the truck driver I had been irritated by the picture's not hanging straight, no matter where I come across a picture that isn't hanging straight I am irritated and I cannot rest until I have put the picture that is in front of me straight; I put the picture straight and said: terrible, these pictures that don't hang straight! Then I sat down again, and the truck driver also sat down again. Can you imagine, dear sir, that pictures on the wall that don't hang straight can drive me out of my mind, can ruin a whole day for me? So, I said to the truck driver, now it's hanging straight again. How did the picture come to be moved? People ask, I think to myself, what does it look like in your hut? And they come into the hut and sit down and watch me. The truck driver watches me. The childlessness that constantly depresses him, I think to myself. People come into the hut and first of all they make the hut filthy, then they make me filthy, make everything filthy, people with their dirty eyes, I think to myself. They set traps when they ask questions and set traps when they don't ask questions. But they also set traps when we answer; if I give an answer, then I've fallen into a trap. People ask me something trivial and then they have lured me into the trap of something of tremendous importance. But people always get me to let them in. I believe I have to let the people in, I open the door to them, I even go on to say that they should sit down. Sit down in the armchair, I say. While they are sitting there, they drink and eat with me and set traps. Trappers, I think to myself. They want to know how, from what, and by what I live, etc., what it is to be a bachelor, etc., who is the person *nearest* to me, and what is he like, etc., it doesn't matter what we answer, a trap has been set for us, even if I do not answer, the trap has been set for me and I fall into it, I have to fall into it. Innumerable traps, if we stay silent. When we invite people in and after they've sat down in our armchairs they thrust us down into our own abyss. They lure us back into earlier times, impose our childhood, youth, age, and so forth upon us, and thrust us into what for ages we had believed we had escaped from. Above all, people lure us back into earlier times. They come to us sentimentalistically. People come into our house, just as they come into my hut, in order to destroy us, to destroy me. In every case, to make us ridiculous, just as the truck driver, after all, only comes into my hut to make me ridiculous. They knock on the door and clap their curiosity, like a deathly piece of nastiness, onto our head. People come in as harmlessness itself and suddenly oppress us with their frightful corporeality, I think to myself. People ask something irrelevant in order to divert us into irrelevance and at the same time they tear down the curtain our own filth is hidden behind. I believe that death is hammering at our temples, I say to the truck driver, I say *come in,* but death does not open the door. I've lived to the point of satiety, I must say that now, I think to myself. Actually I have lived so abundantly that every day sickens me if I just think about it. I can do calculations, I can do calculations as well as a good businessman, but never beyond the limit of calculability. I often sit down with them, with people, dear sir, and talk in their language, and I've eaten the same things as these people, drunk the same things, felt the same hunger, thirst, interests, etc., but my brain is *different.* I have to *be* in isolation. It is absolute nonsense to think that someone like me can simply give up everything that makes one what one is, and sink down into the crowd. The crowd soon recognizes the nonsense and destroys you, or tries to destroy you. The crowd eliminates someone like me, someone who has surrendered himself to them one hundred percent, mercilessly like a foreign body. I do not belong among the crowd, if I hear the crowd, *I belong to myself,* if I hear myself. Since the crowd eliminates me, I have no other choice but to look round for a death in myself, as long as that still interests me. Because this interest too is limited. And then? Since to me death is merely a substitute for the crowd. Whatever is said is all lies, that is the truth, dear sir, the empty phrase is our lifelong prison. From time to time, I say to myself, in all seriousness, everything is mere deception through being alone, through isolation, through me. From truth I deduce lies, just as I deduce lies from the truth, just as I deduce humiliation from myself. Very early on, I say to the truck driver, I gave up asking what the purpose was, because I knew early on that this sort of questioning led to despair, possibly to a humiliating *permanent* madness. To continue to ask means to continue to be mad. Last night I didn't sleep a wink, I say to the truck driver. I lay awake the whole time and I took pleasure in being awake, this was not, as it usually is, an agonizing condition for me to be in, on the contrary I lay there, I thought to myself, and breathed peacefully, from time to time I raised myself up in bed and took a deep breath, and then stretched out flat again. I became aware of a sudden, strange peace in my body, strange, because it seemed to me to be a completely natural peace that had begun the moment I had undressed and climbed into bed, not the slightest trace of my illness. Peace streamed through my arteries and my veins, soon my whole body was nothing but this peace itself. Probably the result of a restlessness in my body that had recently bordered on the unbearable, but not only my body, my mind too was peace itself, and I could think what I liked, I thought, just to give an example, of *encephalitis;* the most ridiculous thing of all was to think that the most ridiculous things could all at once be put in order and thus to think, in the nature of things, of everything that I had willfully destroyed in the early days of my history. Objects. The world around me. I breathed peacefully, and thought peacefully. Everything transparent. Everything logical. Not a sound, nothing that would have disturbed me. As you know, I say to the truck driver, all night long the hut is full of noises. I myself often react catastrophically to natural noises. Even with the windows open I don't hear a single sound. But, in some circumstances, it is precisely this complete *sound*lessness, as *life*lessness, that could have proved fatal to me, I think to myself. But that evening I felt absolutely no fear, perhaps because I was not afraid, everything else was as peaceful as I was myself. I was at peace, I think, whereas otherwise I think of nothing but my unease, and that makes me uneasy. I use a hundred methods for getting to sleep and cannot get to sleep. Dear sir, this may be a circumstance with which you are familiar: you cannot fall asleep, because you want to fall asleep, because you know that you want to fall asleep, etc. At first my mind is set against sleep, yet I want to fall asleep, etc., then my body too is set against sleep, while I want to fall asleep, etc. Because I can no longer be intellectually naive it seems as though I can also no longer be physically naive. Probably my mind and my body are both eternally and urgently at the mercy of nature in the most intense way possible, whereby greater and greater difficulties arise, everything becomes a complication. Most people simply separate mind and body from one another, switch off the mind at one time and the body at another and so, entirely for themselves and in all circumstances, always lead a completely *normal* life. For the longest time now, I have lacked every prerequisite for this. But on that evening, I think to myself, as I watch the truck driver, I had no intention of falling asleep, on the contrary, I wanted to stay awake as long as possible, because what had otherwise always seemed to me to be sinister, as I lay awake, had suddenly, for every possible and conceivable reason, turned into peace for me, nothing but peace and since I live in a state of continual unease, I found, as you can imagine, that this sudden peace was pleasant. Everything was suddenly easy. Because of that I was able, for the longest time, to progress in a certain direction, actually as a person, as you must imagine, in a direction that cannot be defined as a point on the compass. I thought: everything is a vile simplification of the cosmos. You enter infinity and remain unharmed, I thought to myself. I have probably, I say to the truck driver, a sudden observation for me too, overtaxed myself by absolute inactivity, that is by the most intense concentration possible. The truck driver did not understand me. Everything can be explained, I say to him, but at the decisive moment nothing can be explained. Even though I am not at an age when such a thought would be natural, I feel, I think to myself, totally isolated, all this while the truck driver remains silent, because, I think, I have neglected to ensure, in a timely fashion, that I have people around me who are intellectually akin to me, that is, not just emotionally akin, but also intellectually akin, people who think like me, while not having to feel like me, who are, like me, more interested in improbability than in truth, but who are still interested in music, in art, in the products of the imagination. What we lack here, I say to the truck driver, is an artist, a painter and so forth, we don't even have a quick-change artist! I exclaim, but of course the truck driver does not know what I mean by that. So, dear sir, as time has gone by, I have concentrated exclusively on the workers here on the hundreds of factory hands among whom I have been living for nearly three decades. Today, I am older than I am, and basically I have no one, yet I persuade myself that I simply have everything by virtue of my mind. The workers in the paper mill, when all's said and done, are a naturally uncomprehending bunch. A person like Siller, I now say to the truck driver, a man so completely withdrawn into himself, was necessary, indispensable, for watten playing; each of us is similarly necessary and indispensable. Because, if we had not had the schoolmaster, I say, if we had not had you, I say to the truck driver, who knows. But in any case the landlord too was always indispensable. And the landlord's wife and then everything connected with watten playing. Of course it is easy to say I'm not going to play watten any more, but it is also impossible to explain why I am not going to play watten any more. Neither of us knows why I am not going to play watten any more, in the nature of things because of the Siller catastrophe, I say, but also completely independently of the Siller catastrophe. The cause and effect are as familiar to you as they are to me, but, I say, you keep on demanding an explanation from me and that I cannot give you, but on the other hand, as I know, you will keep demanding it from me because I know you. That's the sort of character you are. And, I say to the truck driver, this is connected with the idea that everyone has a right to everything and has to exert that right, everyone to everything, do you take my meaning, what you hear me say is what I mean. At that moment I could no longer bear to stay seated, I stood up, and the truck driver stood up. I put my winter cape around my shoulders, probably because the truck driver was wearing one like it, although I wasn't in the least bit cold, slipped on my rubbers and left the hut. *Walk!* I said, *walk!* and the truck driver saw that I could not walk. Just around the hut, I said. Just around the hut once, I say. The truck driver is too close to me, I say: do keep your distance. The truck driver says: trees dying everywhere! and he points in the direction of the rotten spruce, which, however, at this time of the year, you can no longer see from the hut. As if to show them to myself once more, I show the truck driver my shoes. Here, I say, I've had a large buckle sewn on, look, this large buckle, the largest buckle there is, the shoemaker maintains that a buckle of this size does not exist, but I wouldn't leave him in peace and he did find a buckle of the size I wanted. At first the shoemaker had refused to go into town, I say, but then I forced him to go: in town, I said to the shoemaker, I say to the truck driver, there is absolutely certain to be a buckle like this, and the shoemaker went into town and actually found this buckle. Every shoe has a buckle that is too small, dear sir. I said to the truck driver: in the dark, when I get dressed and it is always dark when I get dressed, when I get dressed or undressed it is dark in the hut, you can see how dark it is in the hut even in broad daylight! I simply cannot see the small buckles. A nervous tremor goes through my whole body, I say to the truck driver, when I *look for* the buckles on my shoes so as to unbuckle them or buckle them up. I am already so old that I cannot find the small buckles that people have on their shoes today. So we must get larger buckles, I said to the shoemaker, and he went into town and found these large buckles, and I had him put these large buckles on all my shoes. Of course the industry saves money, produces these ridiculous little buckles. The large buckles cost more, of course. The industry cuts corners wherever it can. Smaller buckles cost less than larger buckles, I say. The industry cuts corners especially on buckles and laces. Today every shoe has these ridiculous little buckles which you can't find without bending down you cannot find these ridiculous little buckles. But you can buckle or unbuckle these large buckles *immediately* without having to bend right down to the tips of your toes as though you were totally blind. Everybody has these little buckles on their shoes, I say to the truck driver, that's why it takes everybody such a long time to get their shoes on. But, I say, look! I say to the truck driver, I can close this large buckle *immediately,* open and close it *immediately,* one movement of the hand, without having to put my head on the floor, and it's buckled up. Actually, of late everything has been too small for me, that's because my shortsightedness is getting worse, from day to day I grow more shortsighted. People exploit it of course. Shortsightedness is always exploited. Oh, a shortsighted person! people say, and you are already the object of their deceitful intentions. A shortsighted person, they say to each other, and you've lost a pile of money. Industry makes everything too small nowadays, I say to the truck driver, they make everything too short and too tight, and of the very poorest quality. Basically, people go around in clothes that are a swindle, because they are too short, too tight and of poor quality. But people have long ago lost the feeling for quality. For durability. For first-class workmanship. Everything you touch falls apart after only a short while. But industry doesn't think of anything but tossing products onto the market that are worthless after a few days. You slip on a shirt, I say, and it tears, a pair of trousers and they tear, you put on your hat and it tears. It doesn't matter what you put on, it tears in a moment; if you wash it, it falls to bits, etc. If you put new shoelaces in, they break, if you buckle up your shoes the buckles crumble into pieces, if you bend over in a new overcoat it tears, everything tears and breaks and crumbles into pieces: that's progress. Just think, I say to the truck driver, about the door handles you get today, you open a door and you're holding the handle in your hand and it's all very embarrassing, etc. You crank the window down and the window falls on your head, you pick up a bucket full of water and all you're left holding is the handle. And I tell the truck driver the story of my sister's glasses. I say to the truck driver: a year before her death, my sister went to the optician in town to get a new pair of glasses. The wearisome steps you have to take if you want a new pair of glasses, I say. To get an ordinary pair of glasses, my sister went into town twice, three times, four times, because the optician had to test her eyes not once, but three times and four times, even five times. Finally my sister, you remember the dainty little woman, she was shortsighted like me, gets her glasses and she comes home and comes into my room to show me the glasses. I'm sitting at the desk reading Georg Forster's *Voyage Around the World,* I don't want to be disturbed, I say, I'm reading Forster, I say, Forster do you hear! I say, can't you see that I'm reading Forster? I ask, but my sister is not to be put off, she comes into the room and stands there in the room and I cannot throw her out: it's not clear to me why she, who always heeded all my commands, *refuses* to heed my command to leave me in peace, to leave me alone with Forster; then I see why: she's wearing her new glasses. She had just come from town, she said, the glasses were finished, she's wearing her new glasses, her new glasses were finally ready, really, I say, the new glasses, now she can see everything again, as close up as possible, she said, even if the new glasses are not reading glasses as the optician said, they were still glasses for short distances, even if not for the very shortest: she could now see everything a meter away, even a half-meter away. The glasses at last! she repeats, it doesn't bother her that she has had to wait eight weeks for the glasses and has had to go into town almost ten times because of the glasses, that the optician had made a fool of her for such a long time, opticians make a fool of everyone, now she had her glasses and the glasses were good, good and handsome, and she wants to show me her glasses, so she takes them off, and I say she should put the glasses on again, and she puts the glasses on again and the glasses fall to bits. The glasses break into seven or eight pieces. Yes, I say to the truck driver, everything's the same as those glasses. Industry makes everything just for looks and for popular poor taste, you understand! And look, the buckles on my shoes broke off, after I'd buckled and unbuckled them two or three times, and so I've had to have new buckles put on. It was not easy to persuade someone like the shoemaker to put new buckles on my shoes, I say. Of course I often ask myself whether these buckles are not much too big, whether smaller buckles would not have sufficed, larger than the old buckles but not as large as the new ones, half as big, I say. But I don't care about people; what people think doesn't interest me, has never interested me, they can think what they like about my buckles. Actually it is easier to rivet these buckles on to leather shoes, it is much more difficult to rivet them on to rubbers; you know of course that I prefer to walk in rubbers, it's a well-known fact that I much prefer to run around in rubbers. Nobody knows me in anything but rubbers. Rubbers have the greatest advantages. On the other hand I'm ruining my feet. Nothing but sweat makers these rubbers, I say. But at my age and in my situation it is a matter of complete indifference whether I run around in rubbers or in leather shoes: in any case I prefer to run around in rubbers. I am completely indifferent, I say to the truck driver. Actually, I still have dozens of pairs of shoes, all of which I shall give away. *I am not going to give my shoes away yet,* but one day I shall give all my shoes away. I used to buy myself a pair of shoes whenever the opportunity presented itself, wherever I went, the first thing I did was to go into a shoe shop and try on shoes. Tried on dozens of pairs, tried and tried them on, I say, and in every case I bought a pair of shoes. I have bought shoes in Paris, in London, in Cracow, in Warsaw, in Oslo, I say. I bought myself a pair of Canadian boots in Canada. Having traveled around so much in my youth, out of desperation, I think, because I was tired of life, I say to the truck driver, I have in the nature of things the most varied collection of shoes, all my shoes are made in the most diverse styles, the best leathers, I say, the finest linings. To this day, I treat my shoes with Slovakian dubbin, I say. I dub the shoes but I don't put them on again. Because now I only wear rubbers. I hold them under the tap when they are dirty, I say. I always took the greatest pleasure in dubbing my shoes, I say. I could spend half a day dubbing my shoes. I think to myself: I stand in front of the door and dub my shoes. But I shall probably never wear a pair of leather shoes again in my lifetime, I say, because I only walk in rubbers. For years I have been wearing rubbers and I am not ashamed, I am not embarrassed. I even go to funerals in rubbers, more recently in rubber boots. Summer and winter in rubbers, rubber boots. Leather shoes are an anachronism, I think to myself. Of course I ask myself why I had the large buckles put on my leather shoes, for as far as I can see I shall never put on a leather shoe again. But of course it may be that after my death people will put on these leather shoes of mine, and these people will look upon these large buckles as a great distinction, I think. It is also perfectly possible, I say to the truck driver, that someone will live in the hut after my death, will exist here, will exist in the darkness and will then look upon the large buckles on the shoes that I have left behind for him as a great distinction. Look, I say, I bend down, the truck driver watches me, I open the buckle on my right shoe, look, I say, see how easily the buckle is opened, and the truck driver nods, and I say: look, the buckle springs shut again just as quickly, and the truck driver nods, after the buckle has closed. No other buckle springs shut again so quickly, is buckled up again so quickly, I say. It cost me the greatest effort and diplomacy, I say, to persuade the shoemaker that these large buckles were necessary. He may even have thought I was a fool: now he tells people, full of pride, *about the large buckles on my shoes.* Good, I say to the truck driver, let's go back into the hut. The truck driver hadn't for a moment thought of taking his leave and leaving me alone. It's this terrible weather that makes even the healthiest person fall ill, I say. The truck driver has sat down again in his armchair. I watch him. He watches me. Suddenly he tells me about the traveler and about the traveler's tale.

The Traveler

Last night about eleven, the truck driver begins, and the landlord was surprised as well, the traveler, who two months ago discovered Siller the papermaker on a tree in the gravel pit, came into the bar. The traveler, without saying a word and without the landlord's trying to stop him, sat down at the watten table, at which he, the truck driver, had seen no one sit for the whole of October and the first half of November. The situation that arose because of the death of the papermaker and the distress of everyone who knew him, even if they had only the slightest connection with him, were suddenly brought back to the truck driver's mind, in all their strangeness, by the traveler's tale. And also of course by the traveler's lack of sensitivity: scarcely had he sat down at the watten table, ordered beer, bread, pickled sausage, and salt than he started to talk about poor Siller. About the circumstances in which he had found the suicide, the truck driver said, and he spoke in the most thoughtless manner possible, in what was, actually, a terrifying manner. If until then those papermakers who were still in the inn at the time, the truck driver said, who were actually sitting in silence and, in keeping with the weather, in an emotionally numb state, had sought as laboriously as possible, with the means at their disposal on such a depressing evening, to lengthen their stay at the inn, and drink their beer, which had now grown warm, in peace and so shorten the coming night, which would without doubt be a torment to them, they now turned their whole attention to the traveler, who, to their surprise, all at once *completely differently from two months before,* when they had all been under the immediate pressure of Siller's, the papermaker's, suicide, and the traveler, who in the nature of things had been most damagingly put under pressure by the local police officers who sat down with him and plied him with their pointed questions, related the story of Siller's end in every detail, and now, two months later, after so long an emotional and mental gap, the traveler affirmed that he was telling the whole truth. On that Wednesday, I said, we all went to play watten but weren't able to play watten. An excess of the foehn, I said. Everyone went into the woods to play watten, everyone coming from a different direction, going to play watten. You know, I said to the truck driver, I was wandering around in the wood for four hours, four hours!! You were wandering around for two hours, but I wandered around for four hours! And passed the gravel pit again and again. Even the schoolmaster was disoriented, I say. As we now know, the papermaker had also become disoriented. You yourself insisted, I say to the truck driver, that you had become disoriented, totally disoriented, I say. The truck driver's healthy constitution and the ability to orient himself as a result of this healthy constitution saved him, the truck driver, from total disorientation. You are the only one, I say, who emerged from that catastrophic Wednesday completely unharmed, for in truth the *two* hours that you had to walk backwards and forwards in the woods are as nothing compared with the *four* hours that I was wandering about. The schoolmaster, I say, banged his head and fell into the pond as well, as you know, his wife didn't discover the schoolmaster until the next morning, half frozen in front of the front door, I say. And the papermaker hanged himself. We all went to play watten and we nearly all perished together. The papermaker hanged himself. I would have thought that the schoolmaster was more likely to commit suicide than the papermaker, I say to the truck driver, the schoolmaster was the person I always connected with suicide, not Siller. But nature, dear sir, and this is something people always forget, is completely philosophical, and the characters who are most endangered, whom we always assume to be the most unfortunate people, always emerged from the great and even the greatest difficulties, even if they did emerge as *the characters who are most endangered*. But as much as I know about the schoolmaster's life, as little do I know about Siller's life, I say to the truck driver. I know this person from A to Z was what I always thought about the papermaker's life, I say, whereas in reality I knew least of all about the papermaker's life, as I now know. As much as I know about the schoolmaster's life, as little do I know about the papermaker's life, I think to myself. Because it was possible for me to think and, in fact, constantly to think quite mechanically that I was thoroughly familiar with the papermaker, I did not have to bother with the papermaker. I was probably always afraid that the papermaker would occupy my thoughts. True, I always watched Siller, the papermaker, I say, even watched his brain with my brain, but I never really bothered with Siller, whereas on the other hand, perhaps for decades, I did occupy myself exhaustively with the schoolmaster. In truth I did *study, see through and study,* the schoolmaster in all his unconsciousness and I did penetrate him like a human monstrosity. I penetrated this insignificant, this ridiculous person, dear sir, as if he were a human monstrosity. We often maintain, to ourselves above all, and in so doing justify ourselves to ourselves, that we know something through and through, that we have completed something, only so as not to have to bother ourselves with this thing (this person), because we are afraid that we shall be embarrassed by this preoccupation and that this preoccupation will make us totally unreliable with regard to ourselves, dear sir, because we fear the nuisance, something that we have to regard as fatal, caused by occupying ourselves with this matter (this person!), because we despise ourselves. Nothing is indubitable, dear sir. Were I to go and play watten again, I say to the truck driver, the whole thing would be nothing but an elementary disorder and nothing but sorrow, which is basically nothing but wretchedness, which is more or less nothing but madness. We are at the peak of concentration when we are playing. Playing watten. In the theater, dear sir, even the impossible is entertainment, and even the monstrous, as the improbable, is an object of study, everything in the form of hints. People believe that the philosopher can handle his subject, that is, philosophy, whereas he knows absolutely nothing about his subject. But basically none of us knows anything about subjects. When nature anticipates you, I say to the truck driver, although I know that the truck driver does not understand what I am talking about, yet it is precisely to the truck driver that I say: if nature anticipates you, if it takes Siller (or any other person) out of the submissive world, as it did on that Wednesday, with its mysterious weather, because it comes naturally to it and, as we believe, closes an individual nature, has to close it, if it makes, from one moment to the next, a dead man out of a live one, which is not saying a lot, I say, should we not ask: why not by means of its own artificiality? I say, I have often thought *ah, that's a theologian!* who explains everything to you and gives you reassurance for your whole life and *ah, that's a mathematician!* and *ah, that's an artist!* and *ah, that's an irreproachable scientific nature!* more and more *ah, a simple human being!* and *ah, the simplest of all human beings!* who explains everything to you and will give you reassurance for the rest of your life, but, when all is said and done, not a single person has been able to explain anything to me, and not a single person has given me reassurance, has been able to give me reassurance even about the most ridiculous thing, on the contrary, I say, with the passing of time, I have become progressively more and more disturbed. Now, in the nature of things, I ask no more and no one, not another single person, for in reality there is no one you can ask, unless you are a fool. The masses are like water, I say to the truck driver, you only need to make the smallest hole in the gigantic container in which they find themselves, and out they run. I think, dear sir, that some of them have a constant desire to be the others, and it is from this and from nothing else that everything originates. And nothing originates but human misery. Who knows better then you! I think we know very early on that we cannot think with our brain and cannot speak with our language, yet we go on thinking with our brain and speaking with our language all our lives. I say to the truck driver: even if I could suddenly go and play watten again, I would not go and play watten, because now I know that playing watten doesn't get you anywhere either. The years have proved to me that even playing watten doesn't get you anywhere beyond hastening you on towards total nonsense. You can play watten if you like, I say, but you will see that it doesn't lead you to anything but nonsense. Just as you can inhale and see that it leads to nothing. No matter how long you live or how long you play watten. *Chess* players, like *players* on the stage, and all the other *spoilsports* find themselves in the same dilemma. And now you come along and try to persuade me, I say, that I should go and play watten again. I am not going to play watten again, I say. I think: no never again. If you absolutely want to go and play watten again, I say to the truck driver, find another man, go to Urban, talk to the butcher. Poor Siller as the most weak-kneed of us all, I say. I would never have dreamed that a man like that, a man who loved order, could kill himself, could commit suicide. A man who probably always had *cause* but absolutely no *will* to commit suicide. Just as everybody, dear sir, has reason, cause, to kill off his existence, but not the will to do it, and others have the will and not the strength, and again there are others who have the will and the strength but no opportunity. In any case, for the most complicated people, just as for the simplest, everything is a reason, at least once a day. Poor Siller was unable to play watten in twenty years, I think to myself. But his presence was necessary, I say. Are you comfortable? I ask the truck driver, then I say: what did the traveler say then? I hate travelers, I say. I am always extremely suspicious of travelers, and I find them the most repellent people. What did the traveler say? The truck driver said that the traveler had come to the inn from Wels via Lambach, and, just as he was two months ago, he was completely exhausted, as you can imagine, and yesterday, just as he did two months ago, he immediately ordered beer and pickled sausage, salt, and had the landlord (one of the nastiest people, dear sir!) enlighten him about the eagerness as well as the reluctance, so feared by traveling salesmen, of small general-store owners to make purchases, because he, and thus his whole existence, was totally dependent upon them: he immediately asked whether the case of Siller, the papermaker, who at that time was thought to have gone into the Traun, had in the meantime been cleared up. The landlord brought the traveler a second glass of beer and then another and sat down at the watten table with him, the truck driver said. While the truck driver was telling me about the traveler, dear sir, he had the impression that I wasn't listening to a word he was saying, but he suddenly realized that, although I was putting my papers in order, I was paying the greatest attention to what he was saying, and he said: the landlord told the traveler that they had searched the whole length of the Traun for Siller. Everyone thought it possible that he was already carried so far downstream that he would never be found again, the landlord said to the traveler, said the truck driver. For weeks now it had been a habit to talk about the missing papermaker, there was no one who had not talked about the missing Siller, and the missing papermaker was the number one topic of conversation, not just in the immediate vicinity. When people met, the landlord said to the traveler, the truck driver said, they immediately started talking about Siller. He was said to have been wearing only a long pair of brown work pants and a gray work shirt, the two of them, the landlord and the traveler, said; the traveler repeated that he had seen a copy of the Saturday edition of the *Linzer Tageblatt* sticking out of Siller's pants pocket, but when Siller was cut down from the tree, strangely enough, the traveler said, said the truck driver, the paper was no longer in Siller's pants pocket. But I saw with my own eyes, the traveler said, according to the truck driver, that there was a copy of the *Linzer Tageblatt* in Siller's pants pocket. On that Wednesday, the papermaker had gone barefoot from his home to the mill and from the mill across the wooden bridge to play watten, that is to say, he had really gone into the wood, he had hanged himself barefoot. The traveler repeated the word *barefoot* over and over again, said the truck driver. Siller was said to have had eighty schillings on him, enough for a few glasses of beer and for the kitty. People were saying that his marriage must have been an unhappy one and that Siller had nothing to laugh about at the hands of his gloomy wife, etc.

The landlord had kept on saying to the traveler that Siller had met his wife in a tuberculosis sanitarium where he was employed as a stoker, and the traveler kept on saying: aha, in a tuberculosis sanitarium, in a tuberculosis sanitarium, hm. Siller had married the consumptive against the wishes of his parents. And because he had married her, the landlord kept repeating, the truck driver said, he had himself contracted tuberculosis. From time to time he had been infectious, even in the last weeks of his life. I knew about that, dear sir. Children were kept away from him, the landlord is said to have said to the traveler, timid people were afraid to go near him. There were people, the landlord said to the traveler, who would get up and leave when Siller came into the inn. Siller played the accordion and took long walks in the woods, not because I, his doctor, recommended it, but entirely of his own accord, dear sir, he walked quite long distances just to go the shops, always barefoot, he preferred to walk on the banks of the Traun, by the river that was once a beautiful rushing stream but is now dammed up in an ugly fashion: he loved the river and enjoyed investigating the most trivial details of it. Speaking little, but listening attentively, a characteristic connected with his illness, a constant inner need for solitude, undisturbed privacy, characterized him, the awareness that basically he had died once but, thanks to the highest medical art (his own words!), had suddenly come back to life a second time, probably as the same person, but really as someone completely different. He himself always divided his life into two halves, into the one *before* his stay and his operation in the tuberculosis sanitarium and into the second half *afterwards*. In the second half of his life, he treated with indifference the contempt that was cast on him from all sides while he was still alive. He could not have expressed the thought, even though he might have known, that his existence, one of millions and absolutely pointless, was horrible, and yet time and time again it had of itself become compatible with its own superfluity, I wrote in my notebook on the day he was found. Whenever I watched him while we were playing watten, I always had the impression that he regarded himself as finished but that he had to go on existing because he could not change the situation until a certain frightful and indeterminate point of time had been reached, a situation that was a continual and totally unjustified torment for him. This simple person detested crude wit and familiarity, the low clichés of life that the rest of us constantly use to while away the time. For him, playing watten was no longer as it is, after all, for us, nothing but a source of entertainment and a way to waste time, a reckless fragmentation of existence, but an absolute necessity. It was not a coincidence that every Wednesday Siller was the first of us to arrive at the inn, whereas I was always the last. On Wednesday, according to his wife, the papermaker was a different person from what he was on other weekdays, even early in the morning. But to say that he was happy on the days he played watten would be an inadmissible exaggeration. The truck driver, who had been seated at an adjoining table during the traveler's story, said that the traveler made sure of his listeners and told them he had spent days considering whether he should ever again stay at the inn where, the last time he was there, he had suffered so much unpleasantness in connection with Siller: to be plunged into new unpleasantness because of a habit he admittedly found pleasant and, perhaps willfully, to create a still more unpleasant situation, while being in no way forced to do so, for he could, after all, spend the night wherever he wanted to, and he had had to think, even as he was approaching the inn, that in future whenever he entered the "Avenger" he would always, and perhaps for the rest of his life, be connected with Siller the papermaker, with that unfortunate man's suicide (which he had had to be the one to discover): in future, said the traveler, he would probably, even if he himself never thought of it again, had forgotten the whole thing, be confronted with Siller over and over again. Another person, the traveler said, according to the truck driver, would not have stayed at the "Avenger" again. A more or less sinister connection, like the one that existed between him, the traveler, and Siller, the suicide, was a lifelong one, the traveler is reported to have said. True, he had said that anyone might have found Siller. He had also asked himself, when he found the dead man, whether he should not simply keep quiet about it. In that way he would have been spared all the ruthless interrogations, the brutal verbal exchanges with the local police, the abhorrent curiosity of all the people who kept gathering round, all the remarks, suspicions, conjectures, and unpleasantness in this connection. But the traveler is reported to have said that if you kept quiet about a discovery like that, like the discovery of a dead body, then it would weigh on your conscience for the rest of your life. And besides he was not the sort of person to have such a cold heart as to freeze out everything unpleasant, everything repulsive, or even just puzzling. The realization alone that the body had been decomposing for quite a time had made him, the traveler, report his discovery. He had first touched the corpse's bare feet, the traveler confessed, said the truck driver, and had cleaned his hands on the damp mossy ground after his sudden disgust at having done this. The temptation to go through the dead man's pants pockets, turn them inside out as usual, was a great one, said the truck driver. At first sight, the traveler was forced to conclude that it was a younger man, that he had seen the man before, all in all, the traveler had immediately said to himself that it had to be a papermaker from the mill. That the man hanging on the tree was getting on for forty, and that he, the traveler, probably knew him from the inn. Big and unusually long arms, the traveler is reported to have said over and over again. But as he was getting away from the body as quickly as possible, the traveler had asked himself whether he should first report the matter to the landlord or to the police. At the crucial moment, no one ever knows what the legal requirement is in a given situation, and, in a case like that, everyone acts on the basis of emotion. As he told the landlord, he, the traveler, had first hastened in the direction where he supposed the police station to be, but he completely lost his way, said the truck driver. He came back to the gravel pit several times. The traveler walked around and around in the woods for more than an hour until suddenly a flickering light showed him where the inn was. In a wood like this one, dear sir, anyone who does not know it like the back of his hand can become disoriented, and, in fact, carelessness in a wood like this one, which you do not know, and especially at night, and especially when you are terribly worked up, and especially at a time of year like this, can be fatal. The fact was that for some time people had thought Siller had gone into the Traun, the landlord kept saying to the traveler, because everyone from these parts who commits suicide goes into the Traun, they surface at the weir, often in the presence of hundreds of onlookers, papermakers who are looking on, and they can only be brought to the poles and pulled out of the water with the greatest difficulty. As soon as Siller was missed, people went to the weir and waited there. They waited three days. Four days. Not a sign of Siller. It didn't occur to anyone that Siller had not thrown himself into the Traun but had killed himself in some other way. They were convinced that he must have committed suicide. They went up the whole river with poles, the rescue team got into the police skiff and checked the middle of the river, the current, for how often has a body been caught on a wooden post in the middle of the river. Nothing. They posted a man at the weir, and he was still standing there on the sixth and the seventh day. Finally they gave up the search for the papermaker and resigned themselves to the idea that he had been carried far downstream, possibly as far as the area of Wels. They waited for a report on the matter, but there was none. So finally they turned from Siller to his wife. Just as they had given Siller up for lost, the traveler made his discovery, dear sir. You are most probably not unaware that travelers are known for making such discoveries. Travelers find suicides, pieces of jewelry that have been lost, large sums of money and they are, in general, always being brought into contact with the criminal element. This is another reason why we find travelers sinister. I am repelled by travelers, I say to the truck driver. Where there's a traveler, there's a crime, I say. The discovery of Siller by the traveler showed that not every suicide goes into the Traun; in future people will not go to the weir any more but will have to search the woods. I recall that, in the last ten years since Pöll's suicide, the cashier at the Raiffeisen bank, who hanged himself when the scandal over Pöll's indebtedness was at its height, one person in the neighborhood did hang himself. Dear sir, one of my constantly recurring dreams is as follows: I look into the Traun and see hundreds and thousands of corpses in the Traun all close together, they form a yellowish-white mass of bodies under the clear surface of the water, which has something poetic about it. If I see a face among the mass of corpses, I know it. The limpidity of the water and the immobility and melancholy of the mass of corpses under the surface contrast with one another in a truly wonderful way. Because Siller's decomposition was so advanced, they had buried the body in the cemetery without delay, and that means without any formality at all and, in the nature of things, besides the gravedigger, the landlord and the police, and two workmates of Siller, who happened, by pure chance, to be in the neighborhood of the cemetery while the corpse was being brought in, no one witnessed the burial, as the widow, who had hurriedly been informed, had stayed at home. So a traveler came into the inn, a traveler who had been a regular guest at the inn for years, as you tell me, I say to the truck driver and whom I, as you maintain, do not know. Of course I don't know the traveler, I say. These are the facts of the case, the truck driver reports: the traveler had been unable to sleep that night and for this reason, as he told the police, left the inn at about two o'clock, scantily dressed, and went into the wood, because he was afraid that he would not be able to fall asleep *all night.* The traveler was lost for several hours and criss-crossed the woods until he came into the gravel pit. That's where he discovered the corpse. At first the traveler did not want to tell anyone about his discovery, I say, in order to save himself from a whole series of disagreeable experiences, which are, undoubtedly, always connected with a discovery of this sort. Anyone can make a discovery like that, I say, and the truck driver tells me: the traveler, according to his statements, is weighing in his mind: shall I report what I have found? or shall I not report it? He walked backwards and forwards, first he *walked* backwards and forwards, then he *ran* backwards and forwards, he kept asking himself whether it would not be more sensible not to report his discovery. In any case he thought, the truck driver says, that the dead man must have been hanging on the tree for several days and that you could report, without more ado, a dead man who had been hanging on a tree for several days. But the traveler only decided to report the discovery of the body two hours after he had found it, I say. The truck driver: shortly before he found the body, the traveler said to himself, there must have been a man decomposing here. The traveler knows what a decomposing body smells like, the truck driver says. Then, in fact, in the darkness, the traveler did come upon the corpse hanging from a sturdy branch of the tree. Another man, the traveler is supposed to have said to the landlord, would have gone into the inn, not said a word about his discovery and would have retired to his room and had a good night's sleep and disappeared as quickly as possible next morning. Left as quickly as possible next morning, I say, and the truck driver: as soon as he entered the inn the traveler, without a moment's hesitation, immediately awakened the landlord and told him, without showing any excitement, according to the police records, that someone had hanged himself in the wood. The traveler was not in a position to tell the police that the tree that Siller was hanging on was very close to the gravel pit because, in the darkness, he had not seen the gravel pit at all. It's a miracle, I think, that the traveler did not fall into the gravel pit. Two or three steps more, I say, and the traveler would have fallen into the gravel pit. But, as luck would have it, he turned around, he came upon the corpse and immediately turned around. While considering what he should do once he had come upon the man hanging on the tree, the traveler became disoriented. Actually anyone who goes into the wood immediately becomes disoriented, dear sir, I have yet to meet anyone who has not become disoriented in the wood. The traveler no longer knew where to go, but he walked away from the gravel pit even though he was not really conscious of doing so, and *in this way* he approached the inn, but he also had no idea that he was doing so. Basically he hastened towards the rotten spruce, I say, and the truck driver: yes to the rotten spruce. Suddenly he saw a light and thought to himself, that light is in the inn. The next morning people wanted to know who had turned on the light in the inn at about four o'clock in the morning but no one had any idea. At the time the traveler saw the light in the inn, no one had been awake. As the traveler approached the inn, the light went out again, said the truck driver. Of course, someone must have turned the light on, I say. The traveler saw the light, he was not mistaken, said the truck driver. The light was most probably his salvation, the traveler said to the landlord, said the truck driver. There's no doubt in my mind, I say, that if the light had not suddenly been switched on in the inn, and it is clear that a light was switched on, because the traveler saw it and travelers are well known for not having hallucinations, no traveler has ever had a hallucination, then the traveler would not have come to the inn, he would have gone back into the wood, and would possibly have been so exhausted that he would have fallen into the gravel pit. Yes, says the truck driver, the traveler would have fallen into the gravel pit. When the traveler said to the landlord that a dead man, already in the process of decomposition, was hanging on a tree in the wood, the landlord said that the dead man in question was Siller the papermaker. It is known that on the Wednesday he committed suicide Siller had shown no signs of so-called *mental confusion,* but for months people had been talking about Siller's being in a state of *mental confusion,* whenever the conversation turned to Siller, everybody immediately uttered the words *mental confusion,* I say to the truck driver. They all immediately uttered the words *mental confusion.* Anyway, the words *mental confusion* are a dreadful piece of nonsense, I say. If that is all people know, or if they know nothing more at all, then they talk about *mental confusion,* just as everywhere, and in every case, as you know, dear sir, everyone, no matter how well educated, always invokes so-called *mental confusion* when understanding, reason, and feeling have been exhausted. People always cause the greatest mischief with the concept of *mental confusion,* which is not a concept and cannot be a concept, and they always use the words to draw an unscrupulous bottom line under all human, and especially all inhuman, affairs, this unreliable concept, that is in no way a concept, is *always* abused, whole nations, as you know, constantly use the words *mental confusion* as the bottom line in their always appalling bookkeeping. Siller's wife stated, I say, that on the Wednesday in question, her husband appeared to her to be particularly calm, indeed not for a long time had he exercised such a good influence upon her, he had spoken more than usual, not less, as is the case with people who are going mad, those who are slowly going mad and those who suddenly go mad, they suddenly talk too little or else say nothing at all, whereas, on the day in question, Siller talked more than usual, he had told her in the morning that, in the autumn, they were going to take a trip to the Ritten, a plateau near Bolzano, she told the police, that at last they were going together on the autumn trip she had looked forward to, to visit her relatives on the Ritten, acquaintances and playmates from her childhood and her youth, and this was something she had been looking forward to; her husband had already saved quite a large sum of money for the trip, he confessed to her that morning, and had confided in her how large a sum it was, and she had been happy. He had been very sensible while they were eating breakfast, Siller's widow had stated while she was being interrogated. As it was his day for playing watten, she is supposed to have said to him, if he was going to go out barefoot, then he should put on a warmer pair of trousers and a warmer coat, for even if he couldn't stand the heat during the day, which was seldom the case at that time of the year, she had said to him, the nights were all that much colder. But he was not to be talked into wearing warmer clothes. As he himself knew, she is reported to have said to him, the truck driver said, he was liable to fall ill immediately if the slightest lack of attention was paid to the warmth of his clothes, there was no one alive who had to be more protected against chills than he, who, by his nature, had from earliest childhood always been most prone to illness, but who, for years and years, had not allowed himself to be dissuaded from going barefoot. She sewed a couple of buttons on his coat while she was figuring out what it cost on the Ritten, and she kept on thinking of the Ritten and its attractions all the while she was sewing, she said. Her husband had never liked traveling, not even going on the most modest excursion. And now he had agreed that they should both go to the Ritten for a few days, *possibly even two weeks,* he is supposed to have said. She had in mind that they could gradually visit all their relatives, the one who owned a sawmill and the ones who had always earned their livelihood by running a small business, millers, foresters, day laborers. They were going to stay with a master roofer, who is her cousin. The poverty in which the two had lived, in a world where poverty would soon only be known by hearsay, for more than twenty-two years, separated from the mill only by the dirty, sluggish Traun, no longer a rushing stream and so no longer refreshing, childless and living in one of the twelve huts that belonged to the mill, did not seem depressing to her that morning. On the other hand, she stated to the police, there was nothing remarkable about her husband on that day when he usually played watten, I say to the truck driver. There was no reason for a word more or less on that Wednesday when, as usual, her husband said good-bye to his workmates on the wooden bridge. All statements by witnesses always contain the greatest contradictions. In the evening, she went to bed earlier then usual, she stated, before going to sleep she had thought once more about the Ritten, about new underclothes for the journey, while thinking that her husband had gone to play watten. In reality, however, her husband had not gone into the wood with the intention of going to play watten, but with the intention of hanging himself, to which everything attests, I said. What went on in his mind before he hanged himself, no one knows, I say. His workmates, who were asked whether they had noticed anything unusual about Siller that day, replied in the negative. As usual, on the day when he was going to play watten they had talked little while they were working at the machines, and this had nothing to do with the sudden heat, there was one moment when they had had to laugh at a short anecdote that one of their number told, but they had forgotten what the story was about. Siller had also talked to them about his plans to go to the Ritten in the autumn with his wife. Their relationship with him had always been a pleasant one. They liked his frankness, they valued his precision, lack of prejudice, modesty, his absolute incorruptibility. They remembered the good advice he gave them about their families. For twenty years they had been accustomed to his saying good-bye to them on the wooden bridge before he went to play watten, they stated. Every Wednesday at the same time. But there must, and the question was put to them from all sides, have been something unusual, something special about Siller on that particular Wednesday, something quite trivial that was different from usual, but they all denied that there was anything. When they were asked, they pointed out how tiresome it was for them to be asked questions about anything to do with Siller, the suicide. There *must* have been something different from usual in his behavior, in what he said or did not say, the landlord had said to the traveler. Did he walk more slowly than usual? the traveler asked the landlord, the truck driver said, did he say good-bye to his workmates more quickly than usual? abruptly perhaps? The traveler asked the landlord, the landlord asked the traveler, questions like this over and over again, questions no one can answer, said the truck driver.

. . . . .

Being constantly in seclusion, said the truck driver, I had presumably not heard anything of the rumor that had been going around for a long time to the effect that I had not gone to play watten for the last two months simply because, in order to go and play watten and thus get to the inn, I would have to pass through the wood in which Siller, the papermaker, had hanged himself, dear sir, and I think that in the nature of things it is not only for this one reason but for several different reasons, certainly for a whole lot of reasons, which it is really impossible for to me to lay before you here. No, not to go and play watten because the papermaker had hanged himself in the wood that I would have to pass through if I wanted to go and play watten would be nonsensical, I say to the truck driver. I have a whole lot of reasons, which I find impossible to explain, I say. But the truck driver says: come on, come and play watten tomorrow! Once again, he is trying out his art of persuasion, which is, at the moment, more painful for me than it is for him, because it has once more been set in motion with such shamelessness, but he is not in the least conscious of the shamelessness of suddenly saying to me again that I should go and play watten, when I had made it absolutely clear to him, made it clear a hundred times, that in spite of whatever objections he might have, I was not going to play watten any more. A person like this, I think to myself, never feels any shame. It's true, I think to myself, last time I did hold out the prospect of a game of watten to the truck driver, *one day I will play watten with you again,* I said to him, but only to get him to leave. Now he says: last time you said you would go and play watten again. To which I reply: I said to you last time that I would go and play watten because I needed some peace, peace, do you understand, it never for one moment entered my mind to go and play watten with you again. A person like the truck driver gradually reduces a person like me to despair, I think to myself, and brings you to the point where you lie to him, just in order to get some peace. I said I would go and play watten, I say, because you bothered me, disturbed me while I was working, ruined one of my extraordinary thoughts, but not because I really intended to go and play watten again. I am not going to play watten again. Can't you see that I can no longer walk even as far as the rotten spruce, to say nothing of going to play watten again. Three times around the hut and I'm exhausted. Haven't you seen, when we walk around the hut three times, that I'm completely exhausted? Dear sir, people like the truck driver see nothing. Understand nothing, see nothing. When he entered the hut just now he was trying out his art of persuasion, I think. Again, he caught me by surprise. I am engaged on describing *toxoplasmosis,* when in comes the truck driver. Dear sir, you cannot eject a person who is suddenly standing in the room and is about to sit down, even if you haven't invited that person to come into the room and have certainly not invited him to sit down! There's the doctor sitting down, the truck driver may think if he catches me by surprise in the hut, the doctor who has withdrawn from everybody's company for years now, whose practice has been shut down, and whom everybody, no matter where, calls a madman. At first, the truck driver may think, the doctor withdrew from the top floor of the castle (his father's) into the ground floor of the castle, he withdrew from the castle into the hut, and soon, as he (that is, I!) said recently and, dear sir, as the truck driver may think, he (I!) will withdraw from the hut. I watch the truck driver and I know what he is thinking. He thinks, the doctor lives in unimaginable chaos, and you can see at once that he now only lives in the so-called library, everything points to the fact that apart from him (that is, me!) no one has entered the *so-called* library for years. Books, books, books, prescriptions, notes, he thinks, medicines, food and laundry and even the most ridiculous items of practical use are all thrown together in a heap in the *so-called* library, the truck driver thinks, I think to myself, now and again, he thinks, the doctor (I!) goes into his consulting room, as the doctor himself says, just to torture himself. The consulting room, the truck driver thinks, is the only room, except for the *so-called* library, that the doctor goes into. But in the consulting room, too, there is unimaginable chaos, the truck driver thinks. The authorities closed down the doctor's practice illegally, as the doctor himself says, the truck driver thinks. Not a single patient left, the truck driver thinks. It is really infamous to call the room next to the consulting room a library, the truck driver thinks, and I think that's why I too do not call the library the library, but only the *so-called* library. The *so-called* library, the truck driver thinks, I think to myself, in which the books really only play a subsidiary role. To have to hear, the truck driver thinks, I think to myself, the way the doctor always calls the *so-called* library the *so-called* library, and apparently he takes the greatest pleasure in the name. His clothing, coat, pants, as well as his shirt, the truck driver may think, I think to myself, have not been brushed or washed for years and actually there is an unimaginable smell in the *so-called* library. Even if this smell is not unbearable, it is still the smell that is aimed quite consciously by a person at a specific goal, which, in the nature of things, is detested by the masses and which is completely incomprehensible to them, and to everyone, for well-known reasons, a consistently practiced and total dilapidation, dear sir. After a probably sleepless night, the truck driver thinks, I think to myself, in which all possible martyrdoms were visited upon him (me!), he is now occupied in bringing order into manuscripts, prescriptions, bills, records of the human *body* and of the human *brain,* and of cases of illness. He has apparently had breakfast, the truck driver thought as he entered the hut, but in reality he is obsessed with his pile of papers. I myself once said to the truck driver: all these days, these years, are nothing but a single capitulation in the face of this pile of papers, dear sir, the only question left is when to burn this pile. The whole pile has to be burned! I once said to the truck driver. Everything you see here on this pile must be burned. Everything that is lying around. For years, I have thought, I once said to the truck driver, and the truck driver remembers it, I think, all these papers must be burned, because what is written on them is nonsense, actually written on these papers by a madman in his madness, often written on these papers all of a sudden in the night and, my friend, in a language, I said to the truck driver, that I myself no longer understand, my friend. I have kept these papers for decades, dear sir. Now everything should be burned. Now I tell the truck driver that I shall burn all these papers *today.* The fact that there might possibly be a sentence, a remark (or a detailed statement!) of some significance has, time and again, made me keep this pile of papers, dear sir. But even if a significant sentence or even a significant, or just a useful, thought or even a thought that serves the *common* good (or an utterance of that sort!) were contained in these papers, and the possibility exists, the possibility certainly exists, dear sir, I do not believe that it is a good thing *not* to burn this whole pile of medico-philosophical, or purely medical or purely philosophical or practico-medical, practico-philosophical, practico-medico-philosophical papers. Whatever a person has done, whatever he has thought, he should destroy again, and the destruction of what he always believed that he would have to live on for the whole of his life and had thought over and over again that it was that and nothing else that he *could* live on, he should not leave to others and above all not leave to others after his death. The destruction of what you yourself have created, please do not misunderstand me, dear sir, is the least that can be expected of a rational person. But the moment you can no longer think this thought may be the next moment, dear sir, and this is an awful fact. Yes, I say to the truck driver, I will burn these papers. Today, I say. All of them today. All these papers. And not only the papers you see here, but simply every paper: indeed, I still have a vast quantity of papers here in the hut, I say, mainly in the consulting room, mainly in the trash bins of which there are dozens standing around in the consulting room, and in the castle as well, there are piles of papers everywhere, all of which I have written in the course of my life. Observations, I say, throughout the endlessly long and tedious years, I say, I have spent my life incessantly *observing,* basically, my whole life long I have done nothing else but observe, or at least I have done nothing else with a greater intensity, and in the end this has destroyed me, dear sir, and I have gone on covering these papers with writing. No need of help, I say. No humanity, *in*humanity, I say. A ghastly habit, I say. All the ideas I have ever had, nothing but futility, over and over again.

Madness. A crime. For it is not intelligence, dear sir, that we put down on paper, it is absurdity, incapacity, malice. As I wake up, I am thinking about what is going to happen to all these papers. And as I go to sleep, I am occupied with the same thought. One match and all these papers are burned, I say. These thoughts, for the most part, drafts of thoughts, I say, which like all thoughts and drafts of thoughts are thrust into our brains from the world around us, which is, in every case, always a catastrophe, and cast out from our brains into the catastrophic world around us. Burn, I say. With my own hands. I will take all the papers out of all the rooms and down from all the attics and lug them up from all the cellars and burn them. It's all madness, you know, I say. Suddenly: you have always been an early riser, whereas I have always been a late riser. Because you are an early riser you come here at the crack of dawn and take me by surprise. You come here and try to persuade me. It's always the same: you say that I should go and play watten again, and I refuse. I am not going to go and play watten any more, I say. For twenty years I have been going to play watten. Now I am not going to play watten any more. No watten playing, no, I say. And you say that I should do something useful with the castle. I hate anything that is useful. Suddenly anything that was useful became anathema to me. I have no interest in the castle any more, it never interested me. The castle is open, dear sir, nothing but unlocked doors, but no one has been into the castle for two years. I hear people saying, one day the doctor will move into the castle again, I say to the truck driver, but I assure you, I say, that I will never move into the castle again. I accept the hut. I *still* accept the hut. Burn the papers and kick the bucket in the hut, I think to myself. People say, rent the castle, dear sir, open it up for old people or orphans! Make a lunatic asylum out of it! Let prisoners who have been released from prison into it! There is no building more suited to the presentation of plays with a large cast. If only scientists could meet here! Artists! What enormous rooms! What excellent acoustics! What a strange attitude towards people! I never for one moment felt at home in that megalomaniacal building, dear sir. I have no desire to remember the eeriness of the rooms in which every generation of our family has, in the most natural way, as they themselves have said time and again, gone mad, nor do I wish to remember the walls, the furniture, the terrible artificiality! I hate nothing more intensely than people and, day after day, I have entered into so many people, that now I am hopelessly lost because of all the people I have entered into throughout my life. Deeper and deeper into them, first with a boundless affection then deeper and deeper with a boundless hatred. A person turns up, I think to myself, while the truck driver is watching in silence as I make an even greater mess of the pile of papers, and I walk with him I think to myself and he walks with me, this person, I think to myself, we walk a little way together, at the same time, and I hate this person, I hate this person more and more and I observe myself as I hate him and I see that my hatred towards him is utterly natural and also utterly philosophical and that this person simply does not notice that I hate him while I am walking with him and he is walking with me. If am alone, I want to be with people, if I am with people then I want to be alone, this condition has lasted for decades. Sometimes I detest them, sometimes I detest myself for being among them, I know this condition. Always strange expressions, which turn out to be our own clumsy expressions, which we hear, our own boundless clumsiness, our own boundless madness, our own boundless lovelessness, our own boundless hatred, dear sir. But, I say, what I think and what I *imagine* about the truck driver while I am thinking, dear sir, brings me face to face with a humiliating misunderstanding. The people we know longest, the people who are most familiar to us, speak the strangest language. They talk to us out of an incomprehensible *baseness,* dear sir, you understand. I am putting this pile of papers in order because I am desperate, I think to myself, while I am putting the pile of papers in order, and I know that, while I am putting it in order, the truck driver does not think I am putting the pile of papers in order because I am desperate, because he is thinking something quite different. Every thought could be developed silently, I used to think, every thought most silently on into infinity, but it is not possible to develop a thought completely silently on into infinity. But all thoughts can be used for the total destruction of our own life, just as they can be used for the destruction of every life. To have a thought means to remove yourself, for the sake of a thought, first from mankind and its concepts, and then from yourself. Over and over again, the thought that I have long since died. People turn up and we discover that we are indeed *still* alive, that we are not *yet* dead, are *again not yet* dead, dear sir, when a person turns up, and perhaps we are always only alive through contact with a person, when someone speaks to us, when someone slanders us, when someone hates us. Then again, I think that everything is a pretense. Even in the simplest of people, if we suddenly occupy ourselves with them, we find that everything is pretense. At first, I thought only the most complicated people are nothing but pretense, but the simplest too are nothing but pretense. And then the pretense of the simplest people is always the most fearful darkening of our mind. It is warm and I wish it would get cool, and it gets cool and I wish it would get warm. Someone writes me a letter, I think, while I am waiting for a letter from someone else. Do you know that I often think the air itself will suffocate me? Nature appears in all the books as a sort of burlesque, in which thoughts are completely devalued. We live in a world of burlesque, in which the high art of the representation of life and the even higher art of living and existing are ridiculed. When I wake up in the morning I saddle my name with a burlesque existence. Day in day out, I commit suicide in a burlesque manner. Philosophy burlesque. Religion burlesque. A war, a gigantic pile of corpses, dear sir, a whole mendacious part of the earth, today that's all a joke. It is precisely the diversity of characters, I say to the truck driver, the diametrically opposite, like the schoolmaster's and *your* character, like my character and your character, like Siller's character and the landlord's character, like all our characters, one different from the other but, without doubt, they continually awakened our interest; which is why we kept on going to play watten when it was high time that we should have stopped going to play watten. The diversity of our characters livened us up. Because, for example, how could we imagine a greater contrast than the contrast between you and the schoolmaster, I say. Siller the papermaker and me. All these different dispositions, I say. We all grew up, to be sure, in one and the same countryside. Even though in the most diverse circumstances. Certainly our childhood was a common childhood. Later, when the schoolmaster and I went on to secondary school, that is from the countryside of our childhood into the city, the schoolmaster to the high school and I to the middle school, we separated for a few years from our contemporaries among the working-class children, we separated from Siller, as we did from you, I say, you who became an apprentice in Ried only to come back one day like all the rest. We soon took up watten playing, I say. We played two or three times a week. Then only once a week. Wednesday seemed to us the most convenient day. Acquire knowledge, straighten things out, I once said to us all when we were playing watten. Make the general coincident with the particular. We are talking to someone, dear sir, and we know that this person understands us, and yet at the same time we know that everything rests upon a misunderstanding. The question is not, how do I approach this person (everybody), but rather how do I extricate myself from this person (everybody) and get back into myself again, in every case, over and over again. We make remarks to the person (that is to everyone), or else the person (that is everyone) makes remarks to us, and we know, while we are making these remarks, while these remarks are being made to us, that all the time it is only remarks about death that are being made. Young people are always talking about size as a *proportion in nature,* something that nature has to withhold from human beings, as we know if we are no longer young. When we are young, concepts are clear, just as they are unclear when we are old, yet they are always the same concepts, dear sir. These millions of talents, I think, which all lie under the earth and which had all had the advantage of immortality. When I see the way in which a new style of architecture goes on growing up around me, a terribly vulgar architecture, terribly vulgar music, terribly vulgar painting, terribly vulgar history, I think to myself, and this will not impress you, that it is my architecture, music, art, painting, history, and so forth. If we live for a long time in a land like ours, in which, as you know, everything is placed, with the greatest solemnity, at the mercy of stupidity, we very soon find out that we have no choice any more. In this country there is absolutely no work for the brain, it is unemployed. A so-called colleague of mine, you could not know of this, *reported me to the police,* dear sir, while I was having breakfast in a coffeehouse, he was watching me, and immediately afterwards this colleague of mine reported me to the police. An ampoule and the trembling of my hands, dear sir. The word *chronic* wandered like a ghost through the newspapers. Nevertheless, the papermakers continued to come to my consulting room. Just imagine, the papermakers kept coming to me, even though I never had a contract with the state health service, because in the three decades during which I was practicing the state health service kept rejecting me, just because I come from the castle. And I never charged these people, who give me a friendly greeting no matter where I go, a penny. But the intelligentsia, governed as they are by idiocy, have always been most suspicious of anything that was *free of charge,* but word soon got around that my method of treatment was an honest and, simply, a better one that that of my colleague. But this colleague reported me to the police, and I have been forbidden to practice. And, as I have already pointed out to you, I did not want to trouble the high court with the matter. Everybody here suffers from bronchial asthma, the so-called *Asthma bronchiale.* But most of them came to me with their congenital *dyspepsia,* which comes from the mill. And I have always paid special attention to *hematemesis,* which turns up every day in this area, the vomiting up of blood that is familiar to every man who lives around here. And to *hematuria.* Children are often afflicted by *chorea minor,* with animal-like movements of the limbs. *Tetanus, cephalhematosis,* and so forth. Everyone has rickets. They often have *Still's disease, osteoporosis,* and of course there are the thalidomide babies. I have been able to make some progress in my writings, especially recently. My *defunct practice* has helped my writings. The levels of difficulty, however, as you know, continue to rise. Day in day out and over and over again, I put everything that I know to the test, a practice of my father's. I have detested ease my whole life long, just as I have detested glibness; my whole life long I have hated nothing as much as effortlessness. They took away my practice, but no one can take away my brain. Not my brain. Scientific calling, dear sir, you become accustomed to the most detestable concepts. At the same time, I have always been forced to the conclusion that it is precisely doctors who come from the so-called lower, indeed the lowest, classes, poor people's children who have studied medicine are the worst, the most corrupt, doctors. No sooner have they received their degree but they become nothing but moneymaking machines in white coats, ruthless and vile. Merely the title of doctor is in most cases enough for a doctor who has risen from the proletariat; with it he immediately reduces society to a blind, clumsy humility by his dangerous quackery while raising himself up to the most tasteless wealth. My opponents, who are basically unsuccessful, tried to ruin me by every means at their disposal. They took away my practice and actually destroyed me. The first test comes, I say to the truck driver, when one's contemporaries, even if they are known to you only through embarrassment, books, and so forth, begin to die off from natural causes. We can suddenly recognize a person in outline, by observing them over a long period, sometimes for decades, and just at the moment when we have become familiar with them, the person in question (Siller) dies. The pretence of a conversation which is, at bottom, of no interest to us, we pretend that we understand, that we need knowledge, concern, dear sir, we exchange letters with one another merely so as to be able to remain in the background. None of us wants to be bothered. And we look at the way a person, a philosopher, I think to myself, is bothered by his students, and are outraged, when the person who has been tormented is suddenly dead, has been murdered by his own students (by means the teacher has taught his students). We are afraid of everything, and we have reason to fear everything, and in order to live but one day longer we forget over and over again that we are actually afraid of everything. The papermakers, like the untrained *mill hands,* whom I have got to know in the course of my life, something that medicine made possible, are the ones, dear sir, whom I have to thank, I think over and over again, dear sir, for the fact that I did not go mad in the most humiliating and artificial way but in the most natural manner. But from what else could I have ever benefited except from this, my natural madness, to which all my thoughts pertain and by which they are guided? An extraordinary person is an absolutely perfect and decent person, strictly speaking, not outside the ordinary, I think. Whether there is a person to whom I can write what I *have* to write, I have often thought, thought for years, now here is the opportunity and I am stunned. Because there is nothing in your request that says that I should give you a detailed statement! Thinking for me has long since become a frightful, illogical form of headache, as happens in isolated cases where a person has overtaxed his nature for longer than he should have, a mental illness of course that I am bound to call the complete opposite of feeblemindedness. My art, dear sir, is forever a ridiculous one that has to be ashamed of my nature in the most distressing possible manner. But whoever seeks to separate his nature from what he has, for a long time, recognized as the art that is within him is a fool. As far as I am concerned, I know that misfortune is evidence of existence. The fact that someone is there is misfortune, as only the world knows misfortune. Nature leaves the individual alone with his misfortune. As misfortune you are proof that you are there, I say to myself, I think, the fact that you are there is a misfortune. Every proof is a misfortune. Three ideas come to me, dear sir, while the truck driver is sitting opposite me. *Idea 1:* first are my teachings, then am I myself (as a philosopher of science), who has gradually fallen into oblivion in a way that would have driven another person, faced with this degree of falling into oblivion, mad, as you enter an absolutely intolerable darkness, because of an inattention (of thought), gradually and, at first, certainly, without at first being fully conscious of doing so, but with incredible speed, right in the background of my thought mechanism. As though behind my brain there were a second one that dared to think in opposition to the first one, dear sir. True, I thought and talked, I thought and talked incessantly, because as a result of misfortune, you understand, I am the sort of person who simply has to think and talk incessantly and, of course, has to *conceal* what he is thinking and saying, but within me everything was already broken into small pieces. My head and, as a result, my whole body was subject to this state of illness. *Idea 2:* Whereas I actually believed that I was the center of attention, I had long ceased to be the center of attention, because I believed that I was the center of attention. *Idea 3:* without the suggestion of either a mental or a physical fight, I was destroyed in all my activity by the young, by means of the completely silent and completely painless, completely *unrecognizable,* method that I had devised and had taught them. I taught these young people how to destroy a world that should be destroyed, but they did not destroy the world that should be destroyed but destroyed me who had taught them how to destroy the world that should be destroyed. Above all, the "Avenger" is horrible, I say to the truck driver. Equally distant from all who went there to play watten, it stands at precisely that point in the wood, dear sir, that one would think the most unsuitable for an inn. Yet of all the inns in the neighborhood the "Avenger" is the most popular. Although, as everyone knows, it is the ugliest. My reason tells me that the landlord's father, who built the "Avenger," must have said to himself: this is just the spot, the most unsuitable one for an inn, where I shall build an inn in a vulgar and ugly style, I say to the truck driver. As we know, he got the building materials, consisting largely of old railroad ties (he and his wife and children and grandchildren built the inn between the two world wars) from the city, which at the time lay in total ruin, for next to nothing. I cannot build the inn too cheaply for the papermakers, for whom it was intended, he thought, and he calculated right. To the person who is totally isolated it does not seem difficult actually to be among everyone when he wants to and to be in everyone and, in truth, to know the whole frightfulness and hopelessness and ugliness of the frightfulness and hopelessness through and through. You can go through the whole of philosophy just as you can go through this horrible wood filled with the most monstrous possibilities of being harmed, I say to the truck driver. We do indeed believe that every door can be opened until we see that that is not the case. We deceive ourselves. We confuse what is of use to us with nature. Falling asleep is the problem not waking up, very dear sir. Nature justifies, I see, nature, but nature does not justify reason: I see that more and more clearly. But all of us always only speak the language that no one understands. I say to the truck driver: people go to the mountains and climb the highest peaks, and when they are at the top, right up at the top, they talk, as they do down below, of the possibilities that are denied them. But the truck driver does not understand me. Waking up means to be present at a continuous funeral, dear sir, like a softly spoken sentence; the sort of sentence that is intentionally concealed by an intentionally discreet person can also mean the death of millions of people. It's two o'clock, I say to the truck driver, it is certainly dark, but it's two o'clock. As he does not react to what I am saying, my idea of what I dreamed the night before is not disturbed. *The jackdaws,* I think. At first, I thought as I was waking up, I shall go into my consulting room, what a long time it has been since I was in my consulting room! The impression that the smell of decomposition that is seeping out of the consulting room has grown stronger recently, the supposition that there is a body decomposing in the consulting room, I don't know what kind of body, and the thought that a body could *decompose* in the consulting room, not of course a human body in my consulting room, but the simple fact that *something* is decomposing in my consulting room made me decide to open the door to the consulting room, and I went into the consulting room. When the committee was there at the time they were closing down my practice, I think to myself: I shoved the people out of the consulting room with my hands, as fast as lightning with my hands, closed the shutters, put the instruments into the bins, all the instruments into the bins! Actually, I think to myself, as I go into the consulting room, the smell of decomposition that had seeped out of the consulting room all summer and all autumn has not been noticeable for weeks now. It would have been natural to open the consulting room the moment the smell of decomposition reached its height, but I did not go into the consulting room when the smell of decomposition was at its height, I opened it *today* and went in *today.* And then I made the most remarkable discovery. I unlock the door, and I have the greatest difficulty in unlocking it because the keyhole is stopped up by a tangle of insects. When I unlocked the door, I could not have known what had taken place in the consulting room, the consulting room was darkened by filth, everything was filthy, I am looking at it through the truck driver's eyes: filth everywhere. But gradually I could see more and more shreds of skin, dried skin, more and more feathers from a bird that I still had not identified, finally, on the floor, there is the skeleton of a jackdaw, an unusually large jackdaw, the skeleton of a jackdaw. And a little while later, right next to the skeleton of the jackdaw, the skeleton of a second jackdaw. The two jackdaws had a fight, I think to myself, I can see the scene with great clarity through the truck driver's eyes: the two jackdaws had a fight. Everything in the consulting room points to a fight between the two jackdaws. Not crows, don't misunderstand me, dear sir, jackdaws, not *ravens,* jackdaws. The whole consulting room was devastated, and I think to myself, why didn't you hear these two jackdaws, in their mortal struggle, devastating the consulting room. Just imagine! There were even shreds of jackdaw skin sticking to the windows, shreds of skin and feathers everywhere. But how did the jackdaws get into the consulting room? First one and then the other. Apparently seeking refuge, I think to myself. The first jackdaw seeking refuge in the consulting room and the second seeking refuge with the first. But neither of them could escape from the refuge, apparently they *gradually went mad* and suffocated, as I determined, first the smaller jackdaw then the larger. I should have been aware of such a frightful situation, I think to myself, but the jackdaws probably entered the consulting room while I was away playing watten. Fled into the consulting room because they were cold, went mad, suffocated, dried out. Morphine ampoules lying all around, I think to myself, and I think: the jackdaws probably have great quantities of narcotics in their bodies. Went mad, fainted, suffocated, I think to myself. And then the ants ate the jackdaws. On one of the cold summer evenings, the jackdaws sought refuge from the cold in the consulting room, probably because they were frightened. I showed you the skeletons of the two jackdaws at the time,

I suddenly say to the truck driver, do you remember my showing you the skeletons of the two jackdaws? At the time, you were already trying to persuade me to go and play watten. Strange, the two jackdaws, I say. But the truck driver says he knows nothing about jackdaws. Yes, of course, I say, I dreamed the whole thing about the jackdaws, and I also dreamed that I showed you the jackdaws, I say. The truck driver says: *the schoolmaster is a poor fellow.* A poor fellow? I ask. Yes, I say, of course the schoolmaster is a poor fellow. And then it occurs to me that the schoolmaster has never accomplished anything that he hoped to achieve. He never managed to get to the university as he had wished. Study science or music, the schoolmaster had always told himself. But he studied neither science nor music. He would not have made a scientist, I say to the truck driver, nor a musician. The schoolmaster would always have been just a schoolmaster. But even as a schoolmaster the schoolmaster failed, I say. For thirty years he pretended to be a schoolmaster, but in reality he was never a schoolmaster but just a poor fellow, as you quite rightly say, I say to the truck driver. A schoolmaster's fate, there was sympathy for him and less contempt than I had feared. He teaches the children of the mill-hands with reluctance, I think to myself, but he does not have the courage to draw the obvious conclusion that he should suddenly give up teaching. Take his own life, I think to myself. In fact, the schoolmaster's eyes are still fixed on the city even today, I say to the truck driver, although the schoolmaster knows that that is nonsense and that he exposes himself to a double despair in this act of humiliation, despair over his inability and despair over the brutality and ruthlessness of the world around him. In the course of time, the stench of the paper mill has made him ill. But he is more helpless in the face of the stupidity, the dullness, the irresponsibility of the mill hands and the mill hands' children than are the mill hands and the mill hands' children themselves. Once, ten years ago, I think to myself, he believed he could disappear for ever in the metropolis of Vienna, he walked back and forth in Vienna for days and finally he took advantage of the school vacation and joined a Styrian theater company. Theater companies are almost always a bunch of criminals, he thought to himself, now I shall go to earth among a bunch of criminals like that. All year long the company played rustic and suburban farces in a beer tent in the Prater, the stupid Viennese public like farces of this sort. The schoolmaster was used in a number of small parts, he once told me. The director of the company had promised him that he could count on getting a permanent engagement with the company. In the process of playing these trifling pieces, the schoolmaster had forgotten all about his appointment at the school. He was told he would be playing a lead, and this totally deprived him of any sense of reality. One day, fortunately before the end of the vacation, he forgot a cue, and the director threw him unceremoniously out onto the street. Since then he hasn't made even the slightest attempt to change his situation, to *improve* himself. His situation is, without doubt, the most depressing imaginable. Playing watten is probably his salvation, I say. The truck driver says, *Urban is a mean person.* Then something occurs to me: always in his suspenders, he particularly liked to wear a yellow rowing shirt. At his parents' wish, he had originally attended the commercial college in Linz but, the truck driver said of his neighbor, he was thrown out of the commercial college because of *an incredible perversity* and finished his commercial course at home. At nineteen he passed the examination to become a commercial clerk, at that time, no one could have known that the slender, even though ugly nevertheless slender, youth had all the prerequisites necessary to become today's *fat Urban.* The truck driver says that *Schausteller,* the replacement, is a ruthless person. In this connection, it occurs to me: Schausteller was first intended to be apprenticed to a chandler, but he very soon attached himself to a cattle dealer from Ried in the Innkreis, who covered all the provinces west of the Enns. Eight years transporting pigs, I say. Every day in a different place, I say, from one inn to another, in this way even the most incapable person can develop into a businessman and a judge of character, which without a doubt is what Schausteller is. At first he made a small fortune, then a larger one, and soon he had a large fortune, and in the end he also married a rich wife, the owner of one of the most sought-after so-called Maria Theresa concessions. Three legitimate, four illegitimate children, I say. In addition, a so-called *petrified child,* a child that was not carried to term and was petrified in the womb. He is a master at getting on with people, by nature a capable businessman, always practical, uses his initiative, a mind that guides the brutal world of commerce wherever he goes, and he has little time for feelings. Schausteller operates with amazing skill on the verge of fraud. But, in his own words, he has always transacted only business, has never been guilty of fraud. He is friendly in his dealings, I say, with the reliability of an honest man. Stupidly, as he admits, he had illegitimate children by three quite ordinary women and, in so doing, demonstrated the familiar ineptitude of the lowborn. *The landlord is a repulsive man* says the truck driver. This reminds me that I have never heard so much as a single kind word about the landlord. As he suffers from stomach ulcers, which can no longer be operated on (*ulcus ventriculi et duodeni*), the scene, at the moment, grows darker wherever he goes. His movements remind you of an animal that does not really exist, an animal compounded of all the lower animals. What he says is as malicious as what he does not say. For fifteen years, he was a common soldier, only one arm and ruthless like all cripples. Previous convictions for robbery and inflicting grievous bodily harm, an alcoholic. While he is playing watten he repeats the same unappetizing jokes. The truck driver says that *Siller was an unhappy person.* Of me he says, as I know, that I am *a fool,* I ask you, dear sir. Everything is under control and yet everything is uncontrolled. You see someone and think, what a likable person, and then you soon see (as if you had been hit over the head!) what a vile person, what a ridiculous person, what a low type of person. Of course the torment grows and grows, the doctors you visit understand nothing, criticize everything. One moment I think I'm mad, the next that I'm not mad. Madness is a fully instrumented score. But the world around us keeps quiet about it, that is the nature of the world around us, dear sir. The extraordinary people say, with justification, and they are mocked for it, I have my own police, my own anarchy. Day in day out, I negotiate against myself, they say. Make my own laws. Actually lawlessness never prevails in my head, they say. While they are bound to feel that everything is against them, they are *everything* in nature. You have always had a larger radius than the others, a larger and larger radius, they think. The others develop in a completely unoriginal way. Their largest possible confusion is ever present, everywhere, dear sir, their cultural feeblemindedness. As far as the rotten spruce, as far as the smell of the carcass, I say, and the truck driver says: come on, come and play watten tomorrow, doctor. Recently I have often taken to walking without a hat, barefoot like Siller, out of the hut, like a shot, and as far as the rotten spruce and then into the gravel pit. (In my thoughts). Every day one or two kilometers further. (In my thoughts.) Slip into my trousers, like an idiot, I think to myself, leave the hut as a totally normal and free person. Yes, I say to the truck driver, an antenna on the roof, so that you can receive the devil. The truck driver says: if you go and play watten again, doctor, I will tell the others you are going to play watten again. You can hear everything more clearly in the dark, I say, you see nothing, you hear everything more clearly. In desperation, no matter where you are, no matter where you have to stay in this world, I say, you can, from one moment to the next, out of desperation, exit the tragedy (you are in) and enter the comedy (you are in), or vice versa, at any moment exit the comedy (you are in) and enter the tragedy (you are in). For quite a while in the observation of an object (a person), I think to myself, watch and see this person becoming more and more ruthless towards me. One day I am everything all at once, I think to myself, and thus everything in one moment of time. People, I say to the truck driver, facilitate incessant pain. But the body's innards are not connected to nature through the brain but through the head. And this is all so that we should be afraid, dear sir. The schoolmaster was irritated, I say, Siller was irritated in such a way that he actually went mad, I myself have been close to despair in the middle of the wood, and you cannot cast off this despair, as long as you do not know the reason for it. Even in the most taciturn person, dear sir, we come across the following: the moment comes when he relaxes his intensity and he is lost. And his whole life falls about his ears. There is nothing more depressing than watching the way people give up. The depression that hangs over us is so depressing because we have not yet understood the depression, let alone ourselves. Again and again, dear sir, the idea: a person, one of my students, leaps out of the bushes and kills me. The intention was to turn the old suicidal order into a new suicidal order. That is what I am now reproached with. But I am not going to play watten any more. When I enter the hut, I look behind all the furniture, behind the bins themselves, and reassure myself that there is no one there, because during my absence someone could have come into the hut. Only when I am certain that I am alone in the hut do I cut myself two slices of bread and eat it with some hard and some soft cheese. I am also constantly afraid of electricity, in case that interests you, I have only experienced this fear since I came back into the hut on the Wednesday the papermaker hanged himself. Now I think that it was probably for that reason that, in a moment of far-sightedness, I put on my rubbers. Something else occurs to me about the schoolmaster: he has those round, cracked fingernails, as big as coins, which are an indication of a severe case of tuberculosis, from which he doubtless once suffered, or still does, but of which he, as I know, knows nothing. *Shortness of breath on the riverbank,* I remember. You know, the person, my colleague, I say to the truck driver, the doctor who now treats all my patients, persecutes me because he believes that he has not accomplished what I have accomplished, that he is not what I am, I say to the truck driver. He imagines that I am farther along than he is and that he cannot reduce the distance that separates us. All my life, I say to the truck driver, I have hated one-story houses, and then one day I retired to the hut. Delivered myself up to vermin, dear sir. I am not going to play watten any more, I say to the truck driver. And even if I could, I wouldn't, because I can no longer stand the noise I make in the winter when I stick my cane into the frozen snow. It's quite clear to me what you want, I say, and the truck driver says nothing. You want me to go and play watten again. But I am not going to play watten again. I no longer play watten. Tear up the floor of the hut and you will find some horrible things, I say. A person like me is a person full of tricks and is constantly waiting for a person who will destroy his tricks while destroying his head, dear sir.

WALKING

TRANSLATED BY KENNETH J. NORTHCOTT

There is a constant tussle between all the possibilities of human thought and between all the possibilities of a human mind's sensitivity and between all the possibilities of a human character.

Whereas, before Karrer went mad, I used to go walking with Oehler only on Wednesday, now I go walking—now that Karrer has gone mad—with Oehler on Monday as well. Because Karrer used to go walking with me on Monday, you go walking with me on Monday as well, now that Karrer no longer goes walking with me on Monday, says Oehler, after Karrer had gone mad and had immediately gone into Steinhof. And without hesitation I said to Oehler, good, let's go walking on Monday as well. Whereas on Wednesday we always walk in one direction (in the eastern one), on Monday we go walking in the western direction, strikingly enough we walk far more quickly on Monday than on Wednesday, probably, I think, Oehler always walked more quickly with Karrer than he did with me, because on Wednesday he walks much more slowly and on Monday much more quickly. You see, says Oehler, it's a habit of mine to walk more quickly on Monday and more slowly on Wednesday becuse I always walked more quickly with Karrer (that is on Monday) than I did with you (on Wednesday). Because, after Karrer went mad, you now go walking with me not only on Wednesday but also on Monday, there is no need for me to alter my habit of going walking on Monday and on Wednesday, says Oehler, of course, because you go walking with me on Wednesday *and* Monday you have probably had to alter your habit and, actually, in what is probably for you an incredible fashion, says Oehler. But it is good, says Oehler, and he says it in an unmistakably didactic tone, and of the greatest importance for the organism, from time to time, and at not too great intervals, to alter a habit, and he

This translation of *Walking*, which has been changed in minor ways, first appeared in *Conjunctions*, vol. 32 (1999). I should like to acknowledge with gratitude the help and encouragement that I received from Brad Morrow, the editor of *Conjunctions*.

says he is not thinking of just *altering*, but of a *radical alteration* of the habit. You are altering your habit, says Oehler, in that now you go walking with me not only on Wednesday but also on Monday and that now means walking alternately in one direction (in the Wednesday-) and in the other (in the Monday-) direction, while I am altering my habit in that until now I always went walking with you on Wednesday and with Karrer on Monday, but now I go with you on Monday and Wednesday, and thus also on Monday, and therefore on Wednesday in one (in the eastern) direction and on Monday in the other (in the western) direction. Besides which, I doubtless, and in the nature of things, walk differently with you than I did with Karrer, says Oehler, because with Karrer it was a question of a quite different person from you and therefore with Karrer it was a question of quite different walking (and thinking), says Oehler. The fact that I—after Karrer had gone mad and had gone into Steinhof, Oehler says, finally gone into Steinhof—had saved Oehler from the horror of having to go walking on his own on Monday, these were his own words, I would not have gone walking at all on Monday, says Oehler, for there is nothing more dreadful than having to go walking on one's own on Monday and having to walk on one's own is the most dreadful thing. I simply cannot imagine, says Oehler, that you would not go walking with me on Monday. And that I should have to go walking on my own on Monday is something that I cannot imagine. Whereas Oehler habitually wears his topcoat completely buttoned up, I leave my topcoat completely open. I think the reason for this is to be found in his persistent fear of getting chilled and catching a cold when leaving his topcoat open, whereas my reason is the persistent fear of suffocating if my topcoat is buttoned up. Thus Oehler is constantly afraid of getting cold whereas I am constantly afraid of suffocating. Whereas Oehler has on boots that reach up above his ankles, I wear ordinary shoes, for there is nothing I hate more than boots, just as Oehler hates nothing more than regular shoes. It is ill-bred (and stupid!) always to wear regular shoes, Oehler says again and again, while I say it's senseless to walk in such heavy boots. While Oehler has a wide-brimmed black hat, I have a narrow-brimmed gray one. If you could only get used to wearing a broad-brimmed hat like the one I wear, Oehler often says, whereas I often tell Oehler, if you could get used to wearing a narrow-brimmed hat like me. A narrow-brimmed hat doesn't suit your head, only a wide-brimmed one does, Oehler says to me, whereas I tell Oehler, only a narrow-brimmed hat suits your head, but not a wide-brimmed one like the one you have on. Whereas Oehler wears mittens—always the same mittens—thick, sturdy, woolen mittens that his sister knitted for him, I wear gloves, thin, though lined, pigskin gloves that my wife bought for me. One is only really warm in mittens, Oehler says over and over again, only in gloves, only in soft leather gloves like these, I say, can I move my hands as I do. Oehler wears black trousers with no cuffs, whereas I wear gray trousers with cuffs. But we never agree about our clothing and so there is no point in saying that Oehler should wear a narrow-brimmed hat, a pair of trousers with cuffs, topcoats that are not so tight as the one he has on, and so forth, or that I should wear mittens, heavy boots, and so forth, because we will not give up the clothing that we are wearing when we go walking and which we have been wearing for decades, no matter where we are going to, because this clothing, in the decades during which we have been wearing it, has become a fixed habit and so our fixed mode of dress. If we *hear* something, says Oehler, on Wednesday we check what we have heard and we check what we have heard until we have to say that what we have heard is not true, what we have heard is a lie. If we *see* something, we check what we see until we are forced to say that what we are looking at is horrible. Thus throughout our lives we never escape from what is horrible and what is untrue, the lie, says Oehler. If we *do* something, we think about what we are doing until we are forced to say that it is something nasty, something low, something outrageous, what we are doing is something terribly hopeless and that what we are doing is in the nature of things obviously false. Thus every day becomes hell for us whether we like it or not, and what we think will, if we think about it, if we have the requisite coolness of intellect and acuity of intellect, always become something nasty, something low and superfluous, which will depress us in the most shattering manner for the whole of our lives. For, everything that is thought is superfluous. Nature does not need thought, says Oehler, only human pride incessantly thinks into nature its thinking. What must *thoroughly* depress us is the fact that through this outrageous thinking into a nature that is, in the nature of things, fully immunized against this thinking, we enter into an even greater depression than that in which we already are. In the nature of things conditions become ever more unbearable through our thinking, says Oehler. If we think we are turning unbearable conditions into bearable ones, we have to realize quickly that we have not made (have not been able to make) unbearable circumstances bearable or even less bearable but only still more unbearable. And circumstances are the same as conditions, says Oehler, and it's the same with facts. The whole process of life is a process of deterioration in which everything—and this is the most cruel law—continually gets worse. If we look at a person, we are bound in a short space of time to say what a horrible, what an unbearable person. If we look at nature, we are bound to say, what a horrible, what an unbearable nature. If we look at something artificial—it doesn't matter what the artificiality is—we are bound to say in a short space of time what an unbearable artificiality. If we are out walking, we even say after the shortest space of time, what an unbearable walk, just as when we are running we say what an unbearable run, just as when we are standing still, what an unbearable standing still, just as when we are thinking what an unbearable process of thinking. If we meet someone, we think within the shortest space of time, what an unbearable meeting. If we go on a journey, we say to ourselves, after the shortest space of time, what an unbearable journey, what unbearable weather, we say, says Oehler, no matter what the weather is like, if we think about any sort of weather at all. If our intellect is keen, if our thinking is the most ruthless and the most lucid, says Oehler, we are bound after the shortest space of time to say of *everything* that it is unbearable and horrible. There is no doubt that the art lies in bearing what is unbearable and in not feeling that what is horrible is something horrible. Of course we have to label this art the most difficult of all. The art of existing against the facts, says Oehler, is the most difficult, the art that is the most difficult. To exist against the facts means existing against what is unbearable and horrible, says Oehler. If we do not constantly exist *against,* but only constantly *with* the facts, says Oehler, we shall go under in the shortest possible space of time. The fact is that our existence is an unbearable and horrible existence, if we exist *with* this fact, says Oehler, and not *against* this fact, then we shall go under in the most wretched and in the most usual manner, there should therefore be nothing more important to us than existing constantly, even if *in,* but also at the same time *against* the fact of an unbearable and horrible existence. The number of possibilities of existing *in* (*and with*) the fact of an unbearable and horrible existence, is the same as the number of existing against the unbearable and horrible existence and thus *in* (*and with*) and at the same time *against* the fact of an unbearable and horrible existence. It is always possible for people to exist *in* (*and with*) and, as a result, *in all* and *against all* facts, without existing against this fact and against all facts, just as it is always possible for them to exist in (and with) a fact and with all facts and against one and all facts and thus, above all, against the fact that existence is unbearable and horrible. It is always a question of intellectual indifference and intellectual acuity and of the ruthlessness of intellectual indifference and intellectual acuity, says Oehler. Most people, over ninety-eight percent, says Oehler, possess neither indifference of intellect nor acuity of intellect and do not even have the faculty of reason. The whole of history to date proves this without a doubt. Wherever we look, neither indifference of intellect, nor acuity of intellect, says Oehler, everything is a giant, a shatteringly long history without intellectual indifference and without acuity of intellect and so without the faculty of reason. If we look at history, it is above all its total lack of the faculty of reason that depresses us, to say nothing of intellectual indifference and acuity. To that extent it is no exaggeration to say that the whole of history is a history totally without reason, which makes it a *dead* history. We have, it is true, says Oehler, if we look at history, if we look into history, which a person like me is from time to time brave enough to do, a tremendous nature behind us, actually under us but in reality no history at all. History is a historical lie, is what I maintain, says Oehler. But let us return to the individual, says Oehler. To have the faculty of reason would mean nothing other than breaking off with history and first and foremost with one's own personal history. From one moment to the next simply to give up, accepting nothing more, that's what having the faculty of reason means, not accepting a person and not a thing, not a system and also, in the nature of things, not accepting a thought, just simply nothing more and then to commit suicide in this literally single revolutionary realization. But to think like this leads inevitably to sudden intellectual madness, says Oehler, as we know, and to what Karrer has had to pay for with sudden *total madness*. He, Oehler, did not believe that Karrer would ever be released from Steinhof, his madness is too fundamental for that, says Oehler. His own daily discipline had been to school himself more and more in the most exciting and in the most tremendous and most epoch-making thoughts with an ever greater determination, but only to the furthest possible point before absolute madness. If you go as far as Karrer, says Oehler, then you are suddenly decisively and absolutely mad and have, at one stroke, become useless. Go on thinking more and more and more and more with ever greater intensity and with an ever greater ruthlessness and with an ever greater fanaticism for finding out, says Oehler, but never for one moment think too far. At any moment we can think too far, says Oehler, simply go too far in our thoughts, says Oehler, and everything become valueless. I am now going to return once again, says Oehler, to what Karrer always came back to: that there is actually no faculty of reason in this world, or rather in what we call this world, because we have always called it this world, if we analyze what the faculty of reason is, we have to say that there simply is no faculty of reason—but Karrer had already analyzed that, says Oehler—that actually, as Karrer quite rightly said and the conclusion at which he finally arrived by his continued consideration of this incredibly fascinating subject, there is no faculty of reason, only an underfaculty of reason. The so-called human faculty of reason, says Oehler, is, as Karrer said, always a mere underfaculty of reason, even a subfaculty of reason. For if a faculty of reason were possible, says Oehler, then history would be possible, but history is not possible, because the faculty of reason is not possible and history does not arise from an underfaculty or a subfaculty of reason, a discovery of Karrer's, says Oehler. The fact of the underfaculty of reason, or of the so-called subfaculty of reason, says Oehler, does without doubt make possible the continued existence of nature through human beings. If I had a faculty of reason, says Oehler, if I had an unbroken faculty of reason, he says, I would long ago have committed suicide. What is to be understood from, or by, what I am saying, says Oehler, can be understood, what is not to be understood cannot be understood. Even if everything cannot be understood, everything is nevertheless unambiguous, says Oehler. What we call thinking has in reality nothing to do with the faculty of reason, says Oehler, Karrer is right about that when he says that we have no faculty of reason because we think, for to have a faculty of reason means not to think and so to have no thoughts. What we have is nothing but a substitute for a faculty of reason. A substitute for thought makes our existence possible. All the thinking that is done is only substitute thinking, because actual thinking is not possible, because there is no such thing as actual thinking, because nature excludes actual thinking, because it has to exclude actual thinking. You may think I'm mad, says Oehler, but actual, and that means real, thinking is completely excluded. But what we think is thinking we call thinking, just as what we consider to be walking we call walking, just as we say we are walking when we believe that we are walking and are actually walking, says Oehler. What I've just said has absolutely nothing to do with cause and effect, says Oehler. And there's no objection to saying *thinking*, where it's not a question of thinking, and there's no objection to saying *faculty of reason* where there's no possibility of its being a question of faculty of reason and there's no objection to saying *concepts* where they are not at issue. It is only by designating as actions and things actions and things that are in no way actions and things, because there is no way that they can be actions and things, that we get any farther, it is only in this way, says Oehler, that something is possible, indeed that anything is possible. Experience is a fact about which we know nothing and above all it is something which we cannot get to the root of, says Oehler. But on the other hand it is just as much a fact that we always act exactly or at least much more in concert with this fact, which is what I do (and recognize) when I say, these children, whom we see here in Klosterneuburgerstrasse, have been made because the faculty of reason was suspended, although we know that the concepts used in that statement, and as a result the words used in the statement, are completely false and thus we know that *everything* in the statement is false. Yet if we cling to our experience, which represents a zenith, and we can no longer sustain ourselves, then we no longer exist, says Oehler. Offhand, therefore I say, these children whom we see here in Klosterneuburgerstrasse were made because the faculty of reason was suspended. And it is only, because I do *not cling to experience,* that everything is possible. It is only possible in this way to utter a statement like: people simply walk along the street and make a child, or the statement: people have made a child because their faculty of reason is suspended. Oehler says, these people who make a child do not ask themselves anything, is a statement that is completely correct and at the same time completely false, like all statements. You have to know, says Oehler, that every statement that is uttered and thought and that exists is at the same time correct and at the same time false, if we are talking about proper statements. He now interrupts the conversation and says: In fact these people do not ask themselves anything when they make a child although they must know that to make a child and above all to make your own child means making a misfortune and thus making a child and thus making one's own child is nothing short of infamy. And when the child has been made, says Oehler, those who have made it allow the state to pay for it, this child they have made of their own free will. The state has to be responsible for these millions and millions of children who have been made completely of people's own free will, for the, as we know, completely superfluous children, who have contributed nothing but new, millionfold misfortune. The hysteria of history, says Oehler, overlooks the fact that in the case of all the children who are made it is a question of misfortune that has been made and a question of superfluity that has been made. We cannot spare the child makers the reproach that they have made their children without using their heads, and in the basest and lowest manner, although, as we know, they are not mindless. There is no greater catastrophe, says Oehler, than these children made mindlessly and whom the state, which has been betrayed by these children, has to pay for. Anyone who makes a child, says Oehler, deserves to be punished with the most extreme possible punishment and not to be subsidized. It is nothing but this completely false, so-called social, enthusiasm for subsidy by the state—which as we know is not social in the least, and of which it is said that it is nothing but the most distasteful anachronism in existence, and which is guilty of the fact that the crime of bringing a child into the world, which I call the greatest crime of all, says Oehler—that this crime, says Oehler, is not punished but is subsidized. The state should have the responsibility, Oehler now says, for punishing people who make children, but no, it subsidizes the crime. And the fact that all children who are made are made mindlessly, says Oehler, is a fact. And whatever is made mindlessly and above all whatever is made that is mindless should be punished. It should be the job of parliament and of parliaments to propose and carry out laws against the mindless making of children and to introduce and impose the supreme punishment, and everyone has his own supreme punishment, for the mindless making of children. After the introduction of such a law, says Oehler, the world would very quickly change to its own advantage. A state that subsidizes the making of children and not only the mindless making of children without using one's head, says Oehler, is a mindless state, certainly not a progressive one, says Oehler. The state that subsidizes the making of children has neither experience nor knowledge. Such a state is criminal, because it is quite consciously blind, such a state is not up-to-date, says Oehler, but we know that the up-to-date or, let's say, the so-called up-to-date state is simply not possible and thus this, our present, state cannot be in any shape or form a present-day state. Anyone who makes a child, says Oehler, knows that he is making a misfortune, he is making something that will be unhappy, because it has to be unhappy, something that is by nature totally catastrophic, in which again there is nothing else except what is by nature and which is bound to be totally catastrophic. He is making an endless misfortune, even if he makes only one child, says Oehler. It is a crime. We may never cease to say that anyone who makes a child, whether mindlessly or not, says Oehler, is committing a crime. At this moment, as we are walking along Klosterneuburgerstrasse, the situation is that there are so many, indeed hundreds of, children on Klosterneuburgerstrasse, and this prompts Oehler to continue his remarks about the making of children. To make a human being about whom we know that he does not want the life that has been made for him, says Oehler, for the fact that there is not a single human being who wants the life that has been made for him will certainly come out sooner or later, and before that person ceases to exist no matter who it is: to make such a person is really criminal. People in their baseness—disguised as helplessness—simply convince themselves that they want to have their lives, whereas in reality they never wished to have their lives, because they do not wish to perish because of the fact that nothing disgusts them more than their lives and, at root, nothing more than their irresponsible father, whether these fathers have already left their progeny or not, they do not want to perish because of this fact. All of these people convince themselves of this unbelievable lie. Millions convince themselves of this lie. They wish to have their lives, they say, and bear witness to it in public, day in day out, but the truth is that they do not want to have their lives. No one wants to have his life, says Oehler, everyone has come to terms with his life, but he does not want to have it, if he once has his life, says Oehler, he has to pretend to himself that his life is something, but in reality and in truth it is nothing but horrible to him. Life is not worth a single day, says Oehler, if you will only take the trouble to look at these hundreds of people here on this street, if you keep your eyes open where people are. If you walk along this street overflowing with children just once and keep your eyes open, says Oehler. So much helplessness and so much frightfulness and so much misery, says Oehler. The truth is no different from what I see here: frightful. I ask myself, says Oehler, how can so much helplessness and so much misfortune and so much misery be possible? That nature can create so much misfortune and so much palpable horror. That nature can be so ruthless toward its most helpless and pitiable creatures. This limitless capacity for suffering, says Oehler. This limitless capricious will to procreate and then to survive misfortune. In point of fact, right here in this street, this individual sickness, which runs into the thousands. Uncomprehending and helpless, says Oehler, you have to watch, day in day out, the making of masses of new and ever greater human misfortune, so much human ugliness, so much human atrocity, he says, every day, with unparalleled regularity and stupidity. You know yourself, says Oehler, just as I know myself, and all these people are also no different from us, but only unhappy and helpless and fundamentally lost. He, Oehler, to speak radically, stood for the gradual, total demise of the human race, if he had his way, no more children not a single one and thus no more human beings, not a single one. The world would slowly die out, says Oehler. Ever fewer human beings, finally no human beings at all, not a single human being more. But what he has just said, the earth gradually dying out and human beings growing fewer and fewer in the most natural way and finally dying out altogether, is only the raving of a mind that is already totally, and in the most total manner, working with the process of thinking and, in Oehler's own words, a *non*sense. Of course, an earth that was gradually dying out and finally one without human beings would probably be the most beautiful, says Oehler, after which he says, the thought is, of course *non*-sense. But that doesn't alter the fact, says Oehler, that day in day out you have to stand by and see how more and more people are made with more and more inadequacy and with more and more misfortune, who have the same capacity for suffering and the same frightfulness and the same ugliness and the same detestableness as you yourself have, and who, as the years go by, have an even greater capacity for suffering and frightfulness and ugliness and detestableness. Karrer was of the same opinion, says Oehler. Oehler keeps repeating, *Karrer's view was the same* or *Karrer had a similar view* or *Karrer had a different* or *a contrary view* (*or opinion*). Karrer's statement always went: How do these people, who do not know how they get to such a point, and who have never been asked a question that affected them, how do all these people, with whom, if we think about it, we are bound again and again and with the greatest soundness of mind, to identify ourselves, throughout the course of their lives, no matter who they are, no matter what they are, and no matter where they are, how can they, I say, hurl themselves with ever more terrifying speed into, up into, and down into, their ultimate misfortune with all the horrible—that is human—means at their disposal? My whole life long, I have refused to make a child, said Karrer, Oehler says, to add a new human being over and above the person that I am, I who am sitting in the most horrible imaginable prison and whom science ruthlessly labels as human, I have refused to add a new human being to the person who is in the most horrible prison there is and to imprison a being who bears my name. If you walk along Klosterneuburgerstrasse, and especially if you walk along Klosterneuburgerstrasse with your eyes open, says Oehler, the making of children and everything connected with the making of children completely fades away from you. Then everything fades away from you, Oehler quotes Karrer as saying. I am struck by how often Oehler quotes Karrer without expressly drawing attention to the fact that he is quoting Karrer. Oehler frequently makes several statements that stem from Karrer and frequently thinks a thought that Karrer thought, I think, without expressly saying, what I am now saying comes from Karrer. *Fundamentally, everything that is said is a quotation* is also one of Karrer's statements, which occurs to me in this connection and which Oehler very often uses when it suits him. The constant use of the concept *human nature* and *nature* and in this connection *horrible* and *repugnant* and *dreadful* and *infinitely sad* and *frightful* and *disgusting* can all be traced back to Karrer. I think now that I went walking with Karrer on Klosterneuburgerstrasse for twenty years, says Oehler, like Karrer I grew up on Klosterneuburgerstrasse, and we both knew what it means to have grown up on Klosterneuburgerstrasse, this knowledge has underlain all our actions and all our thinking and, especially, the whole time we were walking together. Karrer's pronunciation was the clearest, Karrer's thought the most correct, Karrer's character the most irreproachable, says Oehler. But recently I had already detected signs of fatigue in his person, above all in his mind, on the other hand his mind was unbelievably active, in a way I had never noticed before. On the one hand Karrer's body, which had suddenly grown old, says Oehler, on the other, Karrer's mind, which was capable of incredible intellectual acuity. His sudden physical decrepitude on the one hand, says Oehler, the sudden weirdness and outrageousness of the thoughts in his head on the other. Whereas Karrer's body, especially in the past year, could very often be seen as a body that had already declined and was in the process of disintegrating, says Oehler, the capacity of his mind was at the same time, in its outrageousness, truly terrifying to me. I suddenly had to consider what sorts of outrageousness this mind of Karrer's was capable of, says Oehler, on the other hand how decrepit this body of Karrer's is, a body that is not yet really old. Doubtless, says Oehler, Karrer went mad when he was at the height of his thinking. This is an observation that science can always make in the case of people like Karrer. That they suddenly, at the height of their thinking, and thus at the height of their intellectual capacity, become mad. There is a moment, says Oehler, at which madness *enters*. It is a single moment in which the person affected *is suddenly mad*. Again, Oehler says: in Karrer's case it is a question of a total, final madness. There's no point in thinking that Karrer will come out of Steinhof again as he did eight years ago. We shall probably never see Karrer again, says Oehler. There is every sign, says Oehler, that Karrer will stay in Steinhof and not come out of Steinhof again. The depression caused by a visit to Karrer in Steinhof would probably be so violent, says Oehler, especially for his mind and as a result, in the nature of things, for his thinking, that such a visit would have the most devastating effect, so that there is no point in thinking about a visit to Karrer in Steinhof. Not even if we were to go together to visit Karrer, says Oehler. If I go alone to see Karrer, it will be the ruin of me for weeks, if not for months, if not forever, says Oehler. Even if you visit Karrer, says Oehler to me, it will be the ruin of you. And if we go together, a visit of that sort would have the same effect on both of us. To visit a person in the condition that Karrer finds himself at the moment would be nonsense, because visiting a person who is totally and finally mad makes no sense. Quite apart from the fact, says Oehler, that every visit to Steinhof has depressed me, visiting a lunatic asylum requires the greatest effort, says Oehler, if the visitor is not a fool without feeling or the capacity to think. It makes me feel ill even to approach Steinhof, let alone go inside. The world outside lunatic asylums is scarcely to be borne, he says. If we see hundreds and thousands of people, of whom, with the best will in the world and with the greatest self-abnegation, we cannot say that we are still dealing with human beings, he says. If we always see that things are much worse in lunatic asylums than we imagined they were before we visited a lunatic asylum. Then, when we are in Steinhof, says Oehler, we recognize that the unbearableness of life outside lunatic asylums—which we have always separated from the life and existence and existence from life and the existence and existing inside lunatic asylums—*outside* lunatic asylums is really laughable compared with the insupportability *in* lunatic asylums. If we are qualified to compare, says Oehler, and to declare ourselves satisfied with the justness of the concepts of inside and outside, that is, inside and outside lunatic asylums, and with the justness of the concepts of the so-called intact as distinct from the concepts of the so-called nonintact world. If we have to tell ourselves that it is only a question of the brutality of a moment to go to Steinhof. And if we know that this moment can be any moment. If we know that every moment can be the one when we cross the border into Steinhof. If you had said to Karrer three weeks ago that he would be in Steinhof today, says Oehler, Karrer would have expressed doubt, even if he had taken into consideration the possibility that at any moment he might be back in Steinhof. Here on this very spot, I said to Karrer, says Oehler, and he stops walking: if it is possible to control the moment that no one has yet controlled, the moment of the final crossing of the border into Steinhof, and that is, into final madness, without being able to finish the unfinished statement, says Oehler, Karrer said at that time, he did not understand what was doubtless an unfinished statement, but that he knew what was meant by this unfinished statement. Even Karrer did not succeed where no one has yet succeeded, says Oehler, in knowing the moment when the border to Steinhof is to be crossed and thus the moment the border into final madness is to be crossed. When we do something, we may not think about why we are doing what we are doing, says Oehler, for then it would suddenly be totally impossible for us to do anything. We may not make what we are doing the object of our thought, for then we would first be the victims of *mortal doubt* and, finally, of *mortal despair.* Just as we may not think about what is going on around us and what has gone on and what will go on, if we do not have the strength to break off our thinking about what happens around us and what has happened and what will happen, that is about the past, the present and the future at precisely the moment when this thinking becomes fatal for us. The art of thinking about things consists in the art, says Oehler, of stopping thinking before the fatal moment. However, we can, quite consciously, drag out this fatal moment, says Oehler, for a longer or a shorter time, according to circumstances. But the important thing is for us to know when the fatal moment is. But no one knows when the fatal moment is, says Oehler, the question is, is it possible that the fatal moment has not yet come and will always not yet come? But we cannot rely on this. We may never think, says Oehler, how and why we are doing what we are doing, for then we would be condemned, even if not instantaneously, but instantaneously to whatever degree of awareness we have reached regarding that question, to total inactivity and to complete immobility. For the clearest thought, that which is the deepest and, at the same time, the most transparent, is the most complete inactivity and the most complete immobility, says Oehler. We may not think about why we are walking, says Oehler, for then it would soon be impossible for us to walk, and then, to take things to their logical conclusion. Everything soon becomes impossible, just as when we are thinking why we may not think, why we are walking and so on, just as we may not think how we are walking, how we are not walking, that is standing still, just as we may not think how we, when we are not walking and standing still, are thinking and so on. We may not ask ourselves: why are we walking? as others who may (and can) ask themselves at will why they are walking. The others, says Oehler, may (and can) ask themselves anything, we may not ask ourselves anything. In the same way, if it is a question of objects, we may also not ask ourselves, just as if it is not a question of objects (the opposite of objects). What we see we think, and, as a result, do not see it, says Oehler, whereas others have no problem in seeing what they are seeing because they do not think what they see. What we call perception is really stasis, immobility, as far as we are concerned, nothing. Nothing. What has happened is thought, not seen, says Oehler. Thus quite naturally when we see, we see nothing, we think everything at the same time. Suddenly Oehler says, if we visited Karrer in Steinhof, we would be just as shocked as we were eight years ago, but now Karrer's madness is not only much worse than his madness of eight years ago, now it is final and if we think how shocked we were eight years ago during our visit to Karrer it would be senseless to think for a moment of visiting Karrer now that Karrer's condition is a dreadful one. Karrer is probably not allowed to receive visitors, says Oehler. Karrer is in Pavilion VII, in the one that is most dreaded. What horrible prisons these the most pitiable of all creatures are locked up in, says Oehler. Nothing but filth and stench. Everything rusted and decayed. We hear the most unbelievable things, we see the most unbelievable things. Oehler says: Karrer's world is his own to the same extent that it is ours. I could just as well be walking here with Karrer along Klosterneuburgerstrasse and be talking with Karrer about *you,* if you and not Karrer were in Steinhof at the moment, or if it were the case that they had sent me to Steinhof and confined me there and you were out walking with Karrer through Klosterneuburgerstrasse and talking about me. We are not certain whether we ourselves will not, the very next moment, be in the same situation as the person we are talking about and who is the object of our thought. *I* could just as well have gone mad in Rustenschacher's store, says Oehler, if I had gone into Rustenschacher's store that day in the same condition as Karrer to engage in the argument with Rustenschacher in which Karrer had been engaged and if I, like Karrer, had not accepted the consequences that followed from the argument in Rustenschacher's store and was now in Steinhof. But in fact it is impossible that I would have acted like Karrer, says Oehler, because I am not Karrer, *I would have acted like myself,* just as *you would have acted like yourself* and not like Karrer, and even if I had entered Rustenschacher's store, like Karrer, to begin an argument with Rustenschacher and his nephew, I would have carried on the argument in a quite different manner and of course everything would have turned out differently from what it did between Karrer and Rustenschacher and Rustenschacher's nephew. The argument would have been a different argument, it simply wouldn't have come to an argument, for if I had been in Karrer's position, I would have carried on the argument quite differently and probably not carried it on at all, says Oehler. A set of several fatal circumstances, which are of themselves not fatal at all and only become fatal when they coincide, leads to a misfortune like the one that befell Karrer in Rustenschacher's store, says Oehler. Then we are standing there because we had witnessed it all and react as though we had been insulted. It is unthinkable to me that, if I had been Karrer, I would have gone into Rustenschacher's store that afternoon, but Karrer's intensity that afternoon was a greater intensity and I followed Karrer into Rustenschacher's store. But to ask *why* I followed Karrer into Rustenschacher's store that afternoon is senseless. Then let's say that what we have here is a *tragedy,* says Oehler. We judge an unexpected happening, like the occurrence in Rustenschacher's store, as irrevocable and calculated where there is no justification for the concepts irrevocable and calculated. For nothing is irrevocable and nothing is calculated, but a lot, and often what is the most dreadful, simply happens. I can now say that I am astonished at my passivity in Rustenschacher's store, my unbelievable silence, the fact that I stood by and fundamentally reacted to *nothing,* that I did fear something without knowing (or suspecting) what I feared, but that in the face of such a fear and thus in the face of Karrer's condition, I did nothing. We say that circumstances bring about a certain condition in people. If that is true, then circumstances brought about a condition in Karrer in which he suddenly went finally mad in Rustenschacher's store. I must say, says Oehler, that it was a question of

fear of ceasing to be senselessly patient. We observe a person in a desperate situation, the concept of a desperate situation is clear to us, but we do nothing about the desperate condition of the person, because we can do nothing about the desperate condition of the person, because in the truest sense of the word we are powerless in the face of a person's desperate condition, although we do not have to be powerless in the face of such a person and his desperate condition, and this is something we have to admit, says Oehler. We are suddenly conscious of the hopelessness of a desperate nature, but by then it is too late. It is not Rustenschacher and his nephew who are guilty, says Oehler. Those two behaved as they had to behave, obviously so as not to be sacrificed to Karrer. The circumstance did not, however, arise in a very short space of time, says Oehler, these circumstances always, and in every case, arise as the result of a process that has lasted a long time. The circumstances that led to Karrer's madness in Rustenschacher's store and to Karrer's argument with Rustenschacher and his nephew did not arise on that day nor on that afternoon and not just in the preceding twenty-four or forty-eight hours. We always look for everything in the immediate proximity, that is a mistake. If only we did not always look for everything in the immediate proximity, says Oehler, looking in the immediate proximity reveals nothing but incompetence. One should, in every case, go back *over everything,* says Oehler, even if it is in the depths of the past and scarcely ascertainable and discernible any longer. Of course the most nonsensical thing, says Oehler, is to ask oneself why one went into Rustenschacher's store with Karrer, to say nothing of reproaching oneself for doing so. He was obliged, he says, to repeat that in this case everything, and at the same time nothing, indicated that Karrer would suddenly go mad. If we may not ask ourselves the simplest of questions, then we may not ask ourselves a question like the question why Karrer went into Rustenschacher's store in the first place, for there was absolutely no need to do so if you disregard the fact that, possibly, Karrer's sudden fatigue after our walk to Albersbachstrasse and back again was actually a reason, nor may we ask why I followed Karrer into Rustenschacher's store. But as we do not ask, we may not, by the same token, say that everything was a foregone conclusion, was self-evident. Suddenly, at this moment, what had until then, been possible, would now be impossible, says Oehler. On the other hand what is, is self-evident. What he sees while we are walking, he sees through, and for this reason he does not observe at all, for anything that can be seen through (completely) cannot be observed. Karrer also made this same observation, says Oehler. If we see through something, we have to say that we do not see that thing. On the other hand no one else sees the thing, for anyone who does not see through a thing does not see the thing either. Karrer was of the same opinion. The question, why do I get up in the morning? can (must) be absolutely fatal if it is asked in such a way as to be really asked and if it is taken to a conclusion or has to be taken to a conclusion. Like the question, why do I go to bed at night? Like the question, why do I eat? Why do I dress? Why does everything (or a great deal or a very little) connect me to some people and nothing at all to others? If the question is taken to a logical conclusion, which means that the person who asks a question, which he takes to its logical conclusion *because* he takes it to a conclusion or because he has to take it to a conclusion, also takes it to a conclusion, then the question is answered once and for all, and then the person who asked the question does not exist any longer. If we say that this person is dead from the moment when he answers his own question, we make things too simple, says Oehler. On the other hand, we can find no better way of expressing it than by saying that the person who asked the question is dead. Since we cannot name everything and so cannot think *absolutely,* we exist and there is an existence outside of ourselves, says Oehler. If we have come as far as we have come (in thought), says Oehler, we must take the consequences and we must abandon these (or the) thoughts that have (or has) made it possible for us to come this far. Karrer exercised this faculty with a virtuosity which, according to Karrer, could only be called mental agility, says Oehler. If we suppose that I, and not Karrer, were in Steinhof now, says Oehler, and you were talking to me here, the thought is nonsensical, says Oehler. The chemist Hollensteiner's suicide had a catastrophic effect upon Karrer, says Oehler, it had to have the effect upon Karrer that it did, rendering chaotic, in the most devastating manner, Karrer's completely unprotected mental state in the most fatal manner. Hollensteiner, who had been a friend of Karrer's in his youth, had, as will be recalled, committed suicide just at the moment when the so-called Ministry of Education withdrew funds vital to his Institute of Chemistry. The state withdraws vital funds from the most extraordinary minds, says Oehler, and it is precisely because of this that the extraordinary and the most extraordinary minds commit suicide, and Hollensteiner was one of these most extraordinary minds. I, says Oehler, could not begin to list the number of extraordinary and most extraordinary minds—all of them young and brilliant minds—who have committed suicide because the state, in whatever form, had withdrawn vital funds from them, and there is no doubt, in my mind, that in Hollensteiner's case we are talking about a genius. At the very moment that was most vital to Hollensteiner's institute, and so to Hollensteiner himself, the state withdrew the funds from him (and thus from his institute). Hollensteiner, who had, in his own day, made a great name for himself in chemistry, which is today such an important area of expertise, at a time when no one in this, his own country, had heard of him, even today, if you ask, no one knows the name Hollensteiner, says Oehler, we mention a completely extraordinary man's name, says Oehler, and we discover that no one knows the name, especially not those who ought to know the name: this is always our experience, the people who ought to know the name of their most extraordinary scientist do not know the name or else they do not want to know the name. In this case, the chemists do not even know Hollensteiner's name, or else they do not want to know the name Hollensteiner, and so Hollensteiner was driven to suicide, just like all extraordinary minds in this country. Whereas in Germany the name Hollensteiner was one of the most respected among chemists and still is today, here in Austria Hollensteiner has been completely blotted out, in this country, says Oehler, the extraordinary has always, and in all ages, been blotted out, blotted out until it committed suicide. If an Austrian mind is extraordinary, says Oehler, we do not need to wait for him to commit suicide, it is only a question of time and the state counts on it. Hollensteiner had so many offers, says Oehler, none of which he accepted, however. In Basel they would have welcomed Hollensteiner with open arms, in Warsaw, in Copenhagen, in Oxford, in America. But Hollensteiner didn't even go to Göttingen, where they would have given Hollensteiner all the funds he wanted, because he couldn't go to Göttingen, a person like Hollensteiner is incapable of going to Göttingen, of going to Germany at all; before a person like that would go to Germany he would rather commit suicide first. And at the very moment when he depends, in the most distressing manner, on the help of the state, he kills himself, which means that the state kills him. Genius is abandoned and driven to suicide. A scientist, says Oehler, is in a sad state in Austria and sooner or later, but especially at the moment when it appears to be most senseless, he has to perish because of the stupidity of the world around him and that means because of the stupidity of the state. We have an extraordinary scientist and ignore him, no one is attacked more basely than the extraordinary man, and genius goes to the dogs because in this state it has to go to the dogs. If only an eminent authority like Hollensteiner had the strength and, to as great an extent, the tendency toward self-denial so as to give up Austria, and that means Vienna, and go to Marburg or Göttingen, to give only two examples that apply to Hollensteiner, and could there, in Marburg or in Göttingen, continue the scientific work that it has become impossible for him to continue in Vienna, says Oehler, but a man like Hollensteiner was not in a position to go to Marburg or to Göttingen, Hollensteiner was precisely the sort of person who was unable to go to Germany. But it was also impossible for Hollensteiner to go to America, as we see, for then Hollensteiner, who was unable to go to Germany because the country made him feel uncomfortable and was intensely repugnant to him, would indeed have gone to America. Very, very few people have the strength to abandon their dislike of the country that is fundamentally ready to accept them with open arms and unparalleled goodwill and to go to that country. They would rather commit suicide in their own country because ultimately their love of their own country, or rather their love of their own, the Austrian, landscape, is greater than the strengths to endure their own science in another country. As far as Hollensteiner is concerned, says Oehler, we have an example of how the state treats an unusually clear and important mind. For years Hollensteiner begged for the funds that he needed for his own research, says Oehler, for years Hollensteiner demeaned himself in the face of a bureaucracy that is the most repugnant in the whole world, in order to get his funds, for years Hollensteiner tried what hundreds of extraordinary and brilliant people have tried. To realize an important, and not only for Austria but, without a shadow of doubt, for the whole of mankind, undertaking of a scientific nature with the aid of state funds. But he had to admit that in Austria no one can realize anything with the help of state funds, least of all something extraordinary, significant, epoch-making. The state, to whom a nature like Hollensteiner's turns in the depths of despair, has no time for a nature like Hollensteiner's. Thus a nature like Hollensteiner's must recognize that it lives in a state, and we must say this about the state without hesitation and with the greatest ruthlessness, that hates the extraordinary and hates nothing more than the extraordinary. For it is clear that, in this state, only what is stupid, impoverished, and dilettante is protected and constantly promoted and that, in this state, funds are only invested in what is incompetent and superfluous. We see hundreds of examples of this every day. And this state claims to be a civilized state and demands that it be described as such on every occasion. Let's not fool ourselves, says Oehler, this state has nothing to do with a civilized state and we shall never tire of saying so continually and without cease and on every occasion even if we are faced with the greatest difficulties because of our ceaseless observation, as a repetition of the same thing over and over again, that this is a state where lack of feeling and sense is boundless. It was Hollensteiner's misfortune to be tied by all his senses to this country, not to this state, you understand, but to this country. And we know what it means, says Oehler, to love a country like ours with all of one's senses in contrast to a state that does everything it can to destroy you instead of coming to your aid. Hollensteiner's suicide is one suicide among many, every year we are made aware of the fact that many people whom we value and who have had talent and genius and who were extraordinary or most extraordinary have committed suicide, for we are constantly going to cemeteries, says Oehler, to the funerals of people who, despairing of the state, have committed suicide, who, if we stop to think, have thrown themselves out of windows or hanged themselves or shot themselves because they felt that they had been abandoned by our state. The only reason we go to cemeteries, says Oehler, is to inter a genius who has been ruined by the state and driven to his death, that is the truth. If we strike a balance between the beauty of the country and the baseness of the state, says Oehler, we arrive at suicide. As far as Hollensteiner was concerned, it became clear that his suicide was bound to distress Karrer, after all, the two had had an unbelievable relationship as friends. Only I always thought that Hollensteiner had the strength to go to Germany, to Göttingen, where he would have had everything at his disposal, says Oehler: the fact that he did not have this strength was the cause of his death. It would also have been of no use to have tried even more intensely to persuade him to go to Göttingen at any price, Karrer said, says Oehler. A nature that was not quite as sensitive as Hollensteiner's would of course have had the strength to go to Göttingen, to go anywhere at all, simply to go where all the necessary funds for his scientific purposes would be at his disposal, says Oehler. But for a nature like Hollensteiner's it is, of course, utterly impossible to settle down in an environment, especially for scientific purposes and in any scientific discipline, that is unbearable to that nature. And it would be senseless, says Oehler, to leave a country that you love but in which you are bound, as we can see, gradually to perish in a morass of indifference and stupidity, and go to a country where you will never get over the depression that that country breeds in you, never get out of a state of mind that must be equally destructive: then it would be better to commit suicide in the country you love, if only out of force of habit, says Oehler, rather than in the country that, not to mince words, you hate. People like Hollensteiner are admittedly the most difficult, says Oehler, and it is not easy to keep in contact with them because these people are constantly giving offense—a characteristic of extraordinary people, their most outstanding characteristic, giving offense—but on the other hand there is no greater pleasure than being in contact with such extremely difficult people. We must leave no stone unturned, says Oehler, and we must always, quite consciously, set the highest value on keeping in contact with these extremely difficult people, with the extraordinary and the most extraordinary, because this is the only contact that has any real value. All other contacts are worthless, says Oehler, they are necessary but worthless. It is a shame, says Oehler, that I didn't meet Hollensteiner a lot earlier, but a remarkable caution toward this person, whom I always admired, did not permit me to make closer contact with Hollensteiner for at least twenty years after I had first set eyes on Hollensteiner, and even then our contact was not the intense contact that I would have wished for. People like Hollensteiner, says Oehler, do not allow you to approach them, they attract you and then at the crucial moment reject you. We think we have a close relationship with these people whereas in reality we can never establish a close relationship with people like Hollensteiner. In fact, we are captivated by such people as Hollensteiner without exactly knowing the reason why. On the one hand it is not, in fact, the person, on the other it is not their science, for we do not understand either of them. It is something of which we cannot say what it is and *because of that* it has the greatest effect upon us. For, says Oehler, you have to have gone to elementary school, to secondary school, and to the university with a man like Hollensteiner, as Karrer did, to know what he is. A person like me doesn't know. We comment, with really terrifying helplessness, upon a matter or a case or simply just a misfortune or just simply Hollensteiner's misfortune. I talked to Karrer about this at precisely the place where we are now standing, a few hours after we had attended Hollensteiner's funeral. Just in Döblingen cemetery itself, says Oehler, where we buried Hollensteiner and, in the nature of things, buried him in the simplest way. He wanted to have a very simple funeral, says Oehler, he had once indicated to Karrer, actually very early on when he was only twenty-one, he had indicated that he wanted a very simple funeral and in Döblingen cemetery. Just in Döblingen cemetery itself, says Oehler, there are so many extraordinary people buried, all of whom were destroyed by the state, who perished as a result of the brutality of the bureaucracy and the stupidity of the masses. We comment upon a thing, a case, or simply a misfortune and wonder how this misfortune could have arisen. How was this misfortune *possible*? We deliberately avoid talking about a so-called *human tragedy*. We have a single individual in front of us, and we have to tell ourselves that this individual has perished at the hands of the state and, vice versa, that the state has perished at the hands of this individual. It is not easy to say that it's a question of a misfortune, says Oehler, of this individual's misfortune, or the state's misfortune. It makes no sense to tell ourselves, now, that Hollensteiner could be in Göttingen (or Marburg) now, because Hollensteiner is not in Göttingen and is not in Marburg. Hollensteiner no longer exists. We buried Hollensteiner in Döblingen cemetery. As far as Hollensteiner is concerned we are left behind with our absolute helplessness (of thought). What we do is to exhaust ourselves meditating about insoluble facts, among which we do not understand the process of thought, though we call it thought, says Oehler. We become aware once more of our unease when we occupy ourselves with Hollensteiner, with Hollensteiner's suicide and with Karrer's madness, which I think is directly connected to Hollensteiner's suicide. We even misuse a subject like that of Hollensteiner in relation to Karrer, to bring ourselves satisfaction. A strange ruthlessness, which is not recognizable as ruthlessness, dominates a man like Hollensteiner, says Oehler, and we are inevitably captivated by this ruthlessness if we recognize that it is an incredibly shrewd emotional state, which we could also call a state of mind. Anyone who knew Hollensteiner had to ask himself now and again where Hollensteiner's way of acting would lead. Today we can see quite clearly where Hollensteiner's way of acting has led. Hollensteiner and Karrer together represent the two most unusual people I have known, says Oehler. There is no doubt that the fact that Hollensteiner hanged himself in his institute is demonstrative in character, says Oehler. The shock of Hollensteiner's suicide was, however, like all shocks about suicides, very very short-lived. Once the suicide is buried, his suicide and he himself are forgotten. No one thinks about it any more and the shock turns out to be hypocritical. Between Hollensteiner's suicide and Hollensteiner's funeral a lot was said about saving the Institute of Chemistry, says Oehler, people saying that the funds that had been denied to Hollensteiner would be placed at the disposal of his successor, as if there were one! cries Oehler, the newspapers carried reports that the ministry would undertake a so-called extensive redevelopment of Hollensteiner's institute, at the funeral, people were even talking about the state's making good what it had until then neglected in the Institute for Chemistry, but today, a few weeks later, says Oehler, that's all as good as forgotten. Hollensteiner demonstrates by hanging himself in his own institute the serious plight of the whole domestic scientific community, says Oehler, and the world, and thus the people around Hollensteiner, feigns shock and goes to Hollensteiner's funeral, and the moment Hollensteiner is buried they forget everything connected with Hollensteiner. Today nobody talks about Hollensteiner any more and nobody talks about his Institute of Chemistry, and nobody thinks of changing the situation that led to Hollensteiner's suicide. And then someone else commits suicide, says Oehler, and another, and the process is repeated. Slowly but surely all intellectual activity in this country is extinguished, says Oehler. And what we observe in Hollensteiner's field can be seen in every field, says Oehler. Until now we have always asked ourselves whether a country, a state, can afford to allow its intellectual treasure to deteriorate in such a really shabby way, says Oehler, but nobody asks the question any longer. Karrer spoke about Hollensteiner as a perfect example of a human being who could not be helped because he was extraordinary, unusual. Karrer explained the concept of the eccentric in connection with Hollensteiner with complete clarity, says Oehler. If there had been a less fundamental, a distanced, relationship between him, Karrer, and Hollensteiner, Karrer told Oehler, he, Karrer, would have made Hollensteiner the subject of a paper entitled *The Relationship between Persons and Characters Like Hollensteiner, as a Chemist, to the State, Which is Gradually and in the Most Consistent Manner Destroying and Killing Them.* In fact, there are in existence a number of Karrer's remarks about Hollensteiner, says Oehler, hundreds of slips of paper, just as there are about you, says Oehler to me, there are in existence hundreds of Karrer's slips of paper just as there are about me. It is obvious that these slips of paper written by Karrer should not be allowed to disappear, but it is difficult to get at these notes of Karrer's, if we want to secure Karrer's writings, we have to apply to Karrer's sister, but she doesn't want to hear anything more about Karrer's thoughts. He, Oehler, thinks that Karrer's sister may already have destroyed

Karrer's writings, for as we see over and over again stupid relatives act quickly, as, for example, the sisters or wives or brothers and nephews of dead thinkers, or ones who have gone finally mad, even when it is a case of brilliant characters, as in the case of Karrer, they don't even wait for the actual moment of death or the final madness of the hated object, says Oehler, but acting as their relatives destroy, that is burn, the writings that irritate them for the most part before the final death or the final confinement of their hated thinker. Just as Hollensteiner's sister destroyed everything that Hollensteiner wrote, immediately after Hollensteiner's suicide. It would be a mistake to assume that Hollensteiner's sister would have taken Hollensteiner's part, says Oehler, on the contrary Hollensteiner's sister was ashamed of Hollensteiner and had taken the state's part, the part, that is, of baseness and stupidity. When Karrer went to see her, she threw him out, says Oehler, that is to say she didn't even let Karrer into her house. And to his question about Hollensteiner's writings she replied that Hollensteiner's writings no longer existed, she had burned Hollensteiner's writings because they appeared to her to be the writings of a madman. The fact is, says Oehler, that the world lost tremendous thoughts in Hollensteiner's writings, philosophy lost tremendous philosophical thoughts, science lost tremendous scientific thoughts. For Hollensteiner had been a continuous, thinking, scientific mind, says Oehler, who constantly put his continuous scientific thought onto paper. In fact, in Hollensteiner's case, we were dealing not only with a scientist but also with a philosopher, in Hollensteiner the scientist and the philosopher were able to fuse into one single, clear intellect, says Oehler. Thus, when you talk of Hollensteiner, you can speak of a scientist who was basically really a philosopher, just as you can speak of a philosopher who was basically really a scientist. Hollensteiner's science was basically philosophy, Hollensteiner's philosophy basically science, says Oehler. Otherwise we are always forced to say, here we have a scientist but (regrettably) not a philosopher, or here we have a philosopher but (regrettably) not a scientist. This is not the case in our judgment of Hollensteiner. It is a very Austrian characteristic, as we know, says Oehler. If we get involved with Hollensteiner, says Oehler, we get involved with a philosopher and a scientist at the same time, even if it were totally false to say that Hollensteiner was a philosophizing scientist and so on. He was a totally scientific philosopher. If we are talking about a person, as we are at the moment about Hollensteiner (and if we are talking about Hollensteiner, then basically about Karrer, but very often basically about Hollensteiner and so on), we are nevertheless speaking all the time about a result. We are mathematicians, says Oehler, or at least we are always trying to be mathematicians. When we think, it is less a case of philosophy, says Oehler, more one of mathematics. Everything is a tremendous calculation, if we have set it up from the outset in an unbroken line, *a very simple* calculation. But we are not always in the position of keeping everything that we have calculated intact within our head, and we break off what we are thinking and are satisfied with what we see, and are not surprised for long that we rest content with what we see, with millions upon millions of images that lie on, or under, one another and constantly merge and displace each other. Again, we can say that what appears extraordinary to a person like me, what is in fact extraordinary to me, *because* it is extraordinary, says Oehler, means nothing to the state. For Hollensteiner meant nothing to the state because he meant nothing to the masses, but we shall not get any further with this thought, says Oehler. And whereas the state and whereas society and whereas the masses do everything to get rid of thought, *we* oppose this development with all the means at our disposal, although we ourselves believe most of the time in the senselessness of thinking, because we know that thinking is total senselessness, because, on the other hand, we know that without the senselessness of thinking *we* do not exist or are nothing. We then cling to the effortlessness with which the masses dare to exist, although they deny this effortlessness in every statement that they make, says Oehler, but, in the nature of things, we do not, of course, succeed in being really effortless in the effortlessness of the masses. We can, however, do nothing less than cling to this misconception from time to time, subject ourselves to the misconception, and that means all possible misconceptions, and exist in nothing but misconception. For strictly speaking, says Oehler, everything is misconceived. But we exist within this fact because there is no way that we can exist outside this fact, at least not all the time. Existence is misconception, says Oehler. This is something we have to come to terms with early enough, so that we have a basis upon which we can exist, says Oehler. Thus misconception is the only real basis. But we are not always obliged to think of this basis as a principle, we must not do that, says

Oehler, we cannot do that. We can only say yes, over and over again, to what we should unconditionally say no to, do you understand, says Oehler, that is the fact. Thus Karrer's madness was causally connected with Hollensteiner's suicide, which of itself had nothing to do with madness. Behavior like Hollensteiner's was bound to do damage to a nature like Karrer's if we consider Hollensteiner's relationship to Karrer and vice versa, in the way in which Hollensteiner's suicide harmed Karrer's nature, says Oehler. Karrer had on many occasions, he went on, spoken to Oehler of the possibility of Hollensteiner's committing suicide. But he was talking about a suicide that would come *from within,* not of one that would *be caused externally,* says Oehler, if we disregard the fact that inner and outer are identical for natures like Hollensteiner and Karrer. For, and these are Karrer's words, says Oehler, the possibility that Hollensteiner would commit suicide from an inner cause always existed, but then with the extension of Hollensteiner's institute and with Hollensteiner's obvious successes in his scientific work, simultaneously with the ignoring and the torpedoing of these scientific successes of Hollensteiner's by the world around him, the possibility existed that he would commit suicide from *an external cause.* Whereas, however, it is characteristic and typical of Hollensteiner, says Oehler, that he did finally commit suicide, as we now know, and what we could not know up to the moment that Hollensteiner committed suicide is that it is also typical of Karrer that he did not commit suicide after Hollensteiner had committed suicide but that he, Karrer, went mad. However, what is frightful, says Oehler, is the thought that a person like Karrer, because he has gone mad and, as I believe, has actually gone finally mad, because he has gone finally mad he has fallen into the hands of people like Scherrer. On the previous Saturday, Oehler made several statements regarding Karrer to Scherrer which, according to Scherrer, says Oehler, were of importance for him, Scherrer, in connection with Karrer's treatment, he, Oehler, did not believe that what he had told Scherrer on Saturday, especially about the incident that was crucial for Karrer's madness, the incident in Rustenschacher's men's store, that the very thing that Oehler had told Scherrer about what he had noticed in Rustenschacher's store, shortly before Karrer went mad, still made sense. For Scherrer's scientific work *it did,* for Karrer *it did not.* For the fact that Scherrer now knows what I noticed in Rustenschacher's store before Karrer went mad in Rustenschacher's store makes no difference to Karrer's madness. What happened in Rustenschacher's store, says Oehler, was only the factor that triggered Karrer's final madness, nothing more. For example, it would have been much more important, says Oehler, if Scherrer had concerned himself with the relationship of Karrer and Hollensteiner, but Scherrer did not want to hear anything from Oehler about this relationship, Karrer's relationship to Hollensteiner was not of the slightest interest to Scherrer, says Oehler. I tried several times to direct Scherrer's attention to this relationship, to make him aware of this really important relationship and of the really important events that took place within this year- and decades-long connection between Karrer and Hollensteiner, but Scherrer did not go into it, says Oehler, but, as is the way with these people, these totally unphilosophical and, for that reason, useless psychiatric doctors, he continued to nag away at the happenings in Rustenschacher's store, which are, in my opinion, certainly revealing but not decisive, says Oehler, but he understood nothing about the importance of the Karrer/Hollensteiner relationship. Scherrer kept on asking me *why* we, Karrer and I, went into Rustenschacher's store, to which I replied every time that I could not answer that question and that I simply could not understand how Scherrer could ask such a question, says Oehler. Scherrer kept on asking questions which, in my opinion, were unimportant questions, whereupon, of course, Scherrer received unimportant answers from me, says Oehler. These people keep on asking unimportant questions and for that reason keep on getting unimportant answers, but they are not aware of it. Just as they are not aware of the fact that the questions they ask are unimportant and as a result make no sense, it does not occur to them that the answers they receive to these questions are unimportant and make no sense. If I had not gone on mentioning Hollensteiner's name, says Oehler, Scherrer would not have hit upon Hollensteiner. There is something terribly depressing about sitting opposite a person who, by his very presence, continuously asserts that he is competent and yet has absolutely no competence in the matter at hand. We observe time and again, says Oehler, that we are with people who should be competent and who also assert and claim, indeed they go on claiming, to be competent in the matter for which we have come to them, whereas they are in an irresponsible, shattering, and really repugnant manner incompetent. Almost everybody we get together with about a matter, even if it is of the highest importance, is incompetent. Scherrer, says Oehler, is, in my opinion, the most incompetent when it's a question of Karrer, and the thought that Karrer is in Scherrer's hands, because Karrer is confined in Scherrer's section, is one of the most frightful thoughts. The enormous arrogance you sense, says Oehler, when you sit facing a man like Scherrer. Hardly a moment passes before you ask yourself what Karrer (the patient) really has to do with Scherrer (his doctor)? For a person like Karrer to be in the hands of a person like Scherrer is an unparalleled human monstrosity, says Oehler. But because we are familiar with his condition, it is immaterial to Karrer whether he is in Scherrer's hands or not. After all, the moment Karrer became finally mad it became immaterial whether Karrer was in Steinhof or not, says Oehler. But it is not the fact that a man like Scherrer is totally unphilosophical that is repugnant, says Oehler, although someone in Scherrer's position ought, first and foremost, besides having his medical knowledge, to be philosophical, it is his shameful ignorance. No matter what I say, Sherrer's ignorance repeatedly finds expression, says Oehler. Whenever I said something, no matter what it was, to Scherrer or whenever Scherrer responded to what I had said, no matter what it was, I was constantly aware that Scherrer's ignorance kept coming to light. But even when Scherrer says nothing, we hear nothing but ignorance from him, says Oehler, a person like Scherrer does not need to say something ignorant for us to know that we are dealing with a completely ignorant person. The observation that doctors are practicing in complete ignorance shakes us when we are with them, says Oehler. But among doctors, ignorance is a habit to which they have become accustomed over the centuries, says Oehler. Some exceptions notwithstanding, says Oehler. Scherrer's inability to think logically and thus to ask logical questions, give logical answers, and so forth, says Oehler, it was precisely when I was in his presence that it occurred to me that people like Scherrer can never go mad. As we know, psychiatric doctors do become mentally ill after a while, but not mad. Because they are ignorant of their life's theme these people finally become mentally ill, but never mad. As a result of incapacity, says Oehler, and basically because of their continual decades-long incompetence. And at that moment I again recognized to what degree madness is something that happens only among the highest orders of humanity. That at a given moment madness is *everything.* But to say something like that to Scherrer, says Oehler, would, above all else, be to overestimate Scherrer, so I quickly gave up the idea of saying anything to Scherrer such as what I have just said about the actual definition of madness, says Oehler. Scherrer is probably not the least bit interested in what took place in Rustenschacher's store, says Oehler, he only asked me to go up to Steinhof because he didn't know anything better to do, to ask me about what happened in Rustenschacher's store, says Oehler. Psychiatric doctors like to make a note of what you tell them, without worrying about it, and what you tell them is a matter of complete indifference to them, that is, it is a matter of complete indifference to them, and they do not worry about it. Because a psychiatric doctor has to make inquiries, they make inquiries, says Oehler, and of all the leads the ones they follow are the least important. Of course, the incident in Rustenschacher's store is not insignificant, says Oehler, but it is only one of hundreds of incidents that preceded the incident in Rustenschacher's store and that have the same importance as the one in Rustenschacher's store. Not a question about Hollensteiner, not a question about the people around Hollensteiner, not a question about Hollensteiner's place in modern science, not a question about Hollensteiner's philosophical circumstances, about his notes, never mind about Hollensteiner's relationship to Karrer or Karrer's to Hollensteiner. In the nature of things, Scherrer should have shown an interest in the time Hollensteiner and Karrer spent together at school, says Oehler, in their common route to school, their origins and so on, in their common, and their different, views and intentions and so on, says Oehler. The whole time I was there, Scherrer insisted that I only make statements about the incident in Rustenschacher's store, and on this point with regard to the happenings in Rustenschacher's store, says Oehler, Scherrer demanded the utmost precision from me. He kept saying leave nothing out, says Oehler, I can still hear him saying leave nothing out while I went on talking without a break about the incident in Rustenschacher's store. This incident acted as a so-called trigger incident, I said to Scherrer, says Oehler, but there can be no doubt that it is not a fundamental one. Scherrer did not react to my observation, I made the observation several times, says Oehler, and so I had repeatedly to take up the incident in Rustenschacher's store. That is absolutely grotesque, Scherrer said on several occasions during my description of the incident in Rustenschacher's store. This statement was merely repugnant to me.

Oehler told Scherrer, among other things, that their, Oehler's and Karrer's, going into Rustenschacher's store was totally unpremeditated, we suddenly said, according to Oehler, let's go into Rustenschacher's store and immediately had them show us several of the thick, warm and at the same time sturdy winter trousers (according to Karrer). Rustenschacher's nephew, his salesman, Oehler told Scherrer, who had served us so often, pulled out a whole heap of trousers from the shelves that were all labeled with every possible official standard size and threw the trousers onto the counter, and Karrer had Rustenschacher's nephew hold all the trousers up to the light, while I stood to one side, the left-hand side near the mirror, as you look from the entrance door. And as was his, Karrer's, way, as Oehler told Scherrer, Karrer kept pointing with his walking stick and with greater and greater emphasis at the many thin spots that are revealed in these trousers if you hold them up to the light, Oehler told Scherrer, at the thin spots that really cannot be missed, as Karrer kept putting it, Oehler told Scherrer, Karrer simply kept saying these so-called new trousers, Oehler told Scherrer, while having the trousers held up to the light, and above all he kept on saying the whole time: these remarkably thin spots in these so-called new trousers, Oehler told Scherrer. He, Karrer, again let himself be carried away so far as to make the comment as to why these so-called new trousers—Karrer kept on saying so-called new trousers, over and over again, Oehler told Scherrer—why these so-called new trousers, which even if they were new, because they had not been worn, had nevertheless lain on one side for years and, on that account, no longer looked very attractive, something that he, Karrer, had no hesitation in telling Rustenschacher, just as he had no hesitation in telling Rustenschacher anything that had to do with the trousers that were lying on the counter and that Rustenschacher's nephew kept holding up to the light, it was not in his, Karrer's, nature to feel the least hesitation in saying the least thing about the trousers to Rustenschacher, just as he had no hesitation in saying a lot of things to Rustenschacher that did *not* concern the trousers, though it would surely be to his, Karrer's, advantage not to say many of the things to Rustenschacher that he had no hesitation in telling him, why the trousers should reveal these thin spots that no one could miss in a way that immediately aroused suspicion about the trousers. Karrer told Rustenschacher, Oehler told Scherrer, these very same new, though neglected, trousers which for that reason no longer looked very attractive, though they had never been worn, should reveal these thin spots, said Karrer to Rustenschacher, as Oehler told Scherrer. Perhaps it was that the material in question, of which the trousers were made, was an imported Czechoslovakian reject, Oehler told Scherrer. Karrer used the term Czechoslovakian reject several times, Oehler told Scherrer, and actually used it so often that Rustenschacher's nephew, the salesman, had to exercise the greatest self-control. Throughout the whole time we were in Rustenschacher's store, Rustenschacher himself busied himself labeling trousers, so Oehler told Scherrer. The salesman's self-control was always at a peak from the moment that we, Karrer and I, entered the store. Although from the moment we entered Rustenschacher's store everything pointed to a coming catastrophe (in Karrer), Oehler told Scherrer, I did not believe for one moment that it would really develop into such a, in the nature of things, hideous catastrophe for Karrer, as Oehler told Scherrer. However, I have observed the same thing on each of our visits to Rustenschacher's store, as Oehler told Scherrer: Rustenschacher's nephew exercised this sort of self-control for a long time, for the longest time, and in fact exercised this self-control up to the point when Karrer used the concept or the term Czechoslovakian reject. And Rustenschacher himself always exercised the utmost self-control during all our visits to his business, up to the moment, as Oehler told Scherrer, when Karrer suddenly, intentionally almost inaudibly but in this way all the more effectively, used the term or the concept Czechoslovakian reject. Every time, however, it was the salesman and Rustenschacher's nephew who first objected to the word reject, as Oehler told Scherrer. While the salesman, in the nature of things, in an angry tone of voice said to Karrer that the materials used in the trousers lying on the counter were neither rejects nor Czechoslovakian rejects but the very best of English materials, he threw the trousers he had just been holding up to the light onto the heap of other trousers, while Karrer was saying that it was all a matter of Czechoslovakian rejects, and made a move as if to go out of the store and into the office at the back of the store. It was always the same, Oehler told Scherrer: Karrer says, as quick as lightning, Czechoslovakian rejects, the salesman throws onto the heap the trousers that had just been held up and says angrily the very best English materials and makes a move as if to go out of the store and into the office at the back of the store, and in fact takes a few steps, as Oehler told Scherrer, toward Rustenschacher, but stops just in front of Rustenschacher, turns around and comes back to the counter, standing at which Karrer, holding his walking stick up in the air, says I have nothing against the way the trousers are finished, no I have nothing against the way the trousers are finished, I am not talking about the way the trousers are finished but about the quality of the materials, nothing against the workmanship, absolutely nothing against the workmanship. Understand me correctly, Karrer repeats several times to the salesman, as Oehler told Scherrer, I admit that the workmanship in these trousers is the very best, said Karrer, as Oehler told Scherrer, and Karrer immediately says to Rustenschacher's nephew, besides I have known Rustenschacher too long not to know that the workmanship is the best that anyone could imagine. But he, Karrer, could not refrain from remarking that we were dealing here with trouser materials, quite apart from the workmanship, with rejects and, as one could clearly see, with Czechoslovakian rejects, he simply had to repeat that in the case of these trouser materials we are dealing with Czechoslovakian rejects. Karrer suddenly raised his walking stick again, as Oehler told Scherrer, and banged several times loudly on the counter with his stick and said emphatically: you must admit that in the case of these trouser materials we are dealing with Czechoslovakian rejects! You must admit that! You must admit that! You must admit that! Whereupon Scherrer asks whether Karrer had said you must admit that several times and how loudly, to which I replied to Scherrer, five times, for still ringing in my ears was exactly how often Karrer had said you must admit that and I described to Scherrer exactly how loudly. Just at the moment when Karrer says you must admit that! and you must admit that gentlemen, and you must admit gentlemen that in the case of the trousers that are lying on the counter we are dealing with Czechoslovakian rejects, Rustenschacher's nephew again holds one of the pairs of trousers up to the light and it is, truth to tell, a pair with a particularly thin spot, I tell Scherrer, Oehler says, twice I repeat to Scherrer: with a particularly thin spot, with a particularly thin spot up to the light, I say, says Oehler, every one of these pairs of trousers that you show me here, says Karrer, Oehler tells Scherrer, is proof of the fact that in the case of all these trouser materials we are dealing with Czechoslovakian rejects. What was remarkable and astonishing and what made him suspicious at that moment, Oehler told Scherrer, was not the many thin spots in the trousers, nor the fact that in the case of these trousers we were dealing with rejects, and actually Czechoslovakian rejects, as he kept repeating, all of that was basically neither remarkable nor surprising and not astonishing either. What was remarkable, surprising, and astonishing was the fact, Karrer said to Rustenschacher's nephew, as Oehler told Scherrer, that a salesman, even if he were the nephew of the owner, would be upset by the truth that was told him, and he, Karrer, was telling nothing but the truth when he said that these trousers all had thin spots and that these materials were nothing but Czechoslovakian rejects, to which Rustenschacher's nephew replied, as Oehler told Scherrer, that he swore that in the case of the materials in question they were not dealing with Czechoslovakian rejects but with the most excellent English materials, several times the salesman swore to Karrer that in the case of the materials in question they were dealing with the most excellent English materials, most excellent, most excellent, not just excellent I keep on repeating, Oehler told Scherrer, again and again most excellent and not just excellent, because I was of the opinion that it is decisive whether you say excellent or most excellent, I keep telling Scherrer, actually in the case of the materials in question we are dealing with the most excellent English materials, says the salesman, Oehler told Scherrer, at which the salesman's, Rustenschacher's nephew's, voice, as I had to keep explaining to Scherrer, whenever he said the most excellent English materials, was uncomfortably high-pitched. If Rustenschacher's nephew's voice is of itself unpleasant, it is at its most unpleasant when he says the most excellent English materials, I know of no more unpleasant voice than Rustenschacher's nephew's voice when he says the most excellent English materials, Oehler told Scherrer. It is just that the materials are not labeled, says Rustenschacher's nephew, that makes it possible to sell them so cheaply, Oehler told Scherrer. These materials are deliberately not labeled as English materials, clearly to avoid paying duty, says Rustenschacher's nephew, and in the background Rustenschacher himself says, from the back of the store, as Oehler told Scherrer, these materials are not labeled so that they can come onto the market as cheaply as possible. Fifty percent of goods from England are not labeled, Rustenschacher told Karrer, I told Scherrer, says Oehler, and for this reason they are cheaper than the ones that are labeled, but as far as the quality goes there is absolutely no difference between goods that are labeled and ones that are not. The goods that are not labeled, especially in the case of textiles, are often forty, very often even fifty or sixty, percent cheaper than the ones that are labeled. As far as the purchaser, above all the consumer, is concerned it is a matter of complete indifference whether he is using labeled or unlabeled goods, it is a matter of complete indifference whether I am wearing a coat made of labeled, or whether I am wearing a coat made of unlabeled materials, says Rustenschacher from the back of the store, Oehler told Scherrer. As far as the customs are concerned we are, of course, dealing with rejects, as you say, Karrer, says Rustenschacher, so Oehler told Scherrer. It is very often the case that what are termed Czechoslovakian rejects, and declared as such to the customs authorities, are the most excellent English goods or most excellent goods from another foreign source, Rustenschacher said to Karrer. During this argument between Karrer and Rustenschacher, Rustenschacher's nephew kept holding up another pair of trousers to the light for Karrer, Oehler says to Scherrer. While I myself, so Oehler told Scherrer, totally uninvolved in the argument, was leaning on the counter, as I said totally uninvolved in the argument between Karrer and Rustenschacher. The two continued their argument, Oehler told Scherrer, just as if I were not in the store, and it was because of this that it was possible for me to observe the two of them with the greatest attention, in the process of which my main attention was, of course, focused on Karrer, for at this point I already feared him, Oehler told Scherrer. Once again I tell Scherrer, if you look from the entrance door, I was standing to the left of Karrer, once again I had to say, in front of the mirror, because Scherrer no longer knew that I had already told him once that during our whole stay in Rustenschacher's store I was always standing in front of the mirror. On the other hand, Scherrer did make a note of everything, according to Oehler, he even made a note of my repetitions, said Oehler. It was obviously a pleasure for Karrer to have all the trousers help up to the light, but having all the trousers held up to the light was nothing new for Karrer, and he refused to leave Rustenschacher's store until Rustenschacher's nephew had held all the trousers up to the light, Oehler told Scherrer, basically it was always the same scene when I went to Rustenschacher's store with Karrer but never so vehement, so incredibly intense, and, as we now know, culminating in such a terrible collapse on Karrer's part. Karrer took not the slightest notice of the impatience, the resentment, and the truly incessant anxiety on the part of Rustenschacher's nephew, Oehler told Scherrer. On the contrary, Karrer put Rustenschacher's nephew the salesman more and more to the test with ever new sadistic fabrications conspicuously aimed at him. Rustenschacher's nephew always reacted too slowly for Karrer. You react too slowly for me said Karrer several times, says Oehler to Scherrer, basically you have no ability to react, it is a mystery to me how you find yourself in a position to serve me, how you find yourself in a postion to work in this truly excellent store of your uncle's, Karrer said several times to Rustenschacher's nephew, Oehler told Scherrer. While you are holding two pairs of trousers up to the light, I can hold up ten pairs, Karrer said to Rustenschacher's nephew. How unhappy Rustenschacher was about the argument between Karrer and his, Rustenschacher's, nephew is shown by the fact that Rustenschacher left the store on several occasions and went into the office, apparently to avoid having to take part in the painful argument. I myself was afraid that I would have to intervene in the argument at any moment, then Karrer raised his walking stick again, banged it on the counter, and said, to all appearances we are dealing with a state of exhaustion, it is possible that we are dealing with a state of exhaustion, but I cannot be bothered at all with such a state of exhaustion, cannot be bothered at all, he said to himself, while he was banging on the counter with his walking stick, in the particular rhythm with which he always banged on the counter in Rustenschacher's store, apparently to calm his inner state of excitement, Oehler told Scherrer, and then he, Karrer, began once more to heap his excesses of assertion and insinuation concerning the trousers on the head of the salesman. Rustenschacher certainly heard everything from the back of the store, as Oehler told Scherrer, even if it appeared as though Rustenschacher observed nothing happening between Karrer and his nephew, Rustenschacher's self-control, I told Scherrer, said Oehler, was at an absolute peak, as the argument between Karrer and Rustenschacher's nephew heated up, Rustenschacher had to exercise a degree of self-control that would have been impossible in another human being. *But the way* in which Karrer had behaved at certain times in Rustenschacher's store and because Rustenschacher *knew* how Karrer always *acts in this almost unbearable manner* in Rustenschacher's store and Rustenschacher knew how Karrer always *re*acts to everything, but he knew that he had nevertheless always calmed down in the end, in fact, whenever we had gone into Rustenschacher's store, Rustenschacher had always shown a much greater ability to judge Karrer's state of mind than Scherrer. Suddenly Karrer said to Rustenschacher, Oehler told Scherrer, if you, Rustenschacher, take up a position behind the pair of trousers that your nephew is at this moment holding up to the light for me, immediately behind this pair of trousers that your nephew is holding up to the light for me, I can see your face through this pair of trousers with a clarity with which I do not wish to see your face. But Rustenschacher controlled himself. Whereupon Karrer said, enough trousers! enough materials! enough! Oehler told Scherrer. Immediately after this, however, Oehler told Scherrer, Karrer repeated that with regard to the materials that were lying on the counter they were dealing one hundred percent with Czechoslovakian rejects. Aside from the workmanship, says Karrer, Oehler told Scherrer, as far as these materials were concerned, it was quite obviously a question, even to the layman, of Czechoslovakian rejects. The workmanship is the best, of course, the workmanship is the best, Karrer keeps repeating, that has always been apparent in all the years that I have been coming to Rustenschacher's store. And how long had he been coming to Rustenschacher's store? and how many pairs of trousers had he already bought in Rustenschacher's store? says Karrer, Oehler tells Scherrer, not one button has come off, says Karrer, Oehler told Scherrer. Not a single seam has come undone! says Karrer to Rustenschacher. My sister, says Karrer, has never yet had to sew on a button that has come off, says Karrer, it is true that my sister has never yet had to sew on a single button that has come off a pair of trousers I bought from you, Rustenschacher, because all the buttons that have been sewn onto the trousers I bought from you are really sewn on so securely that no one can tear one of these buttons off. And not a single seam has come undone in all these years in any of the pairs of trousers I have bought in your store! Scherrer noted what I was saying in the so-called shorthand that is customary among psychiatric doctors. And I felt terrible to be sitting here in Pavilion VI in front of Scherrer and making these statements about Karrer, while Karrer is confined in Pavilion VII, we say *confined* because we don't want to say *locked up* or *locked up like an animal,* says Oehler. Here I am sitting in Pavilion VI and talking about Karrer in

Pavilion VII without Karrer's knowing anything about the fact that I am sitting in Pavilion VI and talking about him in Pavilion VII. And, of course, I did not visit Karrer, when I went *into* Steinhof, nor when I came *away from* Steinhof, says Oehler. But Karrer probably couldn't have been visited. Visiting patients confined in Pavilion VII is not permitted, says Oehler. No one in Pavilion VII is allowed to have visitors. Suddenly Rustenschacher says, I tell Scherrer, says Oehler, that Karrer can try to tear a button off the trousers that are lying on the counter. Or try to rip open one of these seams! says Rustenschacher to Karrer, subject all of these pairs of trousers to a thorough examination, says Rustenschacher, and Rustenschacher invites Karrer to tear, to pull, and to tug at all the pairs of trousers lying on the counter in any way he likes, Oehler told Scherrer. Rustenschacher invited Karrer to do whatever he liked to the trousers. Possibly, Rustenschacher was thinking pedagogically at that moment, Oehler said to Scherrer. Then Oehler said to Rustenschacher that he, Karrer, would refrain when so directly invited to tear up all these pairs of Rustenschacher's trousers, Oehler told Scherrer. I prefer not to make such a tear test, said Karrer to Rustenschacher, Oehler told Scherrer. For if I did make the attempt, said Karrer, to rip *open* a seam or even tear a button *off* just one pair of these trousers, people would at once say that I was mad, and I am on my guard against this, because you should be on your guard against being called mad, Oehler told Scherrer. But if I really were to tear these trousers, Karrer said to Rustenbacher and his nephew, I would tear all of these trousers into rags in the shortest possible time, to say nothing of the fact that I would tear all the buttons off all of these trousers. Such rashness to invite me to tear up all these trousers! says Karrer. Such rashness!, Oehler told Scherrer. Then Karrer returned to the thin spots, Oehler told Scherrer, saying that it was remarkable that if you held all of these trousers up to the light, thin spots were to be seen, thin spots that were quite typical of reject materials, says Karrer. Whereupon Rustenschacher's nephew says, one should not, as anyone knows, hold up a pair of trousers to the light, because all trousers if held up to the light show thin spots. Show me one pair of trousers in the world that you can hold up to the light, says Rustenschacher to Karrer from the back. Not even the newest, not even the newest, says Rustenschacher, Oehler told Scherrer. In every case you would find at least one thin spot in a pair of trousers held up to the light, says Rustenschacher's nephew, says Oehler to Scherrer. Suddenly Rustenschacher adds from the back: every piece of *woven goods* reveals a thin spot when held up to the light, a thin spot. To which Karrer replies that every intelligent shopper naturally holds an article that he has chosen to buy up to the light if he doesn't want to be swindled, Oehler told Scherrer. Every article, no matter what, must be held up to the light if you want to buy it, Karrer said. Even if merchants fear nothing so much as having their articles held up to the light, said Karrer, Oehler told Scherrer. But naturally there are trouser materials and thus trousers, I tell Scherrer, that you can hold up to the light without further ado if you are really dealing with excellent materials, I say, you can hold them up to the light without further ado. But apparently, I tell Scherrer, according to Oehler, we were dealing with English materials in the case of the materials in question and not, as Karrer thought, with Czechoslovakian, and hence not with Czechoslovakian rejects, but I do not believe that we were dealing with excellent, or indeed most excellent English materials, I tell Scherrer, for I saw the thin spots myself in all of these trousers, except that naturally I would not have held forth in the way that Karrer held forth about those thin spots in all the trousers, I tell Scherrer. Probably I would not have gone into Rustenschacher's store at all, seeing that we had been in Rustenschacher's store two or three days before the visit to Rustenschacher's store. It was the same the time before last when we went in: Karrer had Rustenschacher's nephew hold the trousers up to the light, but not so many pairs of trousers, after just a short time Karrer says, thank you, I'm not going to buy any trousers, and to me, let's go, and we leave Rustenschacher's store. But now the situation was totally different. Karrer was already in a state of excitement when he entered Rustenschacher's store because we had been talking about Hollensteiner the whole way from Klosterneuburgerstrasse to Albersbachstrasse, Karrer had become more and more excited as we made our way, and at the peak of his excitement, I had never seen Karrer so excited before, we went into Rustenschacher's store. Of course we should not have gone into Rustenschacher's store in such a high state of excitement, I tell Scherrer. It would have been better not to go into Rustenschacher's store but to go back to Klosterneuburgerstrasse, but Karrer did not take up my suggestion of returning to Klosterneuburgerstrasse. I have made up my mind to go into Rustenschacher's store, Karrer says to me, Oehler told Scherrer, and as Karrer's tone of voice had the character of an irreversible command, I tell Scherrer, says Oehler, I had no choice but to go into Rustenschacher's store with Karrer on this occasion. And I could never have let Karrer go into Rustenschacher's store on his own, says Oehler, not in that state. It was clear to me that we were taking a risk in going into Rustenschacher's store, I tell Scherrer, Karrer's state prevented me from saying a word against his intention of going into Rustenschacher's store. If you know Karrer's nature, I tell Scherrer, says Oehler, you know that if Karrer says he is going into Rustenschacher's store it is pointless trying to do anything about it. No matter what Karrer's intention was, when he was in such a condition there was no way of stopping him, no way of persuading him to do otherwise. On the one hand, it was Rustenschacher who let him go into Rustenschacher's store, on the other hand Rustenschacher's nephew, both of them were basically repugnant to him, just as, basically, everyone was repugnant to him, even I was repugnant to him: you have to know that everyone was repugnant to him, even those with whom he consorted of his own volition, if you consorted with him of his own volition, you were not exempted from the fact that everybody was repugnant to Karrer, I tell Scherrer, says Oehler. *There is no one with such great sensitivity. No one with such fluctuations of consciousness. No one so easily irritated and so ready to be hurt,* I tell Scherrer, says Oehler. The truth is Karrer felt he was constantly being watched, and he always reacted as if he felt he was constantly being watched, and for this reason he never had a single moment's peace. This constant restlessness is also what distinguishes him from everyone else, if constant restlessness can distinguish a person, I tell Scherrer, Oehler says. And to be with a constantly restless person who imagines that he is restless even when he is in reality not restless is the most difficult thing, I tell Scherrer, says Oehler. Even when nothing suggested one or more causes of restlessness, when nothing suggested the least restlessness, Karrer was restless because he had the feeling (the sense) that he was restless, because he had reason to, as he thought. The theory according to which a person is everything he imagines himself to be could be studied in Karrer, the way he always imagined, and he probably imagined this all his life, that he was critically ill without knowing what the illness was that made him critically ill, and probably because of this, and certainly according to the theory,

I tell Scherrer, says Oehler, he really was critically ill. *When we imagine ourselves to be in a state of mind,* no matter what, we are in that state of mind, and thus in that state of illness which we imagine ourselves to be in, *in every state that we imagine ourselves in.* And we do not allow ourselves to be disturbed in what we imagine, I tell Scherrer, and thus we do not allow what we have imagined to be negated by anything, especially by *anything external.* What incredible self-confidence, on the one hand, and what incredible weakness of character and helplessness, on the other, psychiatric doctors show, I think, while I am sitting opposite Scherrer and making these statements about Karrer and, in particular, about Karrer's behavior in Rustenschacher's store, says Oehler. After a short time I ask myself why I am sitting opposite Scherrer and making these statements and giving this information about Karrer. But I do not spend long thinking about this question, so as not to give Scherrer an opportunity of starting to have thoughts about my unusual behavior towards him, because I had declared myself ready to tell him as much as possible about Karrer that afternoon. I now think it would have been better to get up and leave, without bothering about what Scherrer is thinking, if I were to leave in spite of my assurance that I would talk about Karrer for an hour or two I thought, Oehler says. If only I could go outside, I said to myself while I was sitting opposite Scherrer, out of this terrible whitewashed and barred room, and go away. Go away as far as possible. But, like everyone who sits facing a psychiatric doctor, I had only the one thought, that of not arousing any sort of suspicion in the person sitting opposite me about my own mental condition and that means about my soundness of mind. I thought that basically I was acting against Karrer by going to Scherrer, says Oehler. My conscience was suddenly *not clear,* do you know what it means to have a sudden feeling that your conscience is not clear with respect to a friend? and it makes things all the worse if your friend is in Karrer's position, I thought. To speak merely of a bad conscience would be to water the feeling down quite inadmissibly, says Oehler, I was ashamed. For there was no doubt in my mind that Scherrer was an enemy of Karrer's, but I only became aware of this *after a long time, after long observation* of Scherrer—whom I have *known* for years, ever since Karrer was first in Steinhof—and it was only because we were acquainted that I agreed to pay a call on him, but he was not so well known to me that I could say this is someone I know, in that case I would not have accepted Scherrer's invitation to go to Steinhof and make a statement about Karrer. I thought several times about getting up and leaving, says Oehler, but then I stopped thinking that way, I said to myself it *doesn't matter.* Scherrer makes me uneasy because he is so superficial. If I had originally imagined that I was going to visit a scientific man, in the shape of a scientific doctor, I soon recognized that I was sitting across from a charlatan. Too often we recognize too late that we should not have become involved in something that unexpectedly debases us. On the other hand, I had to assume that Scherrer is performing a useful function for Karrer, says Oehler, but I saw more and more that Scherrer, although he is described as the opposite and although he himself believes in this opposite, is indeed convinced by it, is an enemy of Karrer's, a doctor in a white coat playing the role of a benefactor. To Scherrer, Karrer is nothing more than an object that he misuses. Nothing more than a victim. Nauseated by Scherrer, I tell him that Karrer says that there really are trousers and trouser materials that can be held up to the light, *but these,* says Karrer and bursts out into a laughter that is quite uncharacteristic of Karrer, because it is characteristic of Karrer's madness, *you don't need to hold these trousers up to the light,* Karrer says, banging on the counter with his walking stick at the same time, *to see that we are dealing with Czechoslovakian rejects.* Now for the first time I noticed quite clear signs of madness, I tell Scherrer, whereupon, as I can see, Scherrer immediately makes a note, says Oehler, because I am watching all that Scherrer is noting down, says Oehler, *Oehler* (in other words, I) is saying at this moment: *for the first time quite clear signs of madness;* I observe *not only how Scherrer reacts, I also observe what Scherrer makes notes of and how Scherrer makes notes.* I am not surprised, says Oehler, that Scherrer underlines my comment *for the first time signs of madness.* It is merely proof of his incompetence, says Oehler. It occurred to me that Rustenschacher was still labeling trousers in the back, I told Scherrer, and I thought it's incomprehensible, and thus uncanny, that Rustenschacher should be labeling so many pairs of trousers. Possibly it was a sudden, unbelievable increase in Karrer's state of excitement that prompted Rustenschacher's incessant labeling of trousers, for Rustenschacher's incessant labeling of trousers was gradually irritating even me. I thought that Rustenschacher really never sells as many pairs of trousers as he labels, I suddenly tell Scherrer, but he probably also supplies other smaller businesses in the outlying districts, in the twenty-first, twenty-second, and twenty-third districts, in which you can also buy Rustenschacher's trousers and thus Rustenschacher also plays the role of a trousers wholesaler for a number of such textile firms in outlying districts. Now, Karrer says, in the case of this pair of trousers that you are now holding right in front of my face instead of holding them up to the light, Oehler tells Scherrer, it is clearly a case of Czechoslovakian rejects. It was simply because Karrer did not insult Rustenschacher's nephew to his face with this new objection to Rustenschacher's trousers, Oehler told Scherrer. Karrer had at first prolonged his visit to Rustenschacher's store because of the pains in his leg, I told Scherrer, says Oehler. Apparently we had walked too far before we entered Rustenschacher's store, and not only too far but also too quickly while at the same time carrying on a most exhausting conversation about Wittgenstein, I tell Scherrer, says Oehler, I mention the name on purpose, because I knew that Scherrer had never heard the name before, and this was confirmed at once, in the very moment that I said the name Wittgenstein, says Oehler, however, at that point Karrer had probably not been thinking about his painful legs for a long time, but simply for the reason that I could not leave him I was unable to leave Rustenschacher's store. This is something we often observe in ourselves when we are in a room (any room you care to mention): we seem chained to the room (any room you care to mention) and have to stay there, because we cannot leave it when we are *upset*. Karrer probably wanted to leave Rustenschacher's store, I tell Scherrer, says Oehler, but Karrer no longer had the strength to do so. And I myself was no longer capable of taking Karrer out of Rustenschacher's store at the crucial moment. After Rustenschacher had repeated, as his nephew had before him, that the trouser materials with which we were dealing were excellent, he did not, like his nephew before him, say most excellent, just excellent, materials and that it was senseless to maintain that we were dealing with rejects or even with Czechoslovakian rejects, Karrer once again says that in the case of these trousers they were apparently dealing with Czechoslovakian rejects, and he made as if to take a deep breath, as it seemed unsuccessfully, whereupon he wanted to say something else, I tell Scherrer, says Oehler, but he, Karrer, was out of breath and was unable, because he was out of breath, to say what he apparently wanted to say. *These thin spots. These thin spots. These thin spots. These thin spots. These thins spots* over and over again. *These thin spots. These thin spots. These thin spots,* incessantly. *These thin spots. These thin spots. These thin spots.* Rustenschacher had immediately grasped what was happening and, on my orders, Rustenschacher's nephew had already ordered everything to be done that had to be done, Oehler tells Scherrer.

The unbelievable sensitivity of a person like Karrer on the one hand and his great ruthlessness on the other, said Oehler. On the one hand, his overwhelming wealth of feeling and on the other his overwhelming brutality. There is a constant tussle between all the possibilities of human thought and between all the possibilities of a human mind's sensitivity and between all the possibilities of a human character, says Oehler. On the other hand we are in a state of constant *completely natural* and not for a moment *artificial* intellectual preparedness when we are with a person like Karrer. We acquire an increasingly radical and, in fact, an increasingly more radically clear view of and relationship to all objects even if these objects are the sort of objects that in normal circumstances human beings cannot grasp. What until now, until the moment we meet a person like Karrer, we found unattainable we suddenly find attainable and transparent. Suddenly the world no longer consists of layers of darkness but is totally layered in clarity, says Oehler. It is in the recognition of this and in the constant readiness to recognize this, says Oehler, that the difficulties of constantly being with a person like Karrer lie. A person like that is, of course, feared because he is afraid (of being transparent). We are now concerned with a person like Karrer because now he has actually been taken away from us (by being taken into Steinhof). If Karrer were not at this moment in Steinhof and if we did not know for certain that he is in Steinhof, were this not an absolute certainty for us, we would not dare to talk about Karrer, but because Karrer has gone finally mad, as we know, which we know not because science has confirmed it but simply because we only need to use our heads, and what we have ascertained by using our own heads and what, furthermore, science has confirmed for us, for there is no doubt that in Scherrer, says Oehler, we are dealing with a typical representative of science, which Karrer always called *so-called* science, we do dare to talk about Karrer. Just as Karrer, in general, says Oehler, called everything so-called, there was nothing that he did not call only so-called, nothing that he would not have called so-called, and by so doing his powers achieved an unbelievable force. He, Karrer, had never said, says Oehler, even if on the contrary he did say it frequently and in many cases incessantly, in such incessantly spoken words and in such incessantly used concepts, that it was not a question of science, always only of so-called science, it was not a question of art, only of so-called art, not of technology, only of so-called technology, not of illness, only of so-called illness, not of knowledge, only of so-called knowledge, while saying that everything was only so-called he reached an unbelievable potential and an unparalleled credibility. When we are dealing with people we are only dealing with so-called people, just as when we are dealing with facts we are only dealing with so-called facts, just as the whole of matter, since it only emanates from the human mind, is only so-called matter, just as we know that everything emanates from the human mind and from nothing else, if we understand *the concept knowledge* and accept it as a concept that we understand. This is what we go on thinking of and we constantly *substantiate* everything on this basis and on no other. That on this basis things, and things in themselves, are only so-called or, to be completely accurate, only so-called so-called, to use Karrer's words, says Oehler, goes without saying. The structure of the whole is, as we know, a *completely simple one* and if we always accept this completely simple structure as our starting point we shall make progress. If we do not accept this completely simple structure of the whole as our starting point, we have what we call a complete standstill, but also *a whole as a so-called whole.* How could I dare, said Karrer, not to call something only so-called and so draw up an account and design a world, no matter how big and no matter how sensible or how foolish, if I were always only to say to myself (and to act accordingly) that we are dealing with what is so-called and then, over and over again, a so-called so-called something. Just as behavior in its repetition as in its absoluteness is only so-called behavior, Karrer said, says Oehler. Just as we have only a so-called position to adopt vis-à-vis everything we understand and vis-à-vis everything we do not understand, but which we think is real and thus true. Walking with Karrer was an unbroken series of thought processes, says Oehler, which we often developed in juxtaposition one to the other and would then suddenly unjoin them somewhere along the way, when we had reached a place for *standing* or a place for *thinking,* but generally at one particular place for *standing and thinking* when it was a question, says Oehler, of making one of my thoughts into a single one, with another one (his) not into a double one, for a double thought is, as we know, impossible and therefore nonsense. There is never anything but one single thought, just as it is wrong to say that there is a thought beside this thought and what, in such a constellation, is often called a secondary thought, which is sheer nonsense. If Karrer had a thought, and I myself had a thought, and it must be said that we were constantly finding ourselves in that state because it had long since ceased to be possible for us to be in any state but that state, we both constantly had a thought, or, as Karrer would have said, even if he didn't say it, a so-called constant thought right up to the moment when we dared to make our two separate thoughts into a single one, just as we maintain that about really great thoughts, that is so-called really great thoughts, which are, however, not thoughts, for a so-called really great thought is never *a* thought, it is a summation of all thoughts pertaining to a so-called great matter, thus there is no such thing as the really great thought, we do not dare, we told ourselves in such a case, says Oehler, when we had been walking together for a long time and had had *one* thought each individually, but side by side, and when we had held on to this thought and seen through it to make these two completely transparent thoughts into one. That was, one could say, nothing but playfulness, but then you could say that everything is only playfulness, says Oehler, that no matter what we are dealing with we are dealing with playfulness is also a possibility, says Oehler, but I do not contemplate that. The thought is quite right, says Oehler, when we are standing in front of the Obenaus Inn, *suddenly* stopping in front of the Obenaus, is what Oehler says: the thought that Karrer will never go out to Obenaus again is quite right. Karrer really will not go out to Obenaus again, because he will not come out of Steinhof again. We know that Karrer will not come out of Steinhof again, and thus we know that he will not go into Obenaus again. *What will he miss by not going?* we immediately ask ourselves, says Oehler, if we get involved with this question, although we know that it is senseless to have asked this question, but if the question has once been asked, let us consider it and approach the response to the question, *What will Karrer miss by not going into Obenaus again?* It is easy enough to ask the question, but the answer is, however, complicated, for we cannot answer a question like, *What will Karrer miss if he does not go into Obenaus again?* with a simple *yes* or a simple *no*. Although we know that it would have been simpler not to have asked ourselves the question (it doesn't matter what question), we have nevertheless asked ourselves the (and thus a) question. We have asked ourselves an incredibly complicated question and done so completely consciously, says Oehler, because we *think* it is possible for us to answer even a complicated question, we are not afraid to answer such a complicated question as *What will Karrer miss if he does not go into Obenaus again?* Because we think we know so much (and in such depth) about Karrer that we can answer the question, *What will Karrer miss if he does not go into Obenaus again?* Thus we do not dare to answer the question, *we know* that we can answer it, we are not risking anything with this question although it is only as we come to the realization that we are risking nothing with this question that we realize that we are risking *everything* and not only with this question. I would not, however, go so far as to say that I can *explain* how I answer the question, *What will Karrer miss if he does not go into Obenaus again?* says Oehler, but I will also not answer the question without explanation and indeed not without explanation of how I have answered the question or of how I came to ask the question at all. If we want to answer a question like the question, *What will Karrer miss if he does not go into Obenaus again?* we have to answer it *ourselves*, but this presupposes a complete knowledge of Karrer's circumstances with relation to Obenaus and thereafter, of course, the full knowledge of everything connected with Karrer and with Obenaus, by which means we arrive at the fact that we cannot answer the question, *What will Karrer miss if he does not go into Obenaus again?* The assertion that we answer the question while answering it is thus a false one, because we have probably answered the question and, as we believe and know, have answered it ourselves, we haven't answered it at all, because we have simply not answered the question ourselves, because it is not possible to answer a question like the question, *What will Karrer miss if he does not go into Obenaus again?* Because we have not asked the question, *Will Karrer go into Obenaus again?* which could be answered simply by yes or no, in the actual case in point by answering no, and would thus cause ourselves no difficulty, but instead we are asking, *What will Karrer miss if he does not go into Obe-*

naus again? it is automatically a question that cannot be answered, says Oehler. Apart from that, we do, however, answer this question when we call the question that we asked ourselves a so-called question and the answer that we give a so-called answer. While we are again *acting* within the framework of the concept of the so-called and are thus *thinking,* it seems to us quite possible to answer the question, *What will Karrer miss if he does not go into Obenaus again?* But the question, *What will Karrer miss if he does not go into Obenaus again?* can also be applied to *me.* I can ask, *What will I miss if I do not go into Obenaus again?* or you can ask yourself, *What will I miss if I do not go into Obenaus again?* but at the same time it is most highly probable that one of these days I will indeed go into Obenaus again and you will probably go into Obenaus again to eat or drink something, says Oehler. I can say *in my opinion* Karrer will not go into Obenaus again, I can even say Karrer will *probably* not go into Obenaus again, I can say *with certainty* or *definitely* that Karrer will not go into Obenaus again. But I cannot ask, *What will Karrer miss by the fact that he will not go into Obenaus again?* because I cannot answer the question. But let's simply make the *attempt* to ask ourselves, *What does a person who has often been to Obenaus miss if he suddenly does not go into Obenaus any more (and indeed never again)?* says Oehler. Suppose such a person simply never goes among the people who are sitting there, says Oehler. When we ask it in this way, we see that we cannot answer the question because in the meantime we have expanded it by an endless number of other questions. If, nevertheless, we do ask, says Oehler, and we start with the people who are sitting in Obenaus. We first ask, *What is or who is sitting in Obenaus?* so that we can then ask, *Whom does someone who suddenly does not go into Obenaus again (ever again) miss?* Then we at once ask ourselves, *With which of the people sitting in Obenaus shall I begin?* and so on. Look, says Oehler, we can ask any question we like, we cannot answer the question if we *really* want to answer it, to this extent there is not a single question in the whole conceptual world that can be answered. But in spite of this, millions and millions of questions are constantly being asked and answered by questions, as we know, and those who ask the questions and those who answer are not bothered by whether it is wrong because they cannot be bothered, so as not to stop, so that there shall suddenly be nothing more, says Oehler. Here, in front of

Obenaus, look, here, up there on the fourth floor, I once lived in a room, a very small room, when I came back from America, says Oehler. He'd come back from America and had said to himself, you should take a room in the place where you lived thirty years ago in the ninth district, and he had taken a room in the ninth district in the Obenaus. But suddenly he couldn't stand it any longer, not in this street any longer, not in this city any longer, says Oehler. During his stay in America, everything had changed in the city in which *he was suddenly living again after thirty years* in what for him was a horrible way. I hadn't reckoned on that, says Oehler. I suddenly realized that there was nothing left for me in this city, says Oehler, but now that I had, as it happened, returned to it and, to tell the truth, with the intention of staying *forever,* I was not able immediately to turn around and go back to America. For I had really left America with the intention of leaving America forever, says Oehler. I realized, on the one hand, that there was nothing left for me in Vienna, says Oehler and, on the other, I realized with all the acuity of my intellect that there was also nothing more left for me in America, and he had walked through the city for days and weeks and months pondering how he would commit suicide. For it was clear to me that I must commit suicide, says Oehler, completely and utterly clear, only not *how* and also not exactly *when,* but it was clear to me that it would be *soon,* because it had to be soon. He went into the inner city again and again, says Oehler, and stood in front of the front doors of the inner city and looked for a particular name from his childhood and his youth, a name that was either loved or feared, but which was known to him, but he did not find a single one of these names. Where have all these people gone who are associated with the names that are familiar to me, but which I cannot find on any of these doors? I asked myself, says Oehler. He kept on asking himself this question for weeks and for months. We often go on asking the same question for months at a time, he says, ask ourselves or ask others but above all we ask ourselves and when, even after the longest time, even after the passage of years, we have still not been able to answer this question because it is not possible for us to answer it, it doesn't matter what the question is, says Oehler, we ask another, a new, question, but perhaps again a question that we have already asked ourselves, and so it goes on throughout life, until the mind can stand it no longer. Where have all these people, friends, relatives, enemies gone to? he had asked himself and had gone on and on looking for names, even at night this questioning about the names had given him no peace. Were there not hundreds and thousands of names? he had asked himself. Where are all these people with whom I had contact thirty years ago? he asked himself. If only I were to meet just a single one of these people. Where have they gone to? he asked himself incessantly, and why. Suddenly it became clear to him that all the people he was looking for no longer existed. These people no longer exist, he suddenly thought, there's no sense in looking for these people because they no longer exist, he suddenly said to himself, and he gave up his room in Obenaus and went into the mountains, into the country. I went into the mountains, says Oehler, but I couldn't stand it in the mountains either and came back into the city again. I have often stood here with Karrer beneath the Obenaus, says Oehler, and talked to him about all these frightful associations. Then we, Oehler and I, were on the Friedensbrücke. Oehler tells me that Karrer's proposal to explain one of Wittgenstein's statements to him on the Friedensbrücke came to nothing; because he was so exhausted, Karrer did not even mention Wittgenstein's name again on the Friedensbrücke. I myself was not capable of mentioning Ferdinand Ebner's name any more, says Oehler. In recent times we have very often found ourselves in a state of exhaustion in which we were no longer able to explain what we intended to explain. We used the Friedensbrücke to relieve our states of exhaustion, says Oehler. There were two statements we wanted to explain to each other, says Oehler, I wanted to explain to Karrer a statement of Wittgenstein's that was completely unclear to him, and Karrer wanted to explain a statement by Ferdinand Ebner that was completely unclear to me. But because we were exhausted we were suddenly no longer capable, there on the Friedensbrücke, of saying the names of Wittgenstein and Ferdinand Ebner because we had brought our walking and our thinking, the one out of the other, to an incredible, almost unbearable, state of nervous tension. We had already thought that this practice of bringing walking and thinking to the point of the most terrible nervous tension could not go on for long without causing harm, and in fact we were unable to carry on the practice, says Oehler. Karrer had to put up with the consequences, I myself was so weakened by Karrer's, I have to say, complete nervous breakdown, for that is how I can unequivocally describe Karrer's madness, as a fatal structure of the brain, that I can no longer say the word Wittgenstein on the Friedensbrücke, let alone say anything about Wittgenstein or anything connected with Wittgenstein, says Oehler, looking at the traffic on the Friedensbrücke. Whereas we always thought we could make walking and thinking *into a single total process,* even for a fairly long time, I now have to say that it is impossible to make walking and thinking into one total process for a fairly long period of time. For, in fact, it is not possible *to walk and to think with the same intensity for a fairly long period of time,* sometimes we walk more intensively, but think less intensively, then we think intensively and do not walk as intensively as we are thinking, sometimes we think with a much higher presence of mind than we walk with and sometimes we walk with a far higher presence of mind than we think with, but we cannot walk and think with the same presence of mind, says Oehler, just as we cannot walk and think with the same intensity over a fairly long period of time and make walking and thinking for a fairly long period of time into a total whole with a total equality of value. If we walk more intensively, our thinking lets up, says Oehler, if we think more intensively, our walking does. On the other hand, we have to walk in order to be able to think, says Oehler, just as we have to think in order to be able to walk, the one derives from the other and the one derives from the other with ever-increasing skill. But never beyond the point of exhaustion. We cannot say we think the way we walk, just as we cannot say we walk the way we think because we cannot walk the way we think, cannot think the way we walk. If we are walking intensively for a long time deep in an intensive thought, says Oehler, then we soon have to stop walking or stop thinking, because it is not possible to walk and to think with the same intensity for a fairly long period of time. Of course, we can say that we succeed in walking evenly and in thinking evenly, but this art is apparently the most difficult and one that we are least able to master. We say of one person he is an excellent thinker and we say of another person he is an excellent walker, but we cannot say of any one person that he is an excellent (or first-rate) thinker and walker at the same time. On the other hand walking and thinking are two completely similar concepts, and we can readily say (and maintain) that the person who walks and thus the person who, for example, walks excellently also thinks excellently, just as the person who thinks, and thus thinks excellently, also walks excellently. If we observe very carefully someone who is walking, we also know how he thinks. If we observe very carefully someone who is thinking, we know how he walks. If we observe most minutely someone walking over a fairly long period of time, we gradually come to know his way of thinking, the structure of his thought, just as we, if we observe someone over a fairly long period of time as to the way he thinks, we will gradually come to know how he walks. So observe, over a fairly long period of time, someone who is thinking and then observe how he walks, or, vice versa, observe someone walking over a fairly long period of time and then observe how he thinks. There is nothing more revealing than to see a thinking person walking, just as there is nothing more revealing than to see a walking person thinking, in the process of which we can easily say that we see how the walker thinks just as we can say that we see how the thinker walks, because we are seeing the thinker walking and conversely seeing the walker thinking, and so on, says Oehler. Walking and thinking are in a perpetual relationship that is based on trust, says Oehler. The science of walking and the science of thinking are basically a single science. How does this person walk and how does he think! we often ask ourselves as though coming to a conclusion, without actually asking ourselves this question as though coming to a conclusion, just as we often ask the question in order to come to a conclusion (without actually asking it), how does this person think, how does this person walk! Whenever I see someone thinking, can I therefore infer from this how he walks? I ask myself, says Oehler, if I see someone walking can I infer how he thinks? No, of course, I *may* not ask myself this question, for this question is one of those questions that *may* not be asked because they *cannot* be asked without being nonsense. But naturally we may not reproach someone who walks, whose walking we have analyzed, for his thinking, before we know his thinking. Just as we may not reproach someone who thinks for his walking before we know his walking. *How carelessly this person walks* we often think and very often *how carelessly this person thinks,* and we soon come to realize that this person walks in exactly the same way as he thinks, thinks the same way as he walks. However, we may not ask *ourselves* how we walk, for then we walk differently from the way we really walk and our walking simply cannot be judged, just as we may not ask ourselves how we think, for then we cannot judge how we think because it is no longer *our* thinking. Whereas, of course, we can observe someone else without his knowledge (or his being aware of it) and observe how he walks or thinks, that is, his walking and his thinking, we can never observe ourselves without our knowledge (or our being aware of it). If we observe ourselves, we are never observing ourselves but someone else. Thus we can never talk about self-observation, or when we talk about the fact that we observe ourselves we are talking as someone we never are when we are not observing ourselves, and thus when we observe ourselves we are never observing the person we intended to observe but someone else. The concept of self-observation and so, also, of self-description is thus false. Looked at in this light, all concepts (ideas), says Oehler, like self-observation, self-pity, self-accusation and so on, are false. We ourselves do not see ourselves, it is never possible for us to see ourselves. But we also cannot explain to someone else (a different object) what he *is* like, because we can only tell him *how we see him,* which probably coincides with what he is but which we cannot explain in such a way as to say *this is how he is.* Thus everything is something quite different from what it is for us, says Oehler. And always something quite different from what it is for everything else. Quite apart from the fact that even the designations with which we designate things are quite different from the actual ones. To that extent all designations are wrong, says Oehler. But when we entertain such thoughts, he says, we soon see that we are lost in these thoughts. We are lost in every thought if we surrender ourselves to that thought, even if we surrender ourselves to one single thought, we are lost. If I am walking, says Oehler, I am thinking and I maintain that I am walking, and suddenly I think and maintain that I am walking and thinking because that is what I am thinking while I am walking. And when we are walking together and *think* this thought, we think we are walking together, and suddenly we think, even if we don't think it together, we *are thinking,* but it is something different. If I think I am walking, it is something different from your thinking I am walking, just as it is something different if we both think at the same time (or simultaneously) that we are walking, if that is possible. Let's walk over the Friedensbrücke, I said earlier, says Oehler, and we walked over the Friedensbrücke because I thought I was thinking, I say, I am walking over the Friedensbrücke, I am walking with you so we are walking together over the Friedensbrücke. But it would be quite different were you to have had this thought, let's go over the

Friedensbrücke, if you were to have thought, let's walk over the Friedensbrücke, and so on. When we are walking, intellectual movement comes with body movement. We always discover when we are walking, and so causing our body to start to move, that our thinking, which *was* not thinking in our head, also starts to move. We walk with our legs, we say, and think with our head. We could, however, also say we walk with our mind. Imagine walking in such an incredibly unstable state of mind, we think when we see someone walking whom we assume to be in that state of mind, as we think and say. This person is walking completely mindlessly, we say, just as we say, this mindless person is walking incredibly quickly or incredibly slowly or incredibly purposefully. Let's go, we say, into Franz Josef station when we know that we *are going to* say, let's go into Franz Josef station. Or we think we are saying let's walk over the Friedensbrücke and we walk over the Friedensbrücke because we have anticipated what we are doing, that is, walking over the Friedensbrücke. We think what we have anticipated and do what we have anticipated, says Oehler. After four or five minutes we intended to visit the park in Klosterneuburgerstrasse, the fact that we went into the park in Klosterneuburgerstrasse, says Oehler, presupposed that we *knew* for four or five minutes that we *would* go into the park in Klosterneuburgerstrasse. Just as when I say *let's go into Obenaus* it means that I have *thought, let's go into Obenaus,* irrespective of whether I go into Obenaus or not. But we are lost in thoughts like this, says Oehler, and it is pointless to occupy yourself with thoughts like this for any length of time. Thus we are always on the point of throwing away thoughts, throwing away the thoughts that we have and the thoughts that we always have, because we are in the habit of always having thoughts, throughout our lives, as far as we know, we throw thoughts away, we do nothing else because we are nothing but people who are always tipping out their minds like garbage cans and emptying them wherever they may be. If we have a head full of thoughts we tip our head out like a garbage can, says Oehler, but not everything onto one heap, says Oehler, but always in the place where we happen to be at a given moment. It is for this reason that the world is always full of a stench, because everybody is always emptying out their heads like a garbage can. Unless we find a different method, says Oehler, the world will, without doubt, one day be suffocated by the stench that this thought refuse generates. But it is improbable that there is any other method. All people fill their heads without thinking and without concern for others and they empty them where they like, says Oehler. It is this idea that I find the cruelest of all ideas. The person who thinks also thinks of his thinking as a form of walking, says Oehler. He says my or his or this train of thought. Thus it is absolutely right to say, let's enter this thought, just as if we were to say, let's enter this haunted house. Because we say it, says Oehler, because we have this idea, because we, as Karrer would have said, have this so-called idea of such a so-called train of thought. Let's go further (in thought), we say, when we want to develop a thought further, when we want to progress in a thought. This thought goes too far, and so on, is what is said. If we think that we have to go more quickly (or more slowly) we think that we have to think more quickly, although we know that thinking is not a question of speed, true it does deal with something, which is walking, when it is a question of walking, but thinking has nothing to do with speed, says Oehler. The difference between walking and thinking is that thinking has nothing to do with speed, but walking is actually always involved with speed. Thus, to say let's walk to Obenaus quickly or let's walk over the Friedensbrücke quickly is absolutely correct, but to say let's think faster, let's think quickly, is wrong, it is nonsense, and so on, says Oehler. When we are walking we are dealing with so-called practical concepts (in Karrer's words), when we are thinking we are dealing simply with concepts. But we can, of course, says Oehler, make thinking into walking and, vice versa, walking into thinking without departing from the fact that thinking has nothing to do with speed, walking everything. We can also say, over and over again, says Oehler, we have now walked to the end of such and such a road, it doesn't matter what road, whereas we can never say, now we have thought this thought to an end, there's no such thing and it is connected with the fact that walking but not thinking is connected with speed. Thinking is by no means speed, walking, quite simply, is speed. But underneath all this, as underneath everything, says Oehler, there is the world (and thus also the thinking) of practical or secondary concepts. We advance through the world of practical concepts or secondary concepts, but not through the world of concepts. In fact, we now intend to visit the park on Klosterneuburgerstrasse; after four or five minutes in the park on Klosterneuburgerstrasse, Oehler suddenly says, we still have some bird food we brought for the birds under the Friedensbrücke in our coat pockets. Do you have the bird food we brought for the birds under the Friedensbrücke in your coat pocket? To which I answer, yes. To our astonishment both of us, Oehler and I, still have, at this moment in the park on Klosterneuburgerstrasse, the bird food in our coat pockets that we brought for the birds under the Friedensbrücke. It is absolutely unusual, says Oehler, for us to forget to feed our bird food to the birds under the Friedensbrücke. Let's feed the birds our bird food now, says Oehler, and we feed the birds our bird food. We throw our bird food to the birds very quickly and the bird food is eaten up in a short time. These birds have a totally different, much more rapid, way of eating our bird food, says Oehler, different from the birds under the Friedensbrücke. Almost at the same moment, I also say: a totally different way. It was absolutely certain, I think, that I was ready to say the words in a totally different way before Oehler made his statement. We say something, says Oehler, and the other person maintains that he has just thought the same thing and was about to say what we had said. This peculiarity should be an occasion for us to busy ourselves with the peculiarity. But not today. I have never walked from the Friedensbrücke onto Klosterneuburgerstrasse so quickly, says Oehler. We, Karrer and I, also intended, says Oehler, to go straight from the Friedensbrücke back onto Klosterneuburgerstrasse, but no, we went into Rustenschacher's store, today I really don't know why we went into Rustenschacher's store but it's pointless to think about it. I can still hear myself saying, says Oehler, *let's go back onto Klosterneuburgerstrasse.* That is back to where we are now standing, because I always went walking with Karrer here, but certainly not to feed the birds, as I do with you. I can still hear myself saying, *let's go back onto Klosterneuburgerstrasse, we'll calm down on Klosterneuburgerstrasse.* I was already under the impression that what Karrer needed above all else was to calm down, his whole organism was at this moment nothing but sheer unrest: I really did call out to him several times, *let's go onto Klosterneuburgerstrasse,* that was what I said, but Karrer wasn't listening, I asked him to go to Klosterneuburgerstrasse, but Karrer wasn't listening, he suddenly stopped in front of Rustenschacher's store, a place I hate, says Oehler, the fact is that I hate Rustenschacher's store, and said, let's go into Rustenschacher's store and we went into Rustenschacher's store, although it was not, in the least, our intention to go into Rustenschacher's store, because when we were still in Franz Josef station we had said to one another, *today we will neither go to Obenaus nor into Rustenschacher's store.* I can still hear us both stating categorically *neither to Obenaus* (to drink our beer) *nor into Rustenschacher's store,* but suddenly we had gone into Rustenschacher's store, says Oehler, and what followed you know. What senselessness to reverse a decision, once taken, on the grounds of reason, as we had to say (afterwards) and replace it with what is often a terrible misfortune, says Oehler. I had never known such a hectic pace as when I was walking with Karrer down from the Friedensbrücke in the direction of Klosterneuburgerstrasse and into Rustenschacher's store, says Oehler. We had never even crossed the square in front of Franz Josef station so quickly. In spite of the people streaming towards us from Franz Josef station, in spite of these people suddenly streaming towards us, in spite of these hundreds of people suddenly streaming towards us, Karrer went towards Franz Josef station, and I thought that we would, as was his custom, sit down on one of the old benches intended for travelers, right in the midst of all the revolting dirt of Franz Josef station, as was his custom, says Oehler, to sit down on one of these benches and watch the people as they jump off the trains and as, in a short while, they start streaming all over the station, but no, shortly before we were going, as I thought, to enter the station and sit down on one of these benches, Karrer turns round and runs to the Friedensbrücke, runs, says Oehler several times, runs, past the "Railroader" clothing store towards the Friedensbrücke and from there into Rustenschacher's store at an unimaginable speed, says Oehler. Karrer actually ran away from Oehler. Oehler was only able to follow Karrer at a distance of more than ten, for a long while of fifteen or even twenty meters; while he was running along behind Karrer, Oehler kept thinking, if only Karrer doesn't go into Rustenschacher's store, *if only he won't be rash enough* to go into Rustenschacher's store, but precisely what Oehler feared, as he was running along behind Karrer, happened. Karrer said, *let's go into Rustenschacher's store,* and Karrer, without waiting for a word from Oehler, who was, by now, exhausted, went straight into Rustenschacher's store, Karrer tore open the door of Rustenschacher's store with an incredible vehemence, but was then able to pull himself together, says Oehler, only, of course, to lose control again immediately. Karrer ran to the counter, says Oehler, and the salesman, without arguing, began at once to show Karrer, to whom he had shown all the trousers the week before, all the trousers, to hold up all the trousers to the light. Look, said Karrer, says Oehler, his tone of voice suddenly so quiet, probably because we are now standing still, I have known this street from my childhood and I have been through everything that this street has been through, there is nothing in this street with which I would not be familiar, he, Karrer knew every regularity and every irregularity in this street, and even if it is one of the most ugly, he loved the street like no other. How often have I said to myself, said Karrer, you see these people day in day out, and it is always the same people whom you see and whom you know, always the same faces and always the same head and body movements as they walk, head and body movements that are characteristic of Klosterneuburgerstrasse. You know these hundreds and thousands of people, Karrer said to Oehler, and you know them, even if you do not know them, because basically they are always the same people, all these people are the same and they only differ in the eyes of the superficial observer (as judge). The way they walk and the way they do not walk and the way they shop and do not shop and the way they act in summer and the way they act in winter and the way they are born and the way they die, Karrer said to Oehler. You know all the terrible conditions. You know all the attempts (to live), those who do not emerge from these attempts, this whole attempt at life, this whole state of attempting, seen as a life, Karrer said to Oehler, says Oehler. You went to school here and you survived your father and your mother here, and others will survive you as you survived your father and mother, said Karrer to Oehler. It was on Klosterneuburgerstrasse that all the thoughts that ever occurred to you occurred to you (and if you know the truth, all your ideas, all your rebukes about your environment, your inner world they all occurred to you here). How many monstrosities is Klosterneuburgerstrasse filled with for you? You only need to go onto Klosterneuburgerstrasse, and all life's misery and all life's despair come at you. I think of these walls, these rooms with which, and in which, you grew up, the many illnesses characteristic of Klosterneuburgerstrasse, said Karrer, in Oehler's words, the dogs and the old people tied to the dogs. The way Karrer made these statements was, in Oehler's words, not surprising in the wake of Hollensteiner's suicide. Something hopeless, depressing, had taken hold of Karrer after Hollensteiner's death, something I had never observed in him before. Suddenly, everything took on the somber color of the person who sees nothing but *dying* and for whom nothing else seems to happen any more but only *the dying* that surrounds him. But Scherrer, according to Oehler, was not interested in all the changes in Karrer's personality that were connected with Hollensteiner's suicide. Do you remember how they dragged you into the entryway of these houses and how they boxed your ears in those entryways, Karrer suddenly says to me in a tone that absolutely shattered me. As if Hollensteiner's death had darkened the whole human or rather inhuman scene for him. How they beat up your mother and how they beat up your father, says Karrer, says Oehler. These hundreds and thousands of windows shut tight both summer and winter, says Karrer, according to Oehler, and he says it as hopelessly as possible. I shall never forget the days before the visit to Rustenschacher's store, says Oehler, how Karrer's condition got worse daily, how everything you had thought was already totally gloomy became gloomier and gloomier. The shouting and the collapsing and the silence on Klosterneuburgerstrasse that followed this shouting and collapsing, said Karrer, says Oehler. And this terrible filth! he says, as though there had never been anything in the world for him but filth. It was precisely the fact that everything on Klosterneuburgerstrasse, that everything remained as it always had been and that you had to fear, if you thought about it, that it would always remain the same and that had gradually made Klosterneuburgerstrasse into an enormous and insoluble problem for him. *Waking up and going to sleep on Klosterneuburgerstrasse,* Karrer kept repeating. *This incessant walking back and forth on Klosterneuburgerstrasse. My own helplessness and immobility on Klosterneuburgerstrasse.* In the last two days these statements and scraps of statements had continually repeated themselves, says Oehler. *We have absolutely no ability to leave Klosterneuburgerstrasse. We have no power to make decisions any more. What we are doing is nothing. What we breathe is nothing. When we walk, we walk from one hopelessness to another. We walk and we always walk into a still more hopeless hopelessness. Walking away, nothing but walking away,* says Karrer, according to Oehler, over and over again. *Nothing but walking away. All those years I thought I would alter something, and that means everything, and walk away from*

Klosterneuburgerstrasse, but nothing changed (because he changed nothing), says Oehler, and he did not go away. *If you do not walk away early enough,* said Karrer, *it is suddenly too late and you can no longer walk away. It is suddenly clear you can do what you like, but you can no longer walk away. No longer being able to alter this problem of not being able to walk away any more occupies your whole life,* Karrer is supposed to have said, and from then on that is all that occupies your life. You then grow more and more helpless and weaker and weaker and all you keep saying to yourself is that you should have walked away early enough, and you ask yourself why you did not walk away early enough. But when we ask ourselves why we did not walk away and why we did not walk away early enough, which means did not walk away at the moment when it was *high time* to do so, we understand nothing more, said Karrer to Oehler. Oehler says: because we did not think intensively enough about changing things when we really should have thought intensively about making changes and in fact did think intensively about making changes, but not intensively enough because we did not think intensively in the most inhuman way about making changes in something, and that means, above all, ourselves, making changes in ourselves to change ourselves and by this means to change everything, said Karrer. The circumstances were always such as to make it impossible for us. Circumstances are everything, we are nothing, said Karrer. What sort of states and what sort of circumstances have I been in, in which I simply have not been able to change myself in all these years because it all boiled down to a question of states and circumstances that could not be changed, said Karrer. Thirty years ago, when you, Oehler, went off to America, where, as I know, most circumstances were really dreadful, Karrer is supposed to have said, I should have left Klosterneuburgerstrasse, but I did not leave it; now I feel this whole humiliation as a truly horrible punishment. Our whole life is composed of nothing but terrible and, at the same time, terrifying circumstances (as states), and if you take life apart it simply disintegrates into frightful circumstances and states, Karrer said to Oehler. And when you are on a street like this for so long a time, so long that you have left the discovery that you have grown old behind you long ago, you can, of course, no longer walk away, in thought yes, but in reality no, but to walk away in thought and not in reality means a double torment, said

Karrer, after you are forty, your willpower itself is already so weakened that it is senseless even to attempt to walk away. A street like Klosterneuburgerstrasse is, for a person of my age, a sealed tomb from which you hear nothing but dreadful things, said Karrer. Karrer is supposed to have said the words *the vicious process of dying* several times, and several times *early ruin*. How I hated these houses, Karrer is supposed to have said, and yet I kept on going into these houses with a lifelong appetite that is nothing short of depressing. All these hundreds and thousands of mentally sick people who have come out of these houses dead over the course of those years, said Karrer. For every dreadful person who has died from one of these houses, two or three new dreadful people are *created into* these houses, Karrer is supposed to have said to Oehler. I haven't been into Rustenschacher's store for weeks, Karrer said the day before he went into Rustenschacher's store, says Oehler. We live in a time when one should be at least twenty or thirty years younger if one is to survive, Karrer said to Oehler. There has never been an artificiality like it, an artificiality with such a naturalness, for which one should not be over forty. No matter where you look, you are looking into artificiality, said Karrer. Two or three years ago, this street was still not so artificial that it terrified me. But I cannot explain this artificiality, said Karrer. Just as I cannot explain anything any more, said Karrer. Filth and age and absolute artificiality, said Karrer. You with your Ferdinand Ebner, Karrer kept on repeating, and I, at first, with my Wittgenstein, then you with your Wittgenstein and I with my Ferdinand Ebner. When in addition one is dependent upon a female person, my sister, said Karrer. But it is frightful after years of absence, suddenly to face all these people (in Obenaus), said Karrer. If things are peaceful around me, then I am restless, the more restless I grow, the more peaceful things are around me, and vice versa, said Karrer. When you are suddenly dragged back into your filth, said Karrer. Into the filth that has doubtless increased in the thirty years, said Karrer. After thirty years it is a much filthier filth than it was thirty years ago, says Karrer. When I am lying in bed, assuming that my sister keeps quiet, that she is not pacing up and down in her room, which is opposite mine, said Karrer, that she is not, as she is in the habit of doing just as I have gone to bed, opening up all the cupboards and all the chests and suddenly clearing out all these cupboards and chests, then I think back on what I was thinking the day before, said Karrer. I close my eyes and lay the palms of my hands on the blanket and go back very intensely over the previous day. With a constantly increasing intensity, with an intensity that can constantly be increased. The intensity can always be increased, it may be that this exercise will one day cross the border into madness, but I cannot be bothered about that, said Karrer. The time when I did bother about it is past, I do not bother about it any more, said Karrer. The state of complete indifference, in which I then find myself, said Karrer, is, through and through, a philosophical state.